BOOK ONE
ESLURA'S CALLING

SACRED

BOOK ONE
ESLURA'S CALLING

SACRED

BY
M.C. BEELER

ILLUSTRATIONS BY SARAH BELOTE

HALF SUN
PRESS

SACRED

BOOK 1: ESLURA'S CALLING

Published by Half Sun Press

Copyright © 2021 by M.C. Beeler

WWW.MARGARETCBEELER.COM

Edited by Mike Myers
Cover Art by Emir Orucevic
Cartography by Alex Wiersum
Interior Illustrations by Sarah Belote
Interior Formatting by We Got You Covered Book Design

ISBN: 978-1-7361238-3-6

HALF SUN
PRESS

CONTENTS

BOOK ONE
ESLURA'S CALLING

SACRED

GAEDION

CAPE HELADRIA

GALECREST

MEADOW of AEZAROS

ACRED CITY

THE
WORLD
of
ESLURA

TREENODE

BLIGHBURROW

VESKADOTH

CHAPTER ONE

THE RIGHTFUL KING

Rumor had it the sun never cast its rays down on Morgaedion, Eslura's prison island. But that day, its warm glow tickled Demise's back. With the Heart of the Book of Fire, one of the four elemental pillars of the land, burning beneath his robes, he felt like the Rulers of old must have felt when they united Eslura under the Sacred banner. For the first time in his life, Demise was more than a Shadow Reaper, a collector of souls; he was a messenger for the rightful king of Eslura.

Demise sauntered through Eslura's most guarded prison gates, cloak whisking behind him. No words were exchanged between him and the prison guard—a ratty-looking man with a beard down to his steel-toed boots. No eyelashes were batted, and no second glances were taken. It was here where a man could disappear from the world forever, never to be bathed in the sun's rays again. And it was to here his king had been banished.

Demise glanced around at the tall, stone walls surrounding the wheel-rutted courtyard of the prison complex—the last sight the unfortunate souls trapped inside would ever see, and where he knew his comrades waited listening for his signal. Demise smiled—everything was going according to plan.

A second set of gates posed even less of a challenge for Demise, who was welcomed with overly courteous bows by a pair of guards cloaked in blue uniforms—the Sacred Guard. *I piss on your cowering reverence*, he thought, *your rightful king waits within these doors.*

The two guards led Demise to the main cell block and down several spiraled flights of stairs deep into the prison labyrinth. Without the Sacred Guard leading the way, Demise might have never escaped the endless maze of dark, musty cells and torture chambers.

The corridor narrowed, and the cold condensed around him. The flickering lights of a few sparsely arrayed torches cast a pale-yellow light on the damp, roughhewn stone walls.

The Guard halted at the bottom landing, which felt like the center of the earth to Demise. His ears popped and he felt himself breathing heavily. Another group of Guards stood against the wall, shoulders erect, stances unwavering, and all but one wore masks to match their garbs. The unmasked one stepped forward. He was a white sea otter, about waist-high to the others. Demise had heard of the infamous Remidigon Otsby, Captain of the Guard, countless times and been warned of his power, though those warnings meant nothing to him on this day.

"Officer Kazke," Remidigon called to one of the guards.

The otter crossed his arms behind his back and puffed his chest out. *You seem unbothered, Remidigon,* Demise thought to himself, *let us count the moments until your act falls flat.* At the otter's call, a guard in a red cloak stepped out from the line, revealing from behind him a cast iron door with a cutout about as tall as a man's forearm in the shape of an *S.* Kazke held a large, metal *S* in his right hand.

Remidigon nodded and Kazke turned back toward the door. He hoisted the *S* above his head, which must have been heavy judging by his grunting and wavering and positioned it inside the empty *S* shape. Several clicks resounded from within, and the door swung open. Remidigon waved Demise forward, and he proceeded alone into the cell block.

The door fell shut behind him, and a symphony of screams and death cries assaulted Demise's ears while the scent of human decay condemned his nostrils as he entered the dimly lit corridor. Prisoners begged for food, water, light, attention, *anything.* Filthy hands stuck out of many of the hundred or so cells that lined the wall, grasping at Demise as he walked past them. One unfortunate soul, a woman with blue scales and pectoral fins where her ears ought to be, made the mistake of reaching out a filthy, skeletal hand and latching onto the ankle of Demise's boot. He cast a flame down on her hand, and she released his boot and wailed in agony, thrashing her blazing hand against the floor to try to put out the flame. Demise watched as the flames spread to the dirty rags she wore, boiling her alive. The other prisoners gripped the bars of their cells and pressed forward to watch the spectacle, their grimy faces cast in orange by the dancing flames. They shrieked and screamed, with horror or delight, Demise could not tell.

That was but a small taste of the Heart's true power, Demise thought as he stared at the howling woman.

He reached a hand out and extended his long, black claws toward the woman as she tried to tear off her burning rags. She looked up and stared into the deep pits that made up Demise's eyes, a nothingness of shadows hallowed by suffering.

Pathetic scum.

Demise retracted his claws, drawing with them a gust of wind from the woman's mouth, sucking her soul from within, and dragging the last bit of life from her.

She collapsed to the floor, a charred corpse. Smoke rolled off her sizzling remains. Had Demise not been used to the putrid stench of death, he would have been retching alongside the prisoners in the cells around him.

Demise opened his clawed fist and examined the swirling ball of air that hovered above his palm. With his other hand, he unhooked a bottle from his belt, pulled the cork with his teeth and let the ball of air be sucked inside. Then he pushed the cork back into the bottle neck. A rush of energy surged in his chest and spread to his limbs. The woman's soul would add another thirty-two moons to his life.

Demise continued toward the last cell on the left. He had been assured no guards would await him there, and as promised, there were none. Demise took a deep breath and straightened his posture.

The old king lay shivering in the corner of the cell. His once flowing white hair was matted and tangled, and a white beard like a nest of thistles lay on his chest. His cell looked even shabbier than those of the vile peasants and thieves whose cells Demise had passed in the corridor. The walls were wet with slime, the bars slung with spider webs, the floor cracked and covered with filth overflowing from a waste bucket in the other corner.

Demise snarled at the sight. *You've disrespected a king. For this, you will pay.*

The old king opened his beady eyes, glistening with rheum in the flickering torchlight. "My son, is that you?" The words caught in his throat and he spat a blistering cough.

Had Demise not been told which cell was his master's, he would not have recognized the man at first glance. He had lost his impressive bulk and his skin was dull and grey.

"Yes, my lord, it is I, Demise." Demise felt a quiver in his voice.

A skimpy cloth covered the old king's waist, leaving his torso bare. Demise could see his rib cage heave in and out. He watched the old man groan and try to sit up.

"Have you brought it?" the king asked.

Of course he had. His king had commanded, and he still served—the deed was done. "Yes, my lord," he replied. The Heart was burning beneath his robes. Its power was unmistakable. Had he not been a shadow reaper, the Heart would have burned him to ashes like the woman in the cell.

"Good," the king said, "show it to me."

Demise reached beneath his robe and his hand instantly met the blistering energy that brooded over its surface.

"Hurry," the king demanded, chains rattling as he shuffled forward toward the bars. Pus and blood glistened on his wrists, ankles, and neck where heavy shackles chafed against his skin. He winced and crawled toward the bars.

Demise knelt and drew the orb-shaped Heart from beneath his robe, displaying it before his king on two open palms. He bowed his head below the Heart, eyes trained to the stone floor.

His king thrust his hands through the bars and tore the Heart from Demise's hands. He raised it above his head, examining every inch of it with a wide, black-toothed grin that split his dry lower lip. A fiery aura swept across the orb. The king cackled, blood dripping into his matted beard.

With a mighty twist of his hands, the king split the Heart in two at its center. Energy flowed between the severed halves; waves of heat surged through the room in a blinding explosion of fiery light. The veins in the king's withered arms glowed red and his eyes sparkled. He laughed mightily, the deep rumble echoing back from the ends of the corridor. Then he jumped up from the floor, stared at Demise with blazing eyes, and flung the charred remains of the once elegant Heart in the air. Its ashes fluttered to the floor like heavy snowflakes.

"Now, you know what must be done," the old king said, his voice full of fire. "Find the girl and bring her to me."

CHAPTER TWO

CAMP TOSSBRIDGE

"**B**eatrice!" If Fran Dildecker knew how to do one thing right, it was startling Bea half to death. Her shrill voice could have woken each and every one of Mountbridge's one thousand two hundred forty-six residents if she willed it to... except for Joe Dildecker. The old man had custom-designed earplugs for a reason.

Bea woke to red eyes and moaning bones. The two pills she downed the night before had failed to soothe her aching body. She rolled over and peeled her eyes against the light that poured in through her thin curtains.

Not wanting to fight her aching body, she spun onto her back and stared up at where the rafters met with the ceiling of her makeshift attic bedroom. Spiderwebs draped across the exposed pipes where the insulation should have been. Fran insisted against installing it, no matter how many freezing nights Bea suffered through.

After a few minutes, she sighed, stood up, and walked over to where a tower of Christmas decoration boxes stood so high, they cast a shadow over her dresser. She pressed her shoulder against the old dresser and pushed it aside with the scraping of wood against wood to reveal a wall marked up by white chalk.

Five hundred and twenty-nine. Bea ticked a new mark with the broken piece of chalk she left stowed beneath the dresser and sat cross-legged before the display. *Has it really been that long?* Her shoulders slouched with defeat. She could not remember the last time her mother spoke. Her voice, her sweet and gentle tone, had succumbed to the passage of time, tucked away in the deepest crevices of her memory. Thankfully, she could remember her mother's face; a look in the mirror or the few photos she had left helped her with that. She reached beneath the dresser and drew out one of the photos, the rest hidden beneath her mattress without Fran's knowledge. She wiped the dust off it and stared at the little, brown-haired girl squeezing her mother's waist.

She wondered where her dad was, what he looked like, what his voice sounded like. He never once appeared in any of her photos. She had so many questions, so many answers she had never found. Her mother never spoke of him and when Bea asked, she quickly brushed the thought of him away.

Bea leaned her head against the wall, tucked the photo back under the dresser, and shut her eyes. *Neither of you are coming back anytime soon, are you?*

That night, she'd had a dream—the first dream she could remember since her mother disappeared. Although her memories of it were shrouded by golden light, she remembered a cave, black and narrow, and as cold as a December morning.

"Beatrice Tidal!" Fran tramped up the flight of stairs leading to her room. Bea opened one eye and sighed, giving up any last hopes of falling back into her dream world. She could imagine Fran's face turning as red as the Santa's that still sat on the mantel place downstairs as she mumbled what a spoiled little brat Bea was. "Have you forgotten what time it is?" *Oh, Fran,* Bea thought, *I've tried.*

Bea had never called upon a higher power for help, but that night, she felt called to the spiritual life. She got down on her hands and knees and prayed for a miracle. Unfortunately for her, no amount of good luck or prayers could save her from the impending doom known as summer camp.

It had been only a few weeks since Fran and Joe experienced their own, personal miracle, though. On a routine trip to the post office, the couple discovered a colorful pamphlet with the words *Camp Tossbridge* emblazoned on its cover nuzzled up in their post box amongst the barrage of bills they refused to pay. Though they had missed the application deadline by four days, Fran's pleading phone call managed to get Bea enrolled in the camp. Bea guessed that the person on the other end of the call had taken pity on Bea for having to live with such a loud and annoying woman.

"Beatrice!" Fran pounded on her door, shaking the water cup on Bea's bedside table. Bea watched the ripples glide across its surface and collide with the glass. She imagined the water was a great sea where Fran, the terrible sea monster who lurked in its depths, waited for heedless swimmers to make their way into her jaws.

"I'm up," Bea moaned. Fran pounded one last time—as if the twenty others were insufficient—and thumped back down the stairs. Bea wondered what sort of ridiculous powder the sea monster would have caked on her face today. Perhaps green? It seemed to be her favorite color.

Bea put on her favorite sundress and slogged down the stairs into the kitchen amongst the army of Santas, reindeer, flashing red and green lights, bushels of garland, and hundreds of other decorations that had not been put away since Christmas and perhaps never would. Her eyes never quite got used to the chaotic house. Though the seasons changed, and the holidays passed, the house stayed in a constant state of Christmas. Fran and Joe insisted that keeping the decorations up year-round best represented their family business, Christmas tree farming. Bea disagreed, however, and decided they were totally mental.

Joe, whose nose was pressed into the columns of the day's newspaper, was already seated at his table when Bea walked in. Fran stood over the stove scooping something that looked like a hash of scrambled eggs, wet leaves, and roadkill onto three plates.

Bea glanced outside the window at the countless orderly rows of evergreen trees that marched off in every direction. If only she could run off and never have to come back.

Fran cleared her throat, interrupting Bea's reverie. "Sit down, girl."

Bea eyed her own table; the yellow one Fran had made Joe lug up from the crawlspace. Fran insisted that Bea needed to be at least six feet away from them at all times—thus, the wobbly old table of her own. Safety was without a doubt Fran's top priority, and Bea was about the biggest threat she had encountered inside the house ever since *the incident.*

A few months before, Bea, determined to uncover the secrets of *the symbol,* had searched every musty corner and crumbling niche of the internet. All that she had learned was that it could be a five-fold, but she knew nothing of its significance or why it always seemed to follow her, though no one else seemed to be able to see it. She had made the mistake of pointing it out once to Fran on the bottom of a grocery bag...*never again.* The next day, the woman dragged her to the Mountbridge Psych Ward.

Bea pulled out the folding, metal chair and sat down at her table, feeling like some sort of chemical experiment gone wrong.

"And this symbol *calls* to you, Beatrice?" she recalled Dr. Lizzar, the thirty-something-year-old woman with a yellow bun as tight as her face, asking with a raised brow. Her frill-topped pen scarred blue streaks across her notebook as she scrambled to jot down every single detail of Bea's uncomfortable fidgeting.

Bea did not answer—she *could not* answer. Dr. Lizzar would not understand; neither would Fran or Joe or any of the doctors the couple would drag her to in the following days and weeks. There was no earthly explanation for such a...*thing.*

Bea shook away the thought of Dr. Lizzar in exchange for a look at the plate of food Fran slapped on the table in front of her. *Eggs.* By now, Bea believed it to be out of pure spite that the woman continued to cook them for her.

"Don't waste it again," Fran growled with a finger just as

thick and greasy as the sausage link Bea downed in one bite. No one smell could churn Bea's stomach more than the smell of eggs. Although she attempted several times, she could not unsmell their sulfury stink. She poked at the goopy, yellow horrors with her fork and tried not to gag.

"You should be grateful you have food on your plate," Fran said. Bea should have known the comment was coming; the old woman said it every time Bea hesitated to stick her fork into whatever plated monstrosity Fran shoved in front of her. *Grateful.* Yes, of course! How could she not be grateful for her wonderfully perfect new caregiver?

But no, *caregiver* was too warm of a title to give Fran Dildecker. The woman had made it known since the day Bea moved in with her a year and one hundred sixty-four days before that Bea was nothing more to her than a subsidy check.

Bea narrowed her eyes at Fran, shoved a forkful of egg into her mouth, and drowned away the noxious taste with half a cup of water.

After what felt like an eternity, Bea finished her meal and headed toward the sink with her plate. As she lathered the chipped stoneware with soap and hot water, she knew what loomed just above her head. She fought the urge to look up at the clock, fearing what it might tell her.

Against her better judgement, she glanced up and found the numbers and hands of the small tree-shaped clock to be missing. Instead, a glowing symbol appeared on the face; its five golden circles woven together in an elegant design.

Her stomach curled and she dropped her plate, scattering shards of glass into the sink.

"Beatrice Tidal!" Fran placed her hand over her heart and gasped at the noise. "What in the world has gotten into you?" Joe tipped his paper down slightly, adjusted his toothpick, and mumbled, "Huh?"

Bea stared at the water pouring out of the faucet. Her hands shook above the broken plate and she felt herself sinking. She caught the lip of the sink and leaned over it. Nausea gripped her stomach and she thought she might throw up.

"You know what," Fran announced. She stood up from her chair, its metal legs scraping against the floor. Bea flinched at the sound and turned around from the sink. "I think it's about time you bring Beatrice to the bus, Joe." Fran looked down at her husband for approval, but he was too busy picking at the stray beard hairs he had missed in his morning shave. Fran swiped the paper out of his hands and whacked him on his bald spot.

"Joseph! Take Beatrice to the community center." Joe winced and stood up. Bea thought by now he would have known better than to ignore the sea monster, but the old man surprised her more and more each day.

"Gather up yer belongins, kid," Joe said, his words cut apart by the toothpick he swirled between his teeth. "You've got a bus ta catch."

Joe pulled the old Dodge Dart around the bend to the community center and parked in one of the few open spaces. A horde of teenagers had already begun to flock around the bus. Their excited laughter seeped in through Bea's open window. She rolled it up, only slightly muffling the noise. To her, the bus might as well have had *Welcome to your one-way ticket straight to the pits!* painted in bright red across its side.

"Summer camp?" Bea mumbled. "She really thinks this is going to solve things?" She stared out the window. Several of her old classmates were scattered around the crowd, none of whom she had been particularly fond of, or vice versa. She felt queasy and clutched her stomach.

"Come on, now," Joe said. He placed a hand on her shoulder and attempted a smile, which looked more like he had a toothache. "Just try to have fun, kid. It ain't all that bad." He shifted the car into drive, Bea's signal to leave. She knew if she did not get out of the car, Fran would arrive in an instant to drag her out by the tips of her toes. With that in mind, Bea grabbed her bag from beneath her seat and climbed out of the truck.

"I'll see ya back here in a week, all right?" Joe said as she started to close the door. *A week*, Bea thought, *a week might as well be an eternity.*

Bea shut the door, slung her backpack over her shoulder, and walked toward the registration table. She glanced behind her and watched Joe pull the truck away, engine sputtering black clouds of smoke into the air. Bea shook her head and continued toward the table.

"Welcome to Camp Tossbridge!" an older blonde teen, who, based on the colorful name tag, was called "*Jamie*," greeted her. "What's your name?"

"Bea," she said toward the ground. A lone ant crawled

across the dirt into a tiny hole and disappeared from her sight.

"Bea, Bea, Bea," Jamie repeated as she ran her finger down a list of names. "Ah, there you are! Beatrice Tidal." She smiled and put a checkmark next to Bea's name. "You're part of the pink group." *Pink.* Oh, how Bea despised the color pink. Jamie plucked a pink circle off her sticker sheet and handed it to Bea. "Just put this on your shirt so that our counselors know who is and isn't a part of their group. Though, I think you're with Reagan Hideaway. She's running a little late." Bea put the sticker on her shirt, and Jamie stepped aside so Bea could step onto the bus.

The other campers stood idly in the center of the aisle. They spoke loudly of their brief break between school and camp. Bea looked at them and wondered if she could just crawl into her backpack and hide. The reality of the coming week caved in on her as she squeezed between a pair of chatting girls and slumped into a ripped seat.

Hot and sticky, it burned her thighs. Sweat rolled down her neck, tickling her back. The bus, a tin can on wheels, had no air conditioning to combat the intense summer heat. Desperate for one last gulp of fresh air, Bea cracked open the window. The rusty metal frame stopped the pane short, leaving her with a thumb's width of breathing room.

Bea curled her hands into fists, and her nails bit deep into her palms. She wished she could pull out the sketchbook tucked into the front pocket of her backpack. On its pages were the many lands she whisked herself away to whenever she could. Places far, far away. With her sketchbook, Bea could empty her mind onto one of its many blank pages and escape. She pulled her bag closer and sighed in relief, knowing that she would soon be able to pour herself into her art.

"Hey, keep it down back there!"

Bea looked up. The bus driver's menacing stare coincidentally met with hers in the rear-view mirror, and his eyes squinted in an irritated glare. Bea's thoughts of escape quickly faded. She tore her gaze away and rested her head on the seat in front of her. Eye contact was more painful than the chaos around her.

She focused on the little cracks in the green vinyl rather than up where she might catch someone else's eyes. The stitching had come apart at the seams, and a one-inch gap sprouted pieces of stuffing. Years of bussing rowdy teens back and forth did not treat it well; the collage of graffiti a testimony to its wear. Its age shown by the many different phrases scribbled on it. Some told of love, some of hate. Some were poetic verse, while others were clearly written by those who had not quite found their voice.

Her eyes drifted toward the bottom of the seatback where they discovered a familiar symbol scribbled in what looked to be yellow sharpie. Its circles were slightly wobbly and the middle one looked more like a capital *D*, but it was there all right.

Again? Her muscles tensed, toes curling in her beat-up tennis shoes.

"Excuse me, is this seat taken?"

Bea jolted from her thoughts as a waft of overpowering citrus perfume filled her nostrils. She put her hand over her mouth to stifle a cough.

"Sorry, I didn't mean to startle you," a voice from under a pile of paisley bags said. "Mind if I sit?"

Seeing there was no escaping her, Bea mustered a weak "sure" and slid a couple of inches toward the window. As her seatmate stepped on the seat to hoist her bags on the rack above them, Bea searched the seatback in front of her for the symbol but found no traces of it.

A moment later, the girl flopped down into the seat next to Bea. She tossed her bright-red hair over her shoulders and turned her freckled face toward Bea. "Oh!" she exclaimed, pointing at Bea's pink sticker. "You're one of my campers. I'm Reagan." She smiled perfectly white teeth at Bea. "You must be…" She fished through her pocket and pulled out a plastic name tag on a string. "Beatrice? Jamie forgot to give you your tag up front." Reagan handed her the name tag. Bea took it apprehensively, hoping her clammy hands would go unnoticed. She hung it around her neck, feeling like a dog.

"You can call me Bea." She gazed around uncomfortably and shifted in her seat, hands reaching for pockets that weren't there.

"Nice to meet you, Bea," Reagan said. She put her knees up against the seatback in front of them and pulled out a thick book. Her hand, adorned with a collection of gold and silver rings, flipped open the cover and she dug into it.

Bea watched Reagan tug at a gold chain that drooped into her striped crop top. After a few pulls, a purple crystal popped up from under her shirt and swung loosely from the chain. Bea stared at the crystal, drawn to its jagged, sparkling surface. She wanted to reach out and touch it, but merely leaned in to get a better look.

"Have you read it?" Reagan flashed the cover of her book, which seemed to show a small eye inside a ring with three other

19

rings in a triangle around it. Bea almost gasped aloud, but soon realized it wasn't *the* symbol and leaned back in her seat.

Face flush from being caught staring, Bea stammered, "U-uh, no." She had regretfully chopped her hair into an uneven bob, which was now too short to hide behind.

"It's okay, fantasy isn't necessarily a genre for everyone." Reagan laughed and went back to reading.

Bea forced a flat smile and turned to gaze out the window. She leaned her head up against the glass and exhaled. Her eyes—glazed over from the past week's sleepless nights—fell shut as the bus engine sputtered to life and the window began to vibrate.

Bea woke to darkness. She reached out her hands and grasped for something, *anything*, to hold onto. Sweat beaded on her neck and forehead. Her fingers trembled; her eyes hunted for light.

The room burst to life, as if a mighty wave had broken through a barrier dam. Bea dropped to her knees and covered her stinging eyes. A ring of fire danced around her, its flames trapping her inside them.

The heat seared her skin. Flames sent sparks into the air with echoing pops, the tiny embers landing on her skin.

Distracted by the blaze, Bea almost did not notice the figure emerge from the conflagration. A man whose features were as dark as the cloak he wore strode powerfully into the circle of flames and stood before her, his white hair rolling out the sides of his hood and over his shoulders.

Bea lifted her head slowly, shielding her eyes from the light. He tilted his hood-shadowed face down to her.

"Beatrice Tidal," the man said, his voice distant and hollow.

"Who are you?" Bea asked.

The man said nothing more. He turned quickly and disappeared whence he had come.

"Wait! How do you know my name?" she called, but the man was gone. The flames faded, leaving Bea to wallow in the void.

THE LAST OLPHIN

Barnaby had come to detest his life. Well, *detest* was a rather harsh word for him. Perhaps *dislike* would be more suitable. He had spent his whole life tucked away inside Tide Tale Alley, shunned by the outside world, and forced to live within the walls of old Pemadee's bookshop.

He was sick of the same sights—the musty books on the overstuffed shelves, the wobbly reading chairs, the scarred oak floor, the storefront window and its view of the crumbling brick wall across the alleyway. He desperately wanted to get out and explore the oceanside city. He had been told it was a grand sight, had even seen it in a local guidebook. But he had never actually been there, of course. An Olphin in the streets of Ovallia would cause a wave of panic.

Barnaby took up his usual seat beside the front door, leaned his broom against the chair, and pulled out a tattered postcard from his pants pocket. The Eslurian Opera House. Nothing fascinated him more than that building—the very building that drew hundreds of Eslurians to Galecrest each year during the High Moon Festival. It was his dream to see its lush gold-embroidered curtains, its myriad rows of plush red seats, its glittering polished wooden stage...

But you won't ever let me see it, will you? He glanced up at the sign on the door, its paper yellowed and crackled. *Olphin Present.* The words were a warning to patrons and a constant reminder to him of who he was and would always be: an Olphin—*the last free Olphin.*

It felt as if the name had been branded onto his forehead, hovering over him like his own personal storm cloud. Barnaby Britto the Olphin. He could never escape. Eslura would never allow such a creature to roam her lands freely. Not after what the Olphins had done.

It was easy for Barnaby to hide the webbing between his fingers and toes and the scales that covered his body, even the little fins on his legs and arms could be hidden by his cloak, but the green fins that sprouted from his cheeks were a sure giveaway of who he truly was.

Nevertheless, thanks to Pemadee, he had been spared, spared from the sentence that imprisoned his people in the depths of Morgaedion nearly fourteen years ago. They had chosen the wrong side of the battle by taking up arms with Obellius, *the monster.* Barnaby was thankful that his lungs still breathed the air of the oceanside city, albeit filtered through the smell of moldy books and varnished wood, and not the dark and musty air of the prison his people had been condemned to. Pemadee had fought for his freedom, and for that he was very grateful.

But as much as Barnaby tried, his thankfulness always seemed to be drowned out by resentment. His life was a constant reminder of what his people did, a constant reminder of betrayal, suffering, and hatred. Yet, he yearned to be free.

There was, however, one thing that made his life just a tad more tolerable: Mauz.

The plump toad had found his way into Barnaby's life as if by magic. Barnaby would do just about anything for that cross-eyed, fairy-winged amphibian. Yes, he was a toad, warts and all, but there was something in the way he puttered about the air, his tiny wings struggling to hold up his round, little body, that Barnaby simply adored.

"Oh, Mauz," Barnaby said as he watched the toad bob up and down near the front counter, his tongue swinging loosely below him, "what in the name of Aezaros are you doing?" He laughed, stuffed the postcard in his pocket, and got up from his seat at the window to walk over to Mauz and pluck the frog from the air. "I've told you, you won't catch anything with your tongue hanging from your mouth like a dead worm. You actually have to *try* at some point." Barnaby pushed the tongue back into Mauz's mouth.

"Barnaby," Pemadee called from his office. "Come here, please."

Barnaby flung Mauz in the air and rushed toward the office, glancing at the broom still propped up against his chair, a reminder of the work he had not finished. "Yes, Mr. Pemadee?" He waited patiently outside the doorway of Pemadee's office, adjusting his glasses and straightening the collar of his shirt.

The shelves in the small office were stuffed with more books than Barnaby believed possible. A sole window on the back wall had also been jammed with books to fit its shape, leaving Pemadee to conduct his research under the light of a hanging lantern. On a side wall, completely surrounded by old tomes, stood a single glass display case containing a translucent grey stone.

Sitting at his cluttered desk in the center of the room, scratching an indecipherable script with a feather quill on a sheet of yellowed paper with one hand and digging his fingers into his bald scalp with the other, was the closest thing to family that Barnaby had ever known. After a moment, he lifted his head from the paper and looked at Barnaby in the doorway. "I need some air," he said, setting the quill down next to his inkpot. "Watch the store while I'm gone and keep on with your duties, understood?" He pushed back from the desk and the wood of his wheelchair squeaked into motion.

"Yes, Mr. Pemadee," Barnaby replied, nodding so feverishly he felt his gills flapping against his cheeks. Pemadee wheeled past him toward the door and Barnaby followed.

The bell chimed as Pemadee rolled out of the store, leaving Barnaby in the doorway. A rush of cool air filled the store in his exiting. Barnaby sucked in as much of it as he could before the door clattered closed. He knew the sea was only a stone's throw away; he could smell the salt, the fish, the sand and the seaweed. Long had he dreamt of plunging into the surf and letting the water filter in and out of his gills. He closed his eyes, envisioned the sea, and sighed.

Croak!

"Peppersnakes, Mauz!" Barnaby shouted. "Don't scare me like that, you know how jumpy I get." He turned away from the door...and his dream of the ocean.

Croak!

Mauz hovered over a piece of paper that the breeze must have swept off Pemadee's desk face-down onto the floor.

"What?" Barnaby asked the toad. Mauz croaked again, lowered himself down on top of the letter, and prodded the paper with his tongue.

"Don't be foolish." Barnaby shook his head. "You know I couldn't do that." Although he desperately wanted to, Pemadee had stressed to Barnaby time and time again that his personal belongings were none of Barnaby's business.

"We'll just put this back on the desk, okay?" Barnaby said. He scooped the paper up and turned to look back at the front door, which had not moved since Pemadee left. "Well," he said, fluttering the paper in his trembling fingers, "you don't think it would hurt to take a little peek, do you, Mauz?"

Mauz croaked and Barnaby flipped the letter over to skim the page, his heart racing in the daring act.

"What's this?" A small, blue candy was stuck to the bottom of the page. Someone had drawn six red arrows pointing to it. Barnaby plucked the candy off the paper, lifted it to his nose, and inhaled its rich, fruity scent.

"You don't suppose Mr. Pemadee would mind if I took just a little lick, do you?" He opened his mouth and plopped the whole candy inside, ran his tongue over its sugary surface, and decided that the flavor was delightfully sweet and delectably tart at the same time. "Mmm...it's quite all right! You want

26

a lick?" Barnaby plucked the candy from his mouth and held it out for Mauz. The toad ran his sticky tongue over its round surface several times. "Good, isn't it?" Barnaby asked. Mauz croaked and Barnaby took the candy from the toad's mouth and tossed it back in his. He sucked on it noisily as he skimmed the page of swooping script. *Dear Mr. Pemadee…*

Boring, boring, nothing of importance… *Olphin!* He stopped and stared at the word to be sure he had read it correctly.

Olphin. The word stuck in his throat like a fish bone. He swallowed nervously and continued to read.

"I'm either going mad, Mauz," he told the toad, "or there's another Olphin in Eslura." He could not believe the words as he spoke them. It must have been a terrible hoax.

Pemadee had never mentioned another Olphin living in Eslura. The news struck Barnaby like a hammer, smashing all he had thought to be true.

"Well, all right, all right," Barnaby said, swatting a hand at Mauz, who was tickling his gill with his tongue, "Give me a second. I know you're excited, but you don't have to get me all slobbery." Barnaby continued reading, his hands shaking with fear or excitement; he had not the spare thought to consider which.

"Whoever wrote this letter says there was an Olphin in Treenode, and it was only marked a few moons ago. You don't suppose they would still be there, do you? I mean, another free Olphin! Whaddya think, Mauz?" Barnaby hoped and prayed that the words were true.

"Stay here, Mauz," Barnaby said, wagging a finger at the toad. He set the letter back down on the floor, where he had found it. "I'll be back soon."

Mauz croaked.

"Oh, Mauz, don't you worry one bit." Barnaby patted Mauz's lumpy head and smiled. "I'll be okay." At least he hoped he would be okay. He scooped up his cloak from the hook by the door and wrestled his arms into it. He pulled his gloves from its pockets and slid them over his webbed hands.

If there was another Olphin in Eslura, Barnaby was determined to find them, even if it meant confronting the dangers of the world outside Tide Tale Alley. As beautiful as the world looked in photos, he knew it was crawling with scoundrels waiting to capture him and bring him to justice. The thought made him quiver.

Barnaby shoved away his fears, pulled his scarf from its hook, and wrapped it around his gills, letting the soft cloth rest over the brim of his nose just below his glasses.

He opened the door and the bell chimed, nearly scaring his little pants off him. The fresh breeze swept through his brown curls.

He stood outside in the alley; the storefront window no longer separating him from the world. He turned back and peered into the store, his home—and his prison—for his entire life. His chair was empty, his broom still propped up against it. His world, his safe space, was all behind him.

He let go of the knob and stepped forward.

CHAPTER FOUR

ESLURA'S CALLING

Bea woke to a hand on her shoulder. She squinted and blinked, adjusting her eyes to the mid-afternoon sunshine, realized that wasn't helping, and raised her hand to her forehead, shielding her eyes from the dazzling rays.

"Hey," Reagan said, smiling, "we're here." Bea looked around the bus. The other campers had already left, leaving a trail of crumpled candy wrappers and salty snack bags in their wake. She could hear them talking outside the bus. Their voices seeped in through the open windows, tearing away at her peace and quiet. She leaned her head against the back of her seat, closed her eyes again, and sighed. Then she got up, moaning of course, and followed Reagan down the aisle and out of the bus.

"Hey," Jamie, now wearing a blue *Camp Tossbridge* shirt, called and trotted over with a wave. "How'd ya sleep?" She smirked. "The other campers are hanging out in the cabins. Lunch is in about a half hour."

Lunch? How did it already get to be time for lunch? The last thing on Bea's mind was food. She was already nauseous from just being there. She grabbed her gut and felt like she might throw up.

"C'mon, I'll show you where to put your stuff," Reagan said. She led Bea under an arched sign that attempted to spell "*Camp Tossbridge,*" but only managed "*C—p T—sbri—e*" through the moss and overgrown vines that were consuming it, and down a path cratered with potholes of sloppy mud and water from the previous night's rainfall.

Wave-like fumes billowed through the air, distorting the several wooden buildings along the way and making Bea feel like she was in some sort of horrific dream. *Is this what not sleeping for a week makes you feel like?* She pressed her hand onto her scalp and found that it was covered with beads of sweat. She wiped them off on her shirt and hoped she didn't look as grimy as she felt.

"That's Gwenlyn Field." Reagan waved toward the field to her right. "It's where we'll be spending the most of our time." The field was the epitome of every camp field Bea had ever imagined. Volleyball nets, horseshoe pits, basketball courts, and picnic tables. A blackened firepit sat at its center. Sitting around a crackling fire sounded pretty nice, but when she factored in the other campers and the smoldering smell of smoke on her clothes, she decided she would rather not.

On the opposite side of Gwenlyn Field, where the ground sloped downward, was a clover-shaped pond overlooked by a large, A-frame lodge with a wraparound porch. The murky-brown water was half covered by lily-pads and cattails that she, at first glance, mistook for corn dogs on long sticks. A group of younger-looking campers leapt into the water without a moment's hesitation, splashing around and cheering as their counselor cannonballed in to join them.

"It's not as gross as it looks," Reagan said with a laugh, "I promise." Bea smirked. She knew. She had swum in her fair share of slimy pond water herself and lived to speak of it.

Bea and Reagan's journey ended on a grassy yard between four rundown shacks in a small clearing. Overgrowth strangled their sides and moss on their roofs bathed in what little sunlight that managed to break through the canopy of pines above. A densely packed maze of wood stretched endlessly around the clearing, reminding Bea of her old home.

"All we ask is that the campers don't venture into the woods by themselves," Reagan said while Bea gazed around at the rustic setting. "You know, just to keep everyone as safe as possible. It gets pretty rocky back there." Bea nodded and turned her attention back to Reagan. "All right, great!" Reagan smiled. "Well, welcome to your new home away from home, Bea." Reagan walked up two steps to the cabin in front of them and tapped her hand on a wooden sign that read *Black Oak Cabin*.

The cabin was tiny, musty, and hot, and smelled of sweaty bodies and mildew. Bea suspected this was due to the sole air conditioner being taped up with a sign that read "*out of order.*" A pill-shaped speaker sitting on a table in the middle of the room blasted upbeat pop music at an obnoxious volume, not that upbeat pop music was not obnoxious at any volume. Bea grimaced and wished she had snagged a pair of Joe's earplugs.

A half-dozen bunk beds, their mattresses sagging from decades of bouncing campers, were pressed against the moldy wooden walls. A couple of them had already been claimed by the duffel bags on top of them. The windows, two of which were boarded up, were darkened by the overgrowth hanging over them outside.

"We don't have a full group this year," Reagan told Bea, "so feel free to choose whichever empty bed you'd like. Each one has its own cubby too, so you can just unpack your stuff in there. If you need anything at all, holler. I'll be right over there in my room." She pointed to the propped-open door on the far side of the room. Through it, Bea could see Jamie already getting settled. She stood on tiptoes on a wobbly stool with a tack between her teeth, attempting to hang a poster of a shirtless man with a cowboy hat.

Reagan joined Jamie, leaving Bea standing in the center of the room, trying to decide which bed was the least bad. Most of the girls chose to clump together, taking up all six beds on the right side of the room, making the decision an easy one for Bea: left side of the room, far left corner.

She unloaded her bag into her cubby and pulled out her sketchbook. The worn leather surface bore the initials *CT* for her mother, Celine Tidal, the woman whose face she had not seen for nearly a year and a half.

She flipped through the pages, perusing the countless worlds unknown to anyone except Bea and her mother. Her 'escapes,' she called them. The places she found herself traveling to when the world failed to bring her comfort—which, given her current predicament, was more often than not.

Lost in the pages of her sketchbook, Bea did not notice the trio of girls prowling toward her corner of the cabin. "Well, well, well," said a voice she recognized immediately. It belonged to Wren Grout, the principal's daughter and self-made leader of the cheer girls, better known as 'the clones,' to most of the students at Mountbridge High School due to their inability to create unique personalities. "I certainly didn't expect to see you here." The lanky girl placed her hand on the bunk above Bea, trapping her as the other girls closed her in. Bea leaned back and tucked the sketchbook under her pillow, hoping that the pages wouldn't get crumpled.

"Wren," Bea said. It was more than she wanted to say.

"Mmm." Ava Grout, Wren's identical twin, pursed her lips. Her face was caked with enough makeup for a weeklong production of *The Rocky Horror Picture Show*. "I'm just as surprised as you are."

"Haha, yeah," Krista Letting, whose nasally voice always sounded like she always had a clump of snot lodged in her throat, snickered. "How is it being Mountbridge High's only dropout?"

"Yeah," Ava chimed in, "where did you disappear to, huh?"

Bea closed her eyes and took a deep breath. Not only did 'the incident' put distance between her and Fran and Joe, but it also caused her to be pulled from school and admitted to Mountbridge Psych Ward. Three days she spent holed up in that cage, three, painfully long and dull days trying to prove her sanity.

"Krista, Ava," Wren fake gasped, "too soon!" Ava put a hand over her mouth to hide her laughter and Krista shrugged. Bea scooted closer to the wall, hoping that if she didn't feed into their comments they would give up and leave her alone.

"Whatcha got there, Bea?" Ava cocked her head.

"Nothing." Bea didn't even convince herself with the lie, let alone the snickering witches.

"What is it, Bea?" Wren leaned in and hissed like the snake she was. "Don't you know it's not nice to keep secrets from your friends?" *Friends*. Bea let the word sit for a moment. *Friends*. She really let it sink in. Friends didn't start rumors that you left school because you were pregnant. They didn't steal your clothes from the pool locker room or throw ketchup on your pants to make it look like you'd…y'know…

"Yeah, c'mon Bea," Krista snorted, reaching her hand down toward the pillow. Bea put her hand on the pillow before Ava could touch it.

"Please, stop," Bea pleaded. The words caught in her throat and came out like a stutter. The girls laughed, though Bea could not hear the sounds coming from their open mouths. All she could hear was the terrible music blasting from Jamie's speaker. It rang in her ears, making her want to bury her head under her pillow and hide with the sketchbook.

"What?" Ava looked down her nose at Bea. "What's wrong, Bea?" The other girls egged Ava on.

"Hey girls." Reagan came up from behind them, breaking through their circle. She put her hands on her hips. "Is everything all right over here?" She looked down at Bea, frowned, and narrowed her eyes at the girls.

Krista pulled her hand away and shoved it into her pocket. "Of course! We were just catching up with Bea. It's been a while." She grinned, showing off her rainbow-colored braces.

*Lying, scheming, little…*Bea bit her lip.

"Mmm," Reagan hummed, her lips pursed. "Why don't you girls go start a line by the door? It's about time we head over to the mess hall for lunch." They gave Bea a final dirty look and walked toward the cabin door. Bea stared at her grey mattress, embarrassed.

"I'm sorry about that," Reagan said. "Between me and you"—she leaned down a bit and cupped her hands around her mouth—"I can't stand them one bit, and yet they keep getting assigned to my group. Two years in a row. You know how painful that is?" Reagan rolled her eyes and Bea muffled a laugh with her fist. "They won't bother you again, I promise." Bea highly doubted her ability to keep that promise, but she looked up and mustered a "thanks" anyways.

Reagan led the group of girls across Gwenlyn Field to the mess hall. Storm clouds hung low in the sky and tiny drops of rain fell on their heads. A line of campers, both older and younger than Bea, had already formed outside the building, huddling beneath the overhang to escape the rain. Some held their trays above their heads as makeshift umbrellas, while others ignored it and eagerly awaited whatever food was attached to the smoky smell that wafted out the window.

The bright, fluorescent lights inside the hall irritated Bea's eyes. Handmade posters decorated the side walls and a splotchy mural of painted handprints covered most of the back wall. A few grumpy-looking staff members lurked in the kitchen, near the front of the room, and doled out their meal.

Bea made her way up the line and placed her tray on the long table in front of the serving staff. One of the lunch ladies, whose green hair was held back by fishnets, grabbed a foil-wrapped burger and a bottle of water from two stainless steel tubs and placed them on her tray.

When Bea turned to face the room, every table was full, and her heart started to race. Her chest tightened, and she felt herself getting ready to hyperventilate. She stood and gaped at the scene, not knowing where to go or whom to sit next to.

"Excuse me?" Someone tapped her shoulder. A boy behind Bea leaned around her and gave her a look as if to say, "*Move it.*" She realized she was still standing at the front of the line, blocking the other campers from getting their food.

She took a step toward the crowd, mustered a smidgen of courage, which was all she had at the time, and squeezed through the maze of circular tables, dodging chairs that scraped across the floor and ducking under hands that jutted out across the tight aisles. At last, she found an empty table in the back corner of the room by the fire door. She sat down and used her napkin to wipe away some splotches of mayonnaise and a small puddle of unrecognizable green sauce on its surface. She then pulled out her sketchbook from her bag, double checked the table was clean, and flipped to a new page.

Two tables over, she heard her name being passed around in conversation. Wren, Krista, Ava, and six other girls were seated at a large table. They cupped their hands and whispered to one another, snickering and looking toward Bea to see if she heard.

She did.

As if it couldn't get any worse, Wren, Krista, and Ava stood up, lifted their trays, and strolled over to Bea's table.

"Hey, Bea." Wren put down her tray. "Whatcha got there?"

Bea closed the cover of the book and went to tuck it under her seat, but Ava crouched quickly and grabbed its cover.

"Whoa, whoa, whoa," Ava said. She had either smeared her lipstick with her food or had ketchup on her face—it was hard to tell. "Aren't you gonna let us see it? All you ever did in school was draw in this thing. Is that why they kicked you out?"

Bea rolled her eyes. She wished she had gotten kicked out, but that just wasn't the case. She scanned the crowd for Reagan, but she was nowhere to be seen.

"Oh!" Krista laughed into Bea's ear. "You're looking for your little friend, aren't you? Well, she's all the way across the room." Krista pointed at Reagan, who stood chatting with another counselor. "Don't you see? Busy with someone other than you."

Bea fought Ava's hold on the book, but the girl dug her long, fake nails into its cover.

"Let go of it, you little—" Ava kicked Bea's chair and jerked the book from Bea's grasping hands. "Sheesh." Ava rolled her eyes. "You'd think she was hiding a million dollars in the thing." Ava flipped through the book's pages seeming to make sure that no hundred-dollar bills were actually tucked inside. "It's just a bunch of stupid drawings? Who cares?" She handed the book to Wren, and the three girls sat down at Bea's table.

Krista nudged Bea with her elbow. "Did your momma teach you how to draw like that?" Thunder rumbled in the distance.

"What a shame! Poor old Ms. Tidal couldn't stand her loser

daughter anymore so she up and left." Ava put her hands on her rouged cheeks and pouted her ketchup lips.

"Girls, please," Wren said, "we don't want to hurt her feelings, do we?" She smirked at Bea and flipped the page in the sketchbook. "Hmm…" She looked over the top of the book. "Speak of the devil herself, Ms. Celine Tidal."

Bea clenched her fists in her lap and tried hard not to swing one at Wren's cheek. She did not want to test her odds against the girls. Her bi-weekly mandatory gym class where she hid in the bathroom half the time did not prepare her for this. She eyed the rest of the campers at the tables around them. No one was paying any attention to the trio or Bea, and her only hope, Reagan, was preoccupied across the room.

"You know what?" Wren tapped her finger on her chin. "She looks just like you, Bea. A little not-quite-there-in-the-head, ya know what I mean?"

"Oo, oo, lemme see!" Krista begged. She scooted forward and tried to look over Wren's shoulder.

"Patience, Krista! You'll get your turn," Wren snapped. She elbowed Krista in the side. Krista wobbled in her chair and nearly fell off.

"Give it back," Bea mumbled.

"Oh, I'm sorry, did you say something, Beatrice? Could you speak a little louder for me? I just can't seem to hear you when you speak like a church mouse." Wren cupped her ear and leaned closer.

"I said…" Bea looked up and leaned across Ava to get face to face with Wren. "Give. It. Back!" She reached for the book, but Ava slapped her hand away.

"Hey!" Wren recoiled, clutching the book to her chest. "Don't be so rude. I'm not done with it yet. I haven't had enough time with Ms. Tidal." Wren pursed her lips and lifted the book to her face. She cleared her throat as if she were about to begin reading. "After all, she spent her whole life hiding away in the woods." Bea grit her teeth. *If the world wasn't full of nasty witches like you, maybe she wouldn't have been hiding in the first place.*

Bea never thought to question her mother's way of living. She never considered it out of the ordinary, either. It wasn't until she moved in with Fran and Joe that she got her first taste of the outside world and its overly harsh judgements and single-minded nature. She despised it more than anything. She had all she needed in the woods with her mother and didn't have to deal with the likes of the trio while she was there. To her, there was no better way to live than in the woods alone with her mother.

A flash of lightning splintered through the sky, and the lights of the mess hall flickered on and off. A few of the younger campers screamed, then giggled and went back to talking.

"You know what they used to say about your mother, Beatrice?" Thunder clapped, and Wren continued, "They used to say that the reason she chose to live all the way out there in those woods was so that the world wouldn't have to deal with her freak show of a daughter."

Bea leapt up and lunged at the book. The lights flickered again, and Bea grabbed the front cover and pulled with all her weight. Wren clung onto the back cover, laughing and pulling. The book ripped in half and Bea felt like her heart did the same.

"Oops." Wren smiled and threw half the book on the table.

"Wren!" Reagan called. *Oh, now you're here.*

"C'mon, let's go!" Wren snapped at Ava and Krista. They got up and ran to the bathroom.

"Hey!" Reagan yelled again, running after them, but she stopped halfway and turned back to Bea.

Bea picked up the back half of the book and ran out the fire escape. The alarm rang, but she didn't care. All she could think was to run. Fast and far. Into the woods, and out of sight. She wanted to be away from Camp Tossbridge, away from those wenches.

Despite the darkness of the black storm clouds blotting out the sun, Bea felt safer in the woods. They reminded her of home, of her mother, of her childhood, of her...everything. Everything she knew was in the woods.

She ran. Ran through the rain, which started as a trickle and turned into a downpour, soaking her hair flat to her head and running down her cheeks like tears. *No, not tears.* She was stronger than that, she told herself. Stronger than them. Stronger than their cruel words. They didn't matter. And she didn't care. She wiped her face. Wiped the rain, not the tears.

She ran down a game trail, jumping over roots, slipping on wet leaves, slapping branches away from her face. Lightning lit the trail and thunder rolled overhead. After she'd run a good while, she tired and leaned against a tree trunk, panting as rain poured over her face and off her nose. She glanced up and spotted a cave beyond a couple of birch trees.

With nowhere left to go, she pushed through the wet leaves,

entered the cave, collapsed onto a large smooth rock and closed her eyes, not sure she ever wanted to get up again. She lay there until her breathing slowed then tried to wring her clothes free of their weight. The storm continued to rage outside, lightning spider-webbed across the sky lighting up the mouth of the cave, and thunder crashed overhead, shaking the rocks around her.

When she opened her eyes, she saw stalactites hanging from the ceiling like crooked teeth. Rotted vines and overgrowth, pale grey from years in the darkness, draped the walls and snaked across the ground. At the back of the cave was a tunnel that led quickly into blackness. Although the musty smell of the cave made her wheeze, it beat standing in the thunderstorm soaking wet.

Bea sat up and buried her face in her hands. She began to sniffle and wiped her nose with her sleeve. As much as she hated to admit it, she did not want to be alone any longer. That's all. She just wanted to be with her mother again, to feel her arms around her again. A year and a half was too long. Where the heck was she?

She cursed the stupid storm, which responded with a powerful gust of wind that whipped through the cave. She wrapped her arms around her to ward off the chill. Then, in a fit of anger, she clenched her fist and slammed it down on the stone. Pain soared through her hand and wrist and up her arm. She clutched her wrist and pulled her hand up to her face to examine the damage. A deep gash welled with blood, throbbing with the beat of her heart. She stared at it for a moment, wondering if she would need stitches, until she suddenly realized that everything around her had gone completely silent.

An ambient golden glow slowly filled the cave. She looked toward the mouth of the cave to see if someone had entered with a flashlight, but no one was there. Bea thought that maybe she was finally going nuts. It had been a long time coming, but she'd expected it, nevertheless. She turned back toward the tunnel to see if the light was coming from the darkness within. A figure stood there, barely visible, but surrounded by a golden aura. Suddenly, Bea smelled a familiar scent, lemon drop, perhaps, with something else like…home.

"Mom?" she asked aloud before she'd had a moment to think of how absurd it sounded. She stood up from the rock and listened as the figure called out, "Beatrice," in a disturbingly familiar voice. Then the figure and its aura turned and began shrinking away into the darkness of the tunnel.

"Wait!" Bea hollered. And then again, "Mom?" She sprinted toward the tunnel, following the diminishing golden glow as it wound into the darkness. She ran as fast as she could, barely able to see in the fading radiance. She stumbled over some loose rocks, nearly bashing her head on the jagged stone wall, and kept on running.

"Wait!" Her voice echoed through the tunnels. She was losing the light and realized she would be hopeless if she'd let it completely disappear. "Wait! Mom!"

*Mom…mom…mom…*echoed back to her from the dimness ahead. And then the light disappeared.

Bea pressed ahead slowly. At first, the tunnel was straight and then it seemed to enter a series of twists and turns, left, right, up then down until she no longer had any idea which way she was going. She thought about turning around, but the way back was cloaked in complete darkness. The golden glow must have gone somewhere, she thought, so she pressed on, feeling the blood trickle down her forearm. It was a stupid thing, she decided, to follow a light down a tunnel. She began to doubt if she'd even seen a light at all, when the tunnel seemed to make a tight downward spiral and a diffused light appeared on the rocky wall ahead. She stumbled forward a little faster toward the light. As she came into it, the rugged rocks became smoother and the tunnel opened up into a large, circular stone cavern, lit by a nearly blinding golden glow emanating from its center. Sure enough, from the depths of the golden aura, Bea's mother emerged, arms spread and waiting.

"Beatrice," her voice, flowing like honey, filled the stillness of the cavern.

Bea stepped forward...her mother disappeared.

"No!" Bea fell to her knees on the hard stone.

The smothering darkness returned, swallowing Bea, and leaving her in the pitch-black void.

Bea knelt there exhausted, not knowing what to do. Her dress was stiff, its once loose hem now chafing her thighs. Her fist ached and throbbed. She dabbed at her wound with the cloth of her dress but found that doing so made it hurt even worse.

She sat back on her bottom and thought about what to do. A small part of her hoped Reagan, or someone, would come find her and bring her back to her cabin. But she also just wanted to be alone with the bats and the spiders and whatever else lived in the dark cavern. She almost wanted to be a bat herself. Life in the darkness could be an escape of its own.

Suddenly, though, a dim light seemed to illuminate her left knee, scraped and bruised as it was from running through the woods. The light came from the wall of the cave to her left where a golden glowing symbol stretched across the surface. Five, intertwining circles. *A five-fold. The symbol.*

"No, it can't…it can't be." Bea shook her head and looked at it again. Still there. She rubbed her eyes until they watered, and yet it remained pulsing, dimmer then brighter, again and again. She couldn't pull her eyes away from it. It was so out of place, yet it was so appropriate that the darn thing would follow her here. She stood up with a groan and walked over to it. It seemed to flow with an energy of its own. As she got closer, a golden mist cascaded out of the wall where the symbol was inscribed. Bea could feel its extreme power on the tips of her fingers, on her face, on her bare arms and legs.

A bright light emanated from the vibrating symbol, forcing her to clamp her eyes shut. She reached out to touch its glowing rings, unable to help herself. The cavern began to tremble, and tiny cracks ran through the once smooth stone walls. She touched the glowing symbol and a shock like lightning ran through her. Her muscles froze and she screamed. She looked down at her hand and realized it was sunk into the stone up to her wrist, the bright glow rising up her arm. It was pulling her in, into the stone wall. Impossible! She put her foot to the base of the wall, tried to pull back, but she was in past her elbow. She wanted to cry for help, but who was around? Who would even believe it? They'd send her back to Mountbridge

44

for 'treatment.' No!

The light flashed, blinding her. The wall had eaten up her arm, and her face was nearly pressed against the cold stone. Shards of wall crumbled from the trembling ceiling and the ground vibrated beneath her feet. She clenched her teeth, pushed with all her strength against the wall with her knees and other hand, but she could not pull away.

"Bea!" a familiar voice shouted from behind her. Bea could barely turn her head. It was pressed so tightly against the wall all she could do was roll her eyes around to see Reagan reaching for her free arm. "Grab my hand!" she yelled. Bea extended her arm back and Reagan grabbed it and pulled. Bea thought her shoulder was coming out its socket, but the rest of her did not move. She felt her cheek against the stone and gritted her teeth…and heard a loud *pop*.

She was tumbling in a black void, plunging into darkness. A roaring wind tossed her around like a leaf falling in an autumn storm. All she could see was the absence of light. She tried to scream, but no sound came out her mouth. She flailed her arms, grasping at emptiness, anything that might stop her fall. She knew that symbol would eventually be trouble. She should have—

A huge flash of golden light nearly blinded her, and she plunged into icy-cold water, a lake, an ocean, or a pond, she knew not which, but it was cold. She was no longer floating in emptiness—she was submerged in water—and that had to be good. She held her breath. Now she just had to find which way was up.

CHAPTER FIVE

LITTLE DRAGONS

Far in the north and nestled between a range of towering peaks, the floating city of Galecrest never escaped a day without a little snow. The silver buildings were cloaked in white, except their spires, which rose up into the low-hanging clouds. Several dozen windmills churned in the wind, and their loud, yet calming sounds masked the commotion of the midday hustle.

Millennium took a deep breath and tucked her chin into her scarf. She stood on her bedroom balcony, her hands resting on the rail, cold wind whipping through the air, and gazed down at her kingdom. Then, she looked to the sky. The winged beasts who normally zipped through the clouds like blurs of red, blue, and green, were nowhere to be seen. *I wonder where it is the dragons have all disappeared to?*

"Millennium," Ferhant called her from the doorway, "the

children have arrived." He stood with his hands clasped behind his back. Though she had known her loyal Sacred Guard since her choosing ceremony, she had yet to see what he actually looked like. A dragon-horned mask covered his face, and long, grey robes draped his figure.

"Excellent." She smiled and pushed the thought of the dragons to the back of her mind. She had other *dragons* to attend to. "Show them in, please."

Ferhant bowed and left the room. A few moments later, he returned with a gaggle of children—her "little dragons."

Each new moon, the children visited her castle for a recounting of some of Eslura's ancient tales.

"Welcome, little dragons!" she said in greeting. "How are we today?" She opened her arms in a broad gesture of welcome. The children responded by rushing to claim a cushion from the six Ferhant had set out in a circle that morning.

"Easy," Millennium laughed and walked to her stool in front of the cushions. "There's a spot for everyone." She waved Ferhant over and he handed her a large, moss-colored tome and left them to their stories.

"Now, where were we again, my little dragons? My old brain cannot seem to recall." Millennium rubbed her chin, cracked open the old book, and flattened its yellowed pages. The children, each one eager to answer her, jumped up and down and flailed their arms.

"Well, all right, all right. We're all a little excited, aren't we? Why don't we just pick up at the beginning of chapter two? How does that sound?" The children cooed with pleasure at her proposal and shuffled to get comfortable on their cushions. Once they had settled, Millennium cleared her throat and began:

"One sour morning, the skies parted ways and opened up to let fall the stone—a gift from gods greater than even than the gods themselves, a tool for creation, but, alas, for destruction as well."

Millennium was just getting her voice warmed up when Ferhant opened the door and entered the room once again, his eyes wide through the slits on his mask.

"Yes, Ferhant?"

"Millennium, please pardon the intrusion, but we must talk…urgently, I'm afraid." Millennium stood from her stool, set the book on it, and followed Ferhant to the hallway.

"Best close the door, madam," the steward said.

Millennium turned to close the door, spying a few of the children flipping through the pages of the book. *Impatient little things*, she thought and clicked it shut.

"What is it, Ferhant?" she asked.

"It's the dragons."

"What about them? They seemed to be absent from the skies this morning when I took air on my balcony."

"Indeed. It appears as though they've fallen into a…a predicament."

"A 'predicament'? Ferhant, please spare me the trouble of deciphering your true meaning, if you would be so kind."

"They are dying."

Dying. Her heart nearly stopped beating, then picked up thrice as fast.

Millennium dashed down the stairs in a flurry. She ran

out of her castle and weaved her way through the bustling city square, shifting her scarf so its soft fibers concealed her identity. Now was not the time to stop for a chat with the locals; under any other circumstance, she would be more than willing to entertain them.

She arrived at the dragons' nests in the lower quarter of the city and found the dragons huddled together and grim faced.

"Oh, my sweet darlings." She knelt beside a yellow and green pair closest to the mouth of the cave and brushed her hands over their scales. They were icy cold to the touch. "Oh my goodness! What's happened?" Every knowledgeable Galecrestian knew that a dragon's scales were naturally scalding. "You poor things. You're freezing. You must be so scared." As a dragon shifter, the Sacred Ruler of the Book of Air, Millennium could feel their pain.

"They look confused," Ferhant said behind her. He appeared to be quite out of breath, leaning his hands on his knees and panting like a dog.

"Ah, Ferhant, you startled me." Millennium put her hand over her heart. "I didn't know you'd followed me."

"My apologies," he said with a bow. "I assumed you would know, considering it is my duty to do just so."

"And the children?" she asked, realizing that she had left in such a hurry that she had forgotten to make arrangements for their supervision.

"Taken care of," Ferhant told her with another bow.

Millennium trusted her Guard implicitly and she turned her attention back to the dragons. "They've lost their powers. They're as cold as stone."

"Impossible." He knelt and cautiously touched the green dragon with his index finger. "This cannot be."

Millennium wished he was right but knew better than to give herself false hope. She stood and looked west toward Zybersia from the cave mouth. "Something has happened to the Book of Fire. Do you agree?"

"There can be no other explanation," Ferhant replied. "Something must have cut them off from the book's energy."

"Have you received any gullys from the Sacred Guard in Zybersia?"

Ferhant shook his head. "No."

Millennium rubbed her chin. With no Sacred Ruler currently presiding over Zybersia—the last having been murdered by the usurper, Obellius Kalaar—it would only be a matter of time before the city fell victim to the shadows. Without the power of the Book, there would be nothing to protect the city against the darkness—the same darkness that threatened to take the lives of the dragons lying before her.

"I must alert the other Rulers immediately. This is far too dangerous to send word by gully. The gods only know what chaos would ensue if that message were to be intercepted. If our assumptions are true, the city must be in complete disarray."

"I fear for the worst," Ferhant said, gazing into the distance.

"Keep watch on the dragons," Millennium told him. "If the situation worsens, send for me immediately. Understood?"

Ferhant bowed, and she left him in the cave's mouth.

Millennium walked hurriedly down the short path toward the lower edge of the city. She decided she would fly to Blighburrow and Ovallia, too, but first she would check on the Book of Fire in Zybersia. At the ledge, she closed her eyes and let herself fall off the ledge, plummeting toward the earth. She felt a surge of energy rush through her as the power of the Book of Air took hold of her.

From the bottom of her spine, a tail coiled out like a snake. Claws stretched outward from her fingertips. Horns thrust from her head, and fur stretched down her back, blustering in the wind. Purple scales rose from her skin, reflecting the sunlight as she steadied on a gust of wind. She soared upward, into the puffy grey clouds. The massive, floating city shrunk to the size of a pebble and disappeared below her as she beamed up toward the heavens.

She flew until the sun fell behind the mountains and a blanket of stars wrapped the sky, stopping only when a flash of golden light nearly blinded her. She covered her eyes with her clawed forefoot and waited. When the light subsided, she felt a new weight in the atmosphere, a feeling she had felt once before many years ago, when the sky had also turned gold, when Eslura last claimed a Sacred Head.

She weighed her options and changed her course, following the source of light toward Farenworth.

CHAPTER SIX

SHADOWS

Bea flailed in the water, paddling and kicking. It was black as night and cold like the empty, loneliness of solitude. When she finally stopped thrashing, the buoyancy of the air in her lungs began to lift her. At last, her head broke through the surface, and she gasped for air, mouth gaping like a beached fish, choking and spitting. She went under again, and she kicked her legs to come back up. It was nighttime, but clear enough to see two moons hanging in the purple sky above her. Her vision was spinning. Certainly, it must have been. There was no such thing as two moons in the sky. She struggled to stay above the surface as she looked for land. After a moment, she spotted some tufts of grass in the moonlight not too far away.

Dress soaked and freezing, Bea shivered as she made her way to the nearby shore. She clambered up on the grassy bank and lay on her back, staring up at the night sky. An army of shimmering stars flanked an unnaturally large golden moon and a much smaller purple moon. She rubbed her eyes, hoping one of the moons would go away, but when she opened them again, both moons stared down at her like she was totally nuts.

Maybe she had passed out on that rock in the cave. Hit her head, perhaps? Her mother, that gold light, those moons, all some sort of bizarre fever dream.

She sat up and looked around. In the sparkling light of the moons, she saw a sprawling lake surrounded by a vast and dense wood. At first, she hoped she wasn't too far from Camp Tossbridge. After all, Reagan had come to try to rescue her, hadn't she? Then she looked up again at those two moons. Why two? Just to make her think that she was crazy? She pinched the skin of her forearm to see if she was dreaming, but the pain was real. The lake was real. The forest was real. The two moons...

A gust of chill wind howled through the woods near the lake and blew over Bea, raising goosebumps on her arms. She hugged herself for warmth, but her dress was soaking wet, and it did little good. She contemplated getting up and walking somewhere when she heard the crack of a stick nearby, then a rustle in the grass. She looked around, trying to keep her cool, and for a moment, she could have sworn she saw a pair of eyes blinking at her through the brush, but on a second glance, there was nothing but grass and woods and the lake.

"Hello?" she called, half hoping no one would answer. The wind whipped up again, tousling her hair. She reached a hand up to fix her part but stopped halfway.

"What?" She held her wrist out in front of her face and stared at it, arms trembling in the chill. Five interlocking golden rings were inscribed on her skin like a fancy tattoo. *How the...?* She felt her throat tightening, her heart speeding; she prepared to run but froze when she heard a loud splash in the lake and saw the water rippling in all directions.

A head popped up gulping for air, arms flailing. Bea crawled backwards towards the brush, staring at the water, and stopping only when she backed into the trunk of a tree. She kept watch on the person as they made their way to the shore. From such a distance, Bea could not pick out the features of their face. She leaned forward and squinted but stopped when a stick snapped beneath her.

The person turned at the sound and peered toward Bea. "Hello?" a familiar voice cried out. *Reagan.*

Bea crawled forward out of hiding and called out. "Reagan?"

"Bea?" Reagan responded. "Is that you?" She jogged over toward the brush and joined Bea at the edge of the forest, her bright-red hair plastered to her face, the crystal on her necklace glimmering in the moonlight. "Oh, thank goodness you're okay!" She clutched Bea's shoulders. "You are okay, right?"

Reagan's rings dug into Bea's shoulders for a second, but she said, "Yeah, I'm all right. Just a little cold is all." She held her right wrist to cover the mark. *Stupid thing, why now?* She clenched her chattering teeth. She couldn't tell Reagan about the symbol. It was too...crazy. She would have to find a way to hide it before the sun came up—if there even was a sun wherever they were.

Reagan released Bea's shoulders and glanced around. She looked up at the moons and seemed to come to the same conclusion as Bea—something was terribly…wrong.

"Weird dream?" Reagan smiled awkwardly.

"I wish."

"Where the heck are we?" Reagan asked.

"I don't know," Bea said. Everything before waking up in the lake felt like more of a dream than the strange, new world around them. All she could recall of the events was a blinding flash of gold light…and her mother.

Reagan shrugged. "Well, we have to figure out where we are and how to get back to Tossbridge."

Tossbridge. Of all the things that Bea did remember, camp regrettably had to be one of them. Though she had no intention of going back there, Bea nodded. "Wait." She glanced around.

"What is it?" Reagan stared at her, then began looking around.

"I don't know," Bea said. "Something just doesn't feel right." She felt cold suddenly, colder than she had in the Dildeckers' attic on a deep winter night. She looked down. Black smoke cascaded across the ground and over their feet, covering them entirely. Thick clouds floated across the sky, engulfing the light of the moons and casting the two girls in an inky darkness. Fear crept over Bea as her vision was reduced to but an inch around her. All was complete silence save for Reagan and Bea's tremulous breathing.

A gust of wind split the clouds, and a sliver of light fell on the far side of the lake, illuminating a plume of smoke.

Reagan crouched beside Bea and whispered, "What is that?"

The question did not have a simple answer, Bea concluded. The cloud of smoke appeared to take the shape of a man, but its constant roiling made it seem ephemeral, perhaps not really there at all. "I don't know, but it doesn't look good."

"It's moving," Reagan said. The plume shifted and began to float around the lake toward them. "Come on, let's get out of here!" She grabbed Bea's hand and pulled her into the woods.

They sprinted down a rough trail, but the smoke caught up with and rose up around them, wrapping around the trees and cloaking everything in darkness. They pressed forward with their hands out in front of them to feel for a clear path.

"Reagan, where are you?" Bea called.

"I'm right here," she said. Bea felt her hand land on her shoulder but could not make her out through the blackness.

"Do you hear that?" Bea heard hooves clomping on packed dirt from up ahead.

Before Reagan could answer, the smoke dissipated slightly, and a cloaked figure on horseback swung around them and stopped at their side.

"Take my hand," the rider said, reaching a gloved hand out for Bea. It was an old man's voice, but she could not see his face beneath his hood.

Bea looked back toward the approaching, swirling smoke figure and realized she had no other choice but to accept his hand. Her fingers laced between his, and he hoisted her up onto the back of the horse. She realized it had no saddle and felt like she was sliding off its bony back. She grabbed the creature's sides next to her knees and realized its hair felt exactly like the AstroTurf on the soccer field at Mountbridge High.

"You too!" He extended his hand toward Reagan, glancing over his shoulder at whatever it was that was gaining on them. Reagan nodded and he pulled her up. She squeezed behind Bea, pressing her against the back of the man's cloak, which was lined with spikes. She shifted her hips back a few inches and wondered what kind of man wore spikes on his back. Maybe he was a biker? Bea thought. She had seen bikers with spikes on their clothes before.

The man clicked his tongue and squeezed with his legs, launching the horse into a full gallop through the trees. The smoke and shadows trailed closely behind, weaving through the trees almost as if they weren't there.

"Lower your heads," the man said with surprising calmness. Bea ducked and felt Reagan's head rest against her back.

The rider shouted, "Rise!" and Bea couldn't help sneaking a peek. He turned his upper body and extended his hand back to Bea's left. Green light erupted from his glove and shot down the path behind them toward the smoke. Bea watched the limbs of the trees on the sides of the path weave together across the path; roots came up from the ground in an explosion of dirt and leaves and wound themselves in the branches to completely block the way behind them. Bea wasn't sure if she was glad that the smoke figure was blocked or terrified that she was riding on a galloping horse with some kind of sorcerer through the woods to an unknown destination.

"Ya!" the man shouted to his horse. He turned forward and nudged the horse with his boot. It sped down the path far faster than the Dildeckers' old Dodge Dart could ever dream to on the highway.

"We are almost there," the man said over his shoulder as if "there" was a place that Reagan and Bea should have known. The thick forest opened to a field, and the sky cleared of its black clouds, allowing the stars and the moons to peer down on them again. Bea leaned to her left to look ahead of them and saw a small village spread out in a meadow.

Bea thought for a moment that her eyes were deceiving her. The houses looked tiny, and their mossy roofs blended in with the graceful roll of the grassy field. Had they simply passed by it, she might have missed the village entirely. As they got closer, the shattered windows, crooked, open doors, and overgrown vines led her to believe that the place had been abandoned for some time. The whole place was a creepy ghost town, though certainly not anywhere near Camp Tossbridge.

They rode through the middle of the town up to a house that stood slightly taller than the rest. Unlike its neighboring structures, it seemed to be untouched by the overgrowth and its windows were intact. Its alabaster white front sparkled like gold in the light of the moons.

"We don't have much time," the man said as they slowed to a stop. Bea still had not seen his face but wasn't really sure she wanted to. He brought his horse to a halt beside the house. "The Shadow Reaper will follow our trail." He dismounted and his hood caught in the wind, revealing his green face. Bea knew she was tired, but when he took off his glove to help her dismount, his hand was definitely green as grass; and, perhaps worse, it was covered with tiny scales.

She hesitated to accept his gesture, but he had saved them from whatever shadow…*thing* was following them. She took it and slid to the ground.

The horse, now illuminated by the light of the moons, was not much of a horse at all. Although its shape resembled those of the horses at Halo Creek Farm outside Mountbridge, its body was made entirely out of dark-green grass, and its ears were leaves. Its mane and tail were vines woven with pink and purple flowers, and its hooves had rough bark like the trunk of a tree.

"Thank you, Kuma," the man said, patting the beast's back. It whinnied with pleasure and then knelt on the ground. Bea watched as the grass on its back merged with the grass on the ground and grew out to match its length, leaving no trace of its ever being a horse…or whatever it was.

She blinked twice, unsure of what she had just witnessed. The horse, once standing tall before them, now sunk into the earth beneath their feet, gone.

"Come, we must move," the man said. He hurried toward the house, which, though bigger than the other houses, looked too small to fit all three of them at once. He rattled the handle on the little door, which was about up to his midsection, and it popped open to a darkened interior.

"Please." The man gestured toward the tiny doorway. Bea and Reagan shared a look of confusion. What could they do? Where else would they go? Surely not back to where the shadows were. "You must hurry," the man said again. Bea looked at her wrist, the symbol, then sank to her knees on the grass and crawled through the door and into the darkness.

CHAPTER SEVEN

TEA GONE COLD

"Harp," Lumikki addressed her loyal Sacred Guard as the two of them walked down the cobbled street, "what do you make of the mark on that merchant's wrist?" She lifted the jar in her hand. It contained a collection of pink and red flower petals and translucent green stones. Amidst the chaos of the afternoon's audience, a traveling merchant, who claimed to reside in Blighburrow, the neighboring forest kingdom, had given her the colorful gift. He had promised its contents would relieve the nagging thoughts that had plagued her all day since what happened that morning with her twin brother, Remidigon, but Lumikki did not believe anything could soothe her dread.

When the merchant had extended his hand to give her the jar, his sleeve had slid up, and she'd noticed a strange marking on his wrist, just above his hand. It was one she had never seen before—two intersecting vertical circles pierced through the middle by what looked to be a fork in a road. Though skin decorations and tattooing were not uncommon in Eslura, she had never seen this particular design before, and it rather vexed her.

Harp shrugged. "I wouldn't have thought anything of it till you asked. Perhaps a new gang has surfaced in Varaar?"

"Hmm," she hummed, peering at the flowers and stones in the jar. "Perhaps. My mind is a bit on edge today." And rightfully so. The two had just parted the bustling town square, where Lumikki had spent a tirelessly long and boring afternoon addressing the petty concerns of the people of Ovallia, or at least she pretended to address them.

On any other occasion, a full schedule outlined with obligations would have energized her. She loved spending time with her people. But today, she found herself distracted by a never-ending stream of horrible thoughts, led by an image of her brother.

Lumikki could not shake the feeling of dread off her shoulders as she entered the lighthouse and ascended the steps to her bedroom.

She nodded toward Harp, who returned the gesture and took up his position outside her door. She entered her room, closed the door, and blew out a sigh she had been building up all day.

The herbal, fruity aroma of tea still lingered in her room. The scent brought her back to her childhood, to memories of nights spent sipping and conversing with her brother and her mother. Now she was the Sacred Ruler of Ovallia, and nothing could ever be so simple again.

Two cups sat on the table in the corner of her room by the open window, untouched and certainly cold by now. Lumikki strode over to the table and lifted the stirring spoon from one of the cups, the cup that would have been her brother's. She raised the spoon to her mouth and licked it clean.

Normally, the taste would have filled her with joy, and it should not have bothered her that her brother had skipped out on their weekly tea date—it would have been nice to talk to him before she addressed the townspeople. But, no matter how hard she tried, Lumikki could not fight the feeling that something was wrong.

Lumikki put the spoon back in the cup, pushed the thoughts of her brother away, and went to her tub to start a bath. *There's no remedy for a troubled mind quite like a warm tub.*

She drew the water and set out the small jar of petals and stones at the base of the tub. Lumikki then lit each of the candles around the tub one by one. Their sweet scents of lavender and rose filled the room, and their radiance flickered softly across the bath water.

Once satisfied, she picked up the jar the merchant had given her, closed her eyes, and held it against her chest. She hoped that the merchant's words were true but doubted him. Then she opened her eyes, twisted the lid off the jar, and poured its colorful contents into the pooling tub. The petals swirled on the top of the water and settled, tinting it with a light-pink hue, and the green stones sank to the bottom.

Lumikki took off her robe—the ocean-themed silk she had received at her coronation—hung it on her towel hook, and slid her body into the tub, letting the warm water lap against her fur. She closed her eyes, took a deep breath, and listened to the waves crashing against her lighthouse castle walls through the open window.

Lumikki had barely settled into the water when she heard a burbling at the window.

"*Luuuummmmmi!*" the singsong voice called. Lumikki sat bolt upright, sloshing a wave of water over the lip of the tub and soaking the floor. Her friend Trelluby's huge head poked through the window, so big that her pectoral fins pressed flat to the sides of her head as she pushed through.

"Trelluby"—Lumikki clutched her chest—"you startled me."

The sea serpent relaxed her paddle-like fins on the sill, knocking several candles onto the floor. "Whoopsies. Sorry, Lumi." Trelluby batted her eyelashes and pursed her lips.

Lumikki splashed some water from the tub onto the little flames. By now, she knew what to expect whenever Trelluby appeared at her window: a fresh batch of the local gossip. "What is it?" she asked, easing herself back down into the water.

"The people are talking," Trelluby said.

"They're always talking," Lumikki said. "What is it this time?" She didn't really need to ask; she knew they were talking about her.

"They know something's up, my little sea star. You're not very good at hiding your emotions."

"I'm just a little distracted is all," Lumikki replied. "A little tired."

"A little? You weren't even listening to the townspeople

today. And even worse, they noticed." Trelluby furrowed her brows. "What is it, love? What's on your mind? You know you can tell me anything, right?"

Of course, Lumikki knew that. Trelluby, unlike any of the other Eslurians, had stood—or at least floated—by her side since the day the Book of Water chose her to take up the role of Sacred Ruler. The sea serpent had been with her through thick and thin.

"It's nothing," Lumikki said. Surely, she was just overreacting. Remidigon probably just forgot...but that was so unlike him.

"Hmm"—Trelluby pondered with a fin to her chin—"I'll bet this has something to do with that Alpin Loomin figure?"

"Trelluby!" Lumikki's cheeks flushed hot. She looked around the room, half expecting Harp to be standing there, wide eyed and mouth gaping at the scandalous rumor. Lucky for her, he was not. Lumikki sighed and sunk down until her whiskers touched the water. "Trelluby, please, watch what you say."

"Oh, Lumi," Trelluby sighed, "I just can't seem to wrap my head around why you like him. He's about the most foul-spirited little thing I've ever met!"

"Well, you haven't read his letters, then, have you?" The gopher had a way with words that went straight to her heart. She often found herself waiting by the window for any sign of a passing gully that might be carrying a letter from him.

"So, it is Alpin?" Trelluby said. The serpent always seemed to know how to get Lumikki's heart bouncing.

"Of course not!" Lumikki had received a letter from him that morning. She had already read through it ten times, rehearsing her most perfect response. He was definitely not the problem. "But," Lumikki said, "you *do* realize that if anyone were to overhear our conversation that I would be put out of a job, and Alpin would be sent to Morgaedion, right?" Trelluby had been there the day Lumikki placed her right paw on the Book of Water, swearing away all hopes and dreams of ever falling in love. Surely her closest friend knew of the laws put in place to keep the Rulers dedicated to their given roles.

Lumikki frowned. Oh, how she wished she had known the toll that the oath would take on her longing heart.

"Hush, hush, my sea star," Trelluby said with a dismissive wave of her fin, accidentally blowing out all the remaining candles in the process. "Your little secret is safe with me." She paused. "So, if it's not Alpin, what is it?"

"It's really nothing, Trelluby. I just"—Lumikki paused—"I haven't heard from Remi in a while, that's all."

"*Remi? That's* what you're worried about?" Trelluby stifled a laugh with her fin. "Hon, I hate to break it to you, but you've got bigger things to worry about than your brother. Isn't he at the prison?"

Lumikki glanced over toward the small table, at the two cups sitting untouched, where she and her brother sat at every last day of the week. Just the two of them, alone, forgetting their responsibilities and catching up on life.

"His tea went cold…" Lumikki frowned at the thought.

"So?" Trelluby rolled her huge eyes. "Everyone's tea goes cold eventually. What's the big deal?"

"I mean he never showed up, Trelluby. It's not like Remi to miss out on tea…at least not without telling me he couldn't make it, that is."

"Lumikki, listen." Trelluby took a deep breath. "Remidigon is the last thing you need to be worried about. I'm sure he is more than fine. He probably just forgot, for gods' sake! He has a lot of responsibility, too, you know. I wouldn't be a prison guard for all the fish in the ocean."

"I don't know, I just…" Lumikki paused and glanced toward the cups again. "I've got a pretty bad feeling."

"You've always got weird feelings, Lumi. I swear, that Book has turned you into one crazy wave of emotions."

Lumikki felt her head grow heavy and she put her paw to her forehead. "Oh, gods." She clutched her stomach. "I don't feel so well." She felt lightheaded, and everything looked blurry.

"Lumi?" Trelluby leaned her head farther into the room, but her voice sounded distant. Lumikki opened her mouth but could not form the words to speak her mind. She tried to stand but toppled over the edge of the tub and onto the floor.

"Uh…Harp!" Trelluby shouted. "Harp!"

The door swung open, thudded against the wall, and her Guard rushed in. She felt him shake her, but she couldn't move. Her head wobbled back and forth as if her neck were made of string.

"It's gonna be okay, Lumi," Trelluby said. "Yes, yes, Harp, hurry. Please do something!"

Harp scurried out of the room for a moment and returned almost immediately. "Drink," he said. Lumikki felt the lip of a vial thrust up against her lip. She opened her mouth and warm liquid ran down her throat. She felt nothing at first, then her stomach convulsed. She gagged and threw up on the rug next to the tub.

"There, there," Trelluby said as Lumikki continued to vomit. Her throat burned, and she wondered if she would ever stop puking, and what sort of medicine Harp had given her.

"Urguh," she groaned. "What was—"

"Dringrys," Harp said from beside her. He was bent cleaning the puddle of vomit. Lumikki almost vomited when he said it. The serum was extracted from fish guts and fed to gullys before flight. The bird-cat hybrids diet consisted heavily of the foul-tasting stuff and they relied on it for overnight flights as it made them lighter. Any other stomach would reject it immediately.

"Sorry, Lumi," Trelluby said, "it was the only way."

"You suggested this?" Lumikki shot Trelluby a glance. Her own friend, subjecting her to this cruel punishment. How awful.

"Well, you didn't give me much of a choice, did you?" Trelluby laughed.

"What happened?" Lumikki said. She spat out another chunk that had stuck in her throat.

"Might I suggest this?" Harp paused his cleaning, picked up the empty jar off of the floor, and handed it to Lumikki.

"You don't mean to say—"

"Poison," Trelluby said.

"It is quite likely, given that the water was pure," Harp said. "I drank some from the sink when we returned."

"Poison?" Lumikki stared at the empty jar, then dropped it on the floor. It shattered, and she put her paws over her mouth.

"Please forgive me. I should have been more careful," he said. "My naivety must have gotten the best of me."

"No." Lumikki meant to apologize and thank her loyal

Guard for cleaning up her various messes, but instead she stood, snatched her robe from its hook, and tied the belt in a bow at her waist. "It's time for me to trust my instinct. I've got to go see Remidigon." Something was wrong, and she could not ignore the signs any longer. First Remidigon missed their tea, and then someone poisoned her. She had to get to the bottom of it.

"Whoa, whoa, whoa, hold your florahorses. You nearly died, my little sea star. How about you just rest a while, okay?"

"No, Trelluby," Lumikki said, her stomach still queasy. "I must act."

"You can't just leave Ovallia on a hunch. Besides, you've got a whole kingdom to look after and—"

"I'm a Sacred Ruler, Trelluby. I will do as I please."

The sea serpent gulped and gave Lumikki a forced smile. "Yes…you must."

Harp stared down at Lumikki with a raised brow. He knew better than to question his Ruler.

"I'll be back before anyone has the chance to notice I've left," Lumikki told them.

"You've got audiences tomorrow," Trelluby said, looking to Harp for help, but finding none. "What about your people?"

"You and Harp will take over for me. Tell them I'm sick." Lumikki faced Trelluby, whose scrunched-up face showed her displeasure. "Just write down what they say and pass it on to me when I get back. And try not to let the city burn down while I'm gone," she said, forcing a smile. "I'd hate to come back and find this place in ruins." She stepped onto the table in the corner and shimmied up onto the windowsill next to Trelluby's head.

"But, but"—Trelluby grappled for words—"don't you think it's a little bit compulsive? I mean, leaving on a whim because of a *feeling*?"

"It's not a feeling, Trelluby," Lumikki said. "Have you forgotten? Someone tried to *kill* me. What if they had done the same to Remi? If I don't go now, I'll never be able to ease my mind."

"Oh, Lumi"—Trelluby shook her head in disapproval—"just be smart for me, okay? That prison isn't somewhere I'd place high up on my 'safe' list. I'd expect those prisoners to have quite a bit of resentment toward a Ruler like you."

"I'll be fine," Lumikki said.

"All right," Trelluby said. "Would ya at least bring me back a souvenir? You know, somethin' to look forward to after listening to all your people's whining."

Lumikki nodded. She adjusted her paws on the ledge and looked down at the water. Then she took a deep breath, closed her eyes, and leapt out the window and into the air, soaring for a moment before tucking her chin and diving into the water. When she splashed into the cold water, her muscles tightened, and her heart slowed. Her nostrils and ears closed as she plummeted toward the bottom. Then, a stream of blue light emitted from her irises and lit up the water ahead of her.

There was a brief moment of silence where everything around her seemed to freeze in place, then a tidal wave rose up from the depths of the ocean and carried her upwards.

The rush of water thrust her back up through the surface and shot her into the air like a rocket. She glanced down and saw her giant friend still clinging to the side of the lighthouse and staring up at her.

Lumikki waved and turned to face the open sea. She rode her wave into the distance, mind set on Morgaedion and her brother.

CHAPTER EIGHT

THE SACRED HEAD

Candles flicked to life in the foyer of the tiny house that was no longer tiny at all. Unlike its teeny facade, the inside of the home felt ten times larger than any Bea had ever been in and held more gold than a dragon's treasure hoard.

In the center of the foyer, stood a luxurious fountain with two golden gophers dancing on top of it. Streams of water shot out of their cupped paws and fell into a larger pool that was lined with gold and bronze tiles. Beyond the fountain, a grand marble staircase wound up to a mezzanine above with a gold-coffered ceiling. A crystal chandelier hung from it like a glistening disco ball high above her head. Bea imagined that all the gold in the room could buy out Fran and Joe's farm ten, possibly twenty times over.

The man, who had yet to discard his cloak, walked hurriedly from one arched window to the next, securing locks and closing the fringed curtains. He pulled a side table, legs screeching on the marble floor, across the room. The plump vase with frilly flowers that sat on top of it toppled onto the floor and shattered, sending shards of glass and murky water across the once spotless floor. Bea and Reagan stood in the foyer wanting no part in the destruction.

"What in the—" a high-pitched voice called. Its accent reminded Bea of a Shakespeare film she'd been forced to watch at school, but at least she could sort of understand this one. She looked up and was quite certain the person with the accent, speaking from the top of the stairs, was…a gopher, a rather tired gopher who was still wiping the z's out of his eyes and dressed in red silk pajamas. He'd stopped halfway down the winding staircase and seemed to be staring at them with a somewhat displeased expression on his buck-toothed face. His whiskers twitched, and he waggled his golden staff aggressively at the man in the cloak.

"What in the name of Eslura are you doing in my home!" He rapped the staff on the stair rail and continued down to the ground floor. "And my vase!" He bent down and peered at the shattered glass. "My beautiful vase! You idiot, Alistair! You've broken my vase!" He turned toward the man, whose name was evidently Alistair, and wielded his staff like a sword, clutched in his little paws.

Bea took a step back toward the door and nearly tripped over Reagan's foot behind her. Angry gophers, especially those that wielded staffs and spoke in Shakespearean accents, were not to be messed with, or at least she assumed they were not.

"Oh good, Alpin," the old man said. "You're awake. I

need your help bolstering the door and the windows, if you don't mind."

The gopher, Alpin, adjusted his monocle and glared at the lizard through it. "Alistair," he said. "Have you lost your mind? What business do you have to be meddling around in my home? Especially at an hour like this!"

The old man—Alistair—ignored the gopher as he pushed a large wooden armoire in front of the door, grunting as it scraped across the floor.

Alpin tapped his staff on the floor impatiently. "Alistair! Would you take that god-awful cloak off and look at me? I'm talking to you! Don't you know it's rude to not look at someone when they're talking to you?"

Seemingly overheated from pushing the armoire, Alistair pulled off his cloak and threw it over the back of an ornately upholstered chair. He was, without any possible doubt, a man-sized lizard. He wore a pristine white lab coat, the pockets of which overflowed with pink and blue and yellow flowers, and a long, spiked tail covered with olive-green scales followed his every move. His reptilian face had sprouted a grey beard and puffy bags sagged beneath his eyes.

"Pardon me," the lizard said upon seeing Bea and Reagan's gaping faces, "I suppose I have not introduced myself, have I?" He smiled a sharp, toothy smile.

Reagan tugged Bea toward the door, whispering in her ear, "Uh…maybe we should leave now?"

Bea didn't know if she could trust the lizard man—*a lizard man!*—but she had to, or else she had to run. But to where? She didn't even know where she was to begin with. She had no other choice than to trust him. Though he did appear to be friendly, and he did save them from the shadows.

"Have no fear. I assure you that I mean you no harm." He bowed slightly. "My name is Alistair Archibald, and I am the Sacred Ruler of the Book of Land."

Alpin hissed through his big teeth. "Yeah, yeah, Sacred Ruler, we get it. But who are these street urchins you've invited into my home? This is not an orphanage."

The remark angered Bea but she held her tongue.

"These are no street urchins, Alpin," Alistair said. "Though I must apologize, for I don't recall asking your names."

Bea and Reagan introduced themselves despite Alpin's glaring at them and sucking his teeth.

"Just because they have names," he said, "does not mean they aren't peasants."

"Excellent," Alistair said, ignoring the petulant gopher, "now that we're all acquainted, I believe we should address our more pressing issue. A Shadow Reaper has found its way back into Eslura, and I don't assume it has just come to say hello."

"A Reaper?" The gopher stopped staring at the Bea and Reagan and raised a brow at Alistair. "Twee! They've been gone for nearly fourteen years. What makes you—"

"If you do not believe me"—Alistair paused to flick his tongue—"take a walk outside that door and look for yourself, but I would heavily advise against it."

The gopher twitched his little nose, which Bea thought for a moment was cute until she remembered that he wasn't a particularly nice gopher. "Well, then," he huffed, "I've gone mad. This whole bloody world has gone mad!"

Bea thought she pretty much agreed with the gopher about that, but she had other questions. "What's a Reaper?" she asked. She figured it was the swirling black smoke figure that had chased them through the woods, but she wanted to know why.

"Any matters concerning the Reaper," Alistair said, "should not be discussed in open halls like these." He narrowed his eyes and peered sidelong at Alpin.

"Don't look at me like that!" Alpin crossed his arms defiantly and glared up at the lizard. "Just because you decided to march into my home uninvited does not make this my issue."

"You are quite right, Alpin," Alistair said with a nod. "This is not your issue—it is all of our issue. In fact, everyone in Eslura should be very concerned. Now, would you kindly take us to a more private room?"

"Twee! Come on, then," the gopher grumbled, his long claws clicking on the marble floor as he led them down a dark corridor to the last door on the right. He clicked the lock and the door creaked open.

"Galabear!" the gopher shouted. He leapt back with a hand to his heart and stood there panting. A large, black, furry beast lay on the floor in the center of the room, its yellow eyes open just enough to peer at them. It had a hunched back and a long and pointy tail Bea thought could probably cut through metal with a mere flick. Its teeth stuck up from its underbite like glistening yellow daggers, and the two long ears that stood up on top of its head made it look like a rabbit that had just eaten a baby elephant.

"What are you doing in here, girl?" Alpin asked.

The beast groaned and rolled over with a loud *thud*.

"Hey," Alpin snapped, "don't you turn away from me while I'm talking to you! We've got guests. Now, be a proper lady and move aside, would you?"

The beast yawned and exhaled a stink like rotten fish and uncooked meat. Bea gagged and clamped her nose shut with her fingers. The beast grumbled again and stretched her long arms and legs, knocking over a table with some books and an unlit candle on it in the process.

"Come on now, ya big loafer, move along. We haven't got all day to be dealing with night hoppers like you." Alpin, who was but pea-size in comparison to his pet, shooed the beast aside. It wobbled past Bea and she thought for a moment that she might like one of the large, fluffy beasts for herself. Perhaps with one of them by her side, the girls from school might finally leave her be.

Alistair walked around the room, lighting the candles and oil lamps on the tables that hadn't been knocked over. The light gradually illuminated a library with more books than Bea had ever seen stuffed into such a small room. Shelves overflowing with tomes reached so high into the air that no ladder could ever dream of reaching their tops. Stacks of books lay piled all over the dusty oak floor, some in stacks even taller than Bea. A fireplace took up the entirety of the back wall. Its mouth, which was shaped like a gopher, was so large that all four of them, excluding Galabear, of course, could have stood inside it with room to spare. But with no logs and dust piled so high they could have been tiny mountains, Bea assumed that the mouth had not held a fire in a long time.

"So," Alpin said, pulling a chair from the table in the center of the room and sitting, "let's hear it. What is a Shadow Reaper doing in Eslura?"

Alistair pulled a chair from the table, took the books off it and set them on the floor, then sat across from Alpin and gestured for Bea and Reagan to do the same. "Well, to be quite frank," the lizard said, "I had hoped we would not need this gathering in the first place, but it seems as though Amelia's foretelling was correct."

"Don't tell me that old hag is back too, I won't believe ya," Alpin said.

"No, Amelia is not back, Alpin." Alistair said it in such a way that Bea thought perhaps he was pained that she was not back. He continued, "Amelia will never be back. Obellius took care of that, as you know."

An awkward silence ensued in which Alpin and Alistair lowered their gazes to the table, leaving Reagan and Bea looking at each other. Bea had no idea what the lizard and gopher were talking about and wondered if Reagan was equally clueless, but she dared not speak and anger the gopher.

At last, Alpin cleared his throat and said quietly, "Okay, then what is it?"

"I wanted to believe she was wrong," Alistair said. "But, alas, I was the one who was wrong. Before her passing, she told me of a vision she had. Even then, she was not clear on what the vision was telling her, but she seemed quite adamant that fourteen years would pass and Obellius would rise again with the power of the Book of Fire."

Alpin crossed his arms and twitched his whiskers. "I find it hard to believe that she would rely on a vision."

"I did as well, until Beatrice arrived. Amelia also foretold that fourteen years would pass before a *new* Sacred Head would be chosen by Eslura. Today, I saw a golden flash erupt in the sky, the same one that preceded Amelia's choosing."

"Twee!" Alpin chirped and rolled his eyes. "That's impossible. She doesn't even have the mark of the Sacred, let alone the mark of the Head."

"Beatrice," Alistair said gazing at her wrist, "may I see your wrist, please?"

Bea tensed and she grabbed her wrist, covering the mark with her opposite hand. *The symbol, they're talking about the symbol.* She felt their eyes burning on her neck as she stared down at where its golden circles were embedded into her skin. She wanted to defend herself, say they had it wrong, that there wasn't anything there, but she looked up and extended her arm, wrist up, across the table, wincing when Alistair clutched it with his cold claws. Alpin leaned forward and stared a second, sucking his big teeth, then exhaling like a leaking balloon and sinking down in his chair. "The Sacred Symbol. You can't be serious."

"I am just as shocked as you are, my friend," Alistair said, "but it seems our Eslura has chosen her next Sacred Head."

"Sacred Head?" Bea looked at the symbol on her wrist, then up at the lizard. "What does that mean? What is it?" She feared the worst.

"Well," Alistair began, rubbing his long grey beard, "I am quite surprised that you do not already know. As Sacred Head, you are the guardian of the Sacred Rulers and their respective Books. It is your job to protect the elemental balance of Eslura."

Sacred Rulers, Books, elemental balance? She didn't even know where or what Eslura was, let alone the first thing about protecting some sort of balance in the strange place. What if she couldn't live up to her new title—whatever the heck it meant? What if they decided she wasn't fit—which she didn't think she was to begin with—and sent her back to the Dildeckers?

"Aargh! So what?" Alpin groaned. "Obellius is rising and a silly girl who has never even heard of the Sacred Head is supposed to stop him? We're doomed! I'll be going back to my hole in the ground. Never should have left to begin with. Good luck, all!"

"I can always count on you for your positivity, Alpin," Alistair said. "However, Beatrice is our Sacred Head, and if Eslura deems it so, then I have more than enough confidence that she will be able to fulfill her role and bring back the Book of Fire to its rightful spot."

Bea's head spun as she stared at the symbol on her wrist. She felt helpless, like a bottle tossed on the waves of a powerful storm, water pouring over and drowning her. Each breath she took felt like another wave crashing down, pulling her beneath the surface and dragging her down.

The thought reminded her of the first time she had visited the ocean. She stood on the sandbar, the water sparkling in the sun and blinding her to where it dropped off into the deep, hundred-foot sea. Clueless, she stepped forward, her mind too focused on the seagulls playing in the distance to see the abyss only a few steps in front of her. She sunk like a rock, the water pulling her down, deeper and deeper into its murky depths.

She was helpless, thrashing her arms as she desperately

yelled incomprehensibly through the thick water. Her heart pounded against her ribcage as the water seeped into her mouth. She flailed and kicked and...

"Beatrice?" Alistair said, pulling her back from her thoughts, up from the abyss. She did not realize how tightly she was clutching her wrist. Her hand was turning red. She released it and looked up at the lizard. All three of them were staring wide-eyed at her.

Alistair opened his mouth as if to say something, but before he could, a loud *clang* came from the fireplace. Black dust cascaded out of its mouth and covered the floor, masking the piles of books beneath its thick veil.

"The Reaper!" Alpin yelped. He leapt out of his seat and hid behind Alistair, who immediately stood from his chair and extended his claws, a green energy flowing between them.

The clattering increased, and more smoke blew down into the room, clogging Bea's nose and burning her eyes. She covered her mouth, passing the symbol before her eyes again. Reagan sneezed loudly.

A single figure emerged from the mouth with their hands held up to protect their face. Alistair lowered his claws, extinguishing the green light, and squinted into the smoke.

"Millennium?" Alistair gasped.

"Twee!" Alpin added.

Alistair invited the woman to sit and pulled a chair over for her while Alpin tried to recover his wits. The woman, whose windswept grey hair reminded Bea of a lion's mane, took slow sips on her freshly brewed tea—insisted upon by Alistair to soothe her after her flight and begrudgingly procured by

Alpin. Her thin lips curled to a smile as warm as the steam that billowed from her cup. She peered around the library curiously, adjusting the puffy, wool scarf around her neck as it partially blocked her view. In the warmth of the room, Bea thought it silly for her to wear such a thick garment, but she didn't dare say anything.

"Alpin, darling," the woman said, chuckling, "I hate to admit it, but you might have more dusty old books in here than I have in my own library."

"It's not really a fair competition," Alpin said, "considering you have Galecrest's entire collection at your disposal."

Millennium smirked and took another sip of tea. She mouthed the words "*perhaps one day*" before setting the cup back down on the table.

"Millennium," Alistair interrupted, "might I ask what brings you here?"

In answering his question, the woman, Millennium, recalled the story of her coming to them. She spoke of a distant kingdom, Galecrest, and its dragons, whose powers seemed to have disappeared overnight. Bea thought she misheard the woman at first. *Dragons?* she thought, fascinated to hear of their existence in the world. She exchanged an astonished glance and brow raise with Reagan. But the part that seemed to catch the lizard's attention the most was her mentioning of a blinding golden flash that streaked across the night sky during her flight.

"So, you saw it as well?" he said, narrowing his eyes at her.

"Well, it nearly sent me flying into a tree!" she said. "All of Eslura simply must have seen it. It lit up the entire sky. I could not imagine how they could miss it."

"I didn't see it," Alpin huffed.

"I hope you were not the only one who missed it," Alistair said. "It would be of great concern to me to know that others know of Beatrice's arrival. At least for now."

Bea shifted in her seat. "W-why?" She looked around, hoping the gopher wouldn't make that angry sound at her.

Alistair cleared his throat. "Not all...um, how should I put this...remember your predecessor fondly." He frowned. "Amelia, though well respected and loved by many, is sadly, and unjustly, in my opinion, remembered mostly for her failure to cast Obellius into oblivion."

Millennium nodded. "Amelia fought her final fight with more strength and courage than I have ever seen in any Eslurian. It was a true heartache to see it all end so tragically."

"Indeed," Alistair said.

"Anyways," she sipped her tea and continued, "I had left for Zybersia to check on the Guard stationed outside of the Sacred Chamber. With Elmryn slain, the Chamber, as you know, no longer holds the same protective power as it used to and relies solely on the strength of the Sacred Guard alone. I fear that something has happened to the Book."

Alistair frowned. "So, then it's true. Amelia knew of it all. First, the Book of Fire, then the arrival of the Sacred Head, and..." He bit his lower lip, seeming to skip over whatever came next. "I thought nothing of her warnings. Like the rest of Eslura, I assumed her mind had succumbed to the shadows. Obellius had a great deal of power over her, not only in physical strength but emotionally as well. It was only logical to conclude that—"

"There's no need to beat yourself up, darling," Millennium said, cutting off his ramblings. "We can only move forward from here, yes? The Book has simply been...misplaced. Surely, with all our efforts we can return it to its rightful Sacred Chamber."

"Twee! You didn't let Alistair finish his little story," Alpin said, "He just happened to *forget* the part about Obellius rising to power again."

"Alistair?" Millennium raised her brow at the lizard. "Is this true?"

Alistair gulped so loud Bea could hear it. "I'm afraid so," he said, "I feared that talking about it would further cement its reality. But seeing that Amelia was right once before, I can only suspect that it is true."

The three Eslurians stared at one another, presumably digesting the new information, when the candles suddenly whisked out and darkness suffocated the room. Bea heard shuffling beside her and squinted, finding Alistair had stood up from his chair and was glancing around the room. He reached for a nearby oil lamp and relit the wick.

"Ah," Millennium said, her face cast in orange, "so it has not only returned to Eslura, but it has also retained its powers. Shadow Reapers do have quite the knack for sucking all light and life out of a situation. But you don't suppose it's found us already, do you?"

"Indeed, I do," Alistair said. He turned to face the gopher. "It is no longer safe here, Alpin. Would you please escort Beatrice and Reagan to Galecrest? With the council room in the Sacred City destroyed, it is the next best place to discuss what to do about the coming darkness. With the High Moon Festival coming up, all Rulers will be present regardless."

"Bah! That stupid thing? I hate crowds." Alpin shook his paws at the lizard. "Also, I am *not* your personal escort. Why don't you take them yourself?"

"Would you like to stay behind and deal with the Shadow Reaper yourself, then?" Alistair said. "Can a gopher of your stature hold off such a monstrosity?" Alpin scrunched his nose and looked to the ground. "And might I remind you that Beatrice is the Sacred Head. It is all of our duty to ensure that she stays safe until she learns to control her powers. If that Shadow Reaper were to get its claws on her, it would be a great trouble for us all. This should not come as a surprise to you."

Powers? Bea thought. She flexed her fingers and wondered what he could possibly mean. Her mind first jumped to the red and blue masked hero from her favorite comic book, but she hadn't been bitten by any spiders—at least she thought… Camp Tossbridge wouldn't be the last place she would expect that to happen—and she couldn't imagine ever being able to fly between buildings like he had. It was all too bizarre, and she was scared of heights anyways.

"*Fine,*" Alpin spat, shaking his staff at the lizard. "But you owe me big for this! And I'm not talkin' just a simple 'thank you.' I'm talking several hundred kaps in my paws, got it?"

"We can discuss your reward when we meet again," Alistair said.

Alpin hobbled over to the fireplace, tapping his staff on the floor and the piles of books to guide him through the darkness. He walked straight into the firebox, brushed his paw against the back wall, and stopped above the surface of a small stone. He pressed his paw slightly and the stone walls slid apart to reveal a secret passageway through the back of the house, at the end of which Bea could see stars and the light of the moons.

"Galabear!" Alpin whistled through his paw. The giant beast came bounding back into the room and bent down by his side. Alpin climbed onto Galabear's back and gestured for Bea and Reagan to join him. "You heard the lizard. Off we go!"

CHAPTER NINE

BEYOND THE SHOP WINDOW

Barnaby stood beside the shop door, his pectoral fins trembling and his gills quivering. The sounds of the outside world filled his ears and he felt like he might faint, collapse on the ground in the alley and stay there, paralyzed, until Pemadee came back and dragged him inside. His hands were slick with sweat and his chest was tight.

"Okay, Barnaby," he told himself. "Nice and easy steps. You got thi—" Something shoved him in the back, flinging him forward. He nearly lost his balance.

"Quit standin' in the middle of the road, aye?" a burly man shouted, edging around him and quickly disappearing out the other side of the alley.

Barnaby collected himself and tightened his hood, which had been knocked askew by the man. He unraveled his scarf and wrapped it again, double and triple checking that no gill or scale or fin was visible. He took a deep breath and was ready to step into the outside world. If *ready* meant utterly terrified, that is.

One step at a time, Barnaby slowly rounded the corner of the alley, poking his head out and looking into the busy town square.

"Whoa," he gasped, stepping back into the safety of the alley as civilians brushed past. He pressed himself against the wall and took several more deep breaths before attempting again.

Ovallia, a city he had known only through a few photos in books, came to life before him, and he was determined to be a part of it. He stepped out from the alley, pumped out his chest, and walked toward the market at the center of the city.

Tall, marble columns surrounded the market square, which was open to the glistening sky. As Barnaby approached it, he stared up at it in wonder. *The sky!* He gasped. *It's really up there.* Just over the tops of the buildings ahead, he saw the stone head of the enormous statue of Bellbour. It looked just like it did in the guidebooks, except much larger. The man stood over the bridge connecting Ovallia to mainland Eslura, a constant reminder of the city's first Sacred Ruler. Barnaby stared at it a moment in disbelief, basking in the rays of the sun until he realized he was wasting time and plunged into the market square.

Civilians coursed through the crowded market carrying empty woven baskets ready to be filled with the day's catch. The scent of boiled clams, lobsters, oysters, and all the like wafted through the air and made Barnaby's stomach coil in hunger. He imagined their savory flavors dancing on his tongue and smiled. People laughed and haggled; vendors shouted their wares; children shrieked with joy; a juggler on a unicycle tossed six flaming balls in the air and caught them again without ever looking down. Barnaby straddled the narrow pathways between the townsfolk, tourists, and many stalls offering exotic fruits, meat on a stick, unique hand-crafted thingamabobs and colorful whatsits.

Barnaby eyed a wagon of purple fruits and swiped one when its shopkeeper turned to chat with a neighboring vendor. He bit a chunk off the fist-sized delight, puckered his lips at the pungent tartness, and swallowed.

"Hey," the shopkeeper bellowed. He leaned over the wagon and snapped his fingers at Barnaby. "You got a presp for that, kid?" Barnaby whipped around to face him, staring at his uneven mustache. "Yeah, you," the man growled. "You gonna pay or what?"

Broke, Barnaby dropped the fruit and ran.

"Hey!" the man shouted behind him. "Thief, thief! Somebody call the Guard!"

The Guard, Barnaby felt his heart drop. The word could only be associated with one thing: the *Sacred* Guard. Pemadee had stressed night upon night that the Sacred Guard was not to be fooled with. They were stone-cold warriors trained in Morgaedion to protect the cities, and more importantly the Rulers that resided there. The Guard held the power to send anyone they pleased to the depths of Morgaedion, and Barnaby knew they wanted nothing more than to send an Olphin like him there.

Barnaby fled to the outskirts of the market and stumbled

upon what he assumed to be the realm of the fishermen. Dozens of docks stretched out into the sparkling waters surrounded by glorious ships, some tall and many-masted while others were mere skiffs. Scruffy men and burly creatures fiddled with nets, wound ropes around cleats and shoulders, and carried barrels and buckets up and down the piers. Seagulls dove courageously down and fought for food against the battering hands of the fishermen, some escaping with mouths full, while others just flapped away squawking angrily.

Beside the piers, wicker huts lined the beach, their doors propped open for passersby to smell their fresh comestibles and eye their handcrafted wares. Palm trees cast shade down on the civilians who sprawled out on the sand, their backs browned by the sun.

When Barnaby had run far enough that he could no longer see the market, he sat down against the trunk of a shady palm tree and caught his breath. He ran his gloved hands through the tiny sand pebbles and watched them sift through his fingers. *Sand.* He had heard of it, seen it in photos, but never once felt its grainy softness.

He glanced around to make sure no one was watching him, and, seeing that no one was, he took off his shoes and dug his webbed toes into the sand. Though it was warm and soft, a chill ran up his spine and through his gills. He sighed and leaned his head against the tree.

He gazed out across the bay at Ovallia's famous lighthouse, which sat like a king on a throne atop the rocky shore. Its marble tower was circled with blue rings and stood more than a hundred feet tall. Its blue beacon shone brilliantly from its lantern room even in the midday sun, and its metal cupola gleamed like fire.

In a guidebook, Barnaby had read that the Book of Water sat guarded within its chambers. A Sacred Book created eons ago by two gods of unfathomable power from a tiny yet mighty stone—or so the fables told. The Sacred Book of Water was one of the four famed tomes that ruled the lands of Eslura, and it was right in that tall lighthouse with its Ruler, Lumikki Otsby.

"Mauz!" Barnaby said. "You've got to—" He suddenly realized his companion was not there to share his excitement. It wasn't the same without him, and he missed the little toad already. "Peppersnakes," he sighed and pulled out his postcard from his pocket. He looked down at the postcard, trying to distract himself from his companion's absence, but what good did a journey do if there was no Mauz?

Barnaby stood and brushed himself off.

"Hey, look out!" a boy shouted as he collided into him. The blow knocked Barnaby down face first into the sand. The postcard fluttered out of his hands and onto the beach.

"Sorry, I'm so sorry," Barnaby said, pulling himself to his knees. He dusted the sand off his cheeks and readjusted his displaced scarf and cloak.

The blonde-haired boy looked about his age and wore a blue silk robe—the traditional water-resistant garment of the Ovallian people. He scowled and narrowed his eyes at Barnaby. "*Olphin*," he hissed through gritted teeth. "You're the Olphin!"

Barnaby turned his head to hide his scales. He glanced at the crowd gathering around him, hoping that no one heard the boy. Luckily, it seemed no one did. He reached for his postcard, but the boy was too quick. He snatched it up before Barnaby could grab it.

"No, wait," Barnaby pleaded, holding his hands up apologetically. "Please."

"The Eslurian Opera House?" The boy raised a brow and held the postcard to his face, pinched between his fingers like a dead rat. "You've got to be kidding me."

"Please," Barnaby begged. He dropped his head in defeat. "Give it back."

The boy laughed and a malicious smile crawled up his cheeks. "You won't be needing this. The Opera House is no place for an *Olphin*." In one swipe, he tore the postcard from corner to corner, and Barnaby felt his heart rend. Tears welled in his eyes.

"What?" The boy bent face-to-face with Barnaby, a false sense of comfort in his tone. "You didn't really think they'd allow a freak like you in there, did you? I'm only helping you out." He laughed and let the shreds of the postcard trickle down onto the sand.

"You'd better head back to Pemadee's," the boy whispered, "before something very *nasty* happens to you."

"There!" someone shouted. Barnaby looked up and saw two blue-cloaked Sacred Guards striding towards him. With their seashell-covered face masks hiding their mouths, it was impossible to tell which of the two had shouted.

Barnaby got up, picked up his shoes, shoved past the boy, and fled down the beach. He took a sharp turn through a couple of palm trees and disappeared into the shadows of an alley, ducking under the low-hanging roofs and dodging the milling civilians who stood in his way. He slowed to a casual scamper, afraid to look back.

The alley poured into the market square, and he wove into the crowd, squeezed through the stalls once again, and found himself heading back to the same, familiar alley he knew. The one he grew up staring out into, the one outside Tide Tale Alley Books.

But no, Barnaby decided he would not head back to the shop. His quest surely did not lead him out the door only to take him back within the same day. He looked both ways down the alley—no Guard, he must have lost them—set his gaze on the giant statue that loomed up above the tops of the buildings. *Bellbour.* His only way out of the city was over that bridge.

Adjusting his scarf, he headed toward the man.

CHAPTER TEN

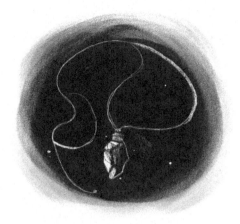

THE EYEARKE STONE

Reagan grabbed onto Galabear's fur. With no saddle to hold her in place, she feared she might fall off. Bea and Alpin sat in front of her, and the gopher's paws guided the giant beast through the dark forest.

"Hey." Bea pointed into the woods at the side of the path. "Someone's following us." Reagan turned and saw a cloaked figure, a woman, based on her shape and the moonlit cheekbones beneath her hood. She was leaping from branch to branch behind them.

"Oh, great," Alpin hissed. "C'mon, girl, we've got company." He nudged his heel into Galabear's side, and she lurched into a gallop, snapping their heads back.

Reagan watched the woman fall behind, rustling through the leaves and fading into the distance. "I think we lost her," she said. She turned forward again and realized her statement was far from the truth.

The woman swooped down from the trees and landed in front of Galabear. The giant creature reared and roared, tossing Reagan, Bea, and Alpin off her back, then took off into the woods with her tail tucked beneath her legs.

"Galabear!" Alpin yelped. He ran a few steps into the trees where his pet fled, and the woman grabbed him. She pressed a dagger to his furry chest. "You—" he shouted but stopped when she moved her blade up just beneath his little snout.

"No one speaks, no one moves," the woman hissed. Alpin squirmed, trying to get away from the knife, but the woman yelled, "I said, no one moves!" and he stopped.

"All right, all right" he grumbled.

"Speaking," she growled from beneath her bandana. Alpin pursed his lips and the woman pushed him down onto the forest floor.

Reagan looked toward Bea. She was still her counselor, her protector, even though they were far from Camp Tossbridge. But the woman stepped toward Reagan instead, pointing her gleaming blade at her. "You," she said. "Follow me, and I'll let your friends live."

As if it were not strange enough that Bea was some kind of royalty in this increasingly weird and seemingly dangerous place, Reagan was completely baffled that anyone should even pay her any attention at all here. "Okay, okay," she said. She glanced toward Bea, whose eyes were wide, and at Alpin, who stood beside her sucking his teeth, then followed the woman into the woods. She had a noticeable limp, but it did nothing to slow her stride.

"Hands up, walk straight," the woman said, pressing the blade to Reagan's back and pushing her forward. They walked for several minutes into the woods to a clearing, where there was a tall beast that resembled a kangaroo in every way except that it was as big as a horse, had floppy rabbit ears, large eyes, and a tail that split in two near its end.

"That was too easy," the woman announced. "Almost pathetic. And to imagine someone else could have gotten their hands on you before I did." She didn't seem to be expecting Reagan to reply, only spewing her mind. Reagan knew better than to speak up and defend herself. The woman's blade was still out and glistening in the moonlight, a constant reminder of what could be lodged in her throat.

"On your knees," the woman demanded, shoving Reagan to the ground before she had a chance to move herself.

Reagan could not hold her tongue any longer. "What do you want with me?" If she were to die there, she would at least like to know the reason why, even if it were for nothing more than the pleasure of killing.

Her captor ignored the question. She grabbed Reagan's wrists and pulled them behind her back, nearly breaking her arms in the process. A rope tightened around them and Reagan yelped.

This is it. This is how I go. This woman is going to kill me. Reagan wanted to scream, to call for help, but found her voice cut short by a hand pressing a wet cloth that smelled like nail polish remover over her mouth. She needed to stay alive for Bea, needed to do whatever it was she could to get back to her.

She struggled against the woman, her attempts at freedom

95

growing less purposeful with each second the cloth stayed over her mouth. Her vision went fuzzy, eyelids heavy, too heavy. She felt her limbs go limp and her body collapsed into the woman.

Reagan shifted uncomfortably, blinking her eyes open at the dark, sandy ground. Everything spun, making her feel like she might throw up. She tried to move, but found her arms were bound tightly behind her back, burning her wrists. Her mind ran in circles as she bounced up and down on her stomach and tried to remember what happened.

Hooves trod through the sand below her, thrashing her head to and fro on top of the beast's powerful thigh. She groaned and rolled her stiff neck, sore muscles battling her along the way.

She looked to the side and found herself eye to eye with a dead animal. Flies swarmed around its bunny-like face, its tongue lolling from its long snout. Its eyes were open wide and empty, locked onto Reagan's as if to tell her *"run."*

She shrieked and launched herself away from the dead animal, tumbling off the back of the hooved beast. Unable to brace her fall, she landed on her side on the ground, knocking the air out of her. She wheezed; her cheek pressed into the sand.

"Hey!" her hooded captor shouted, and the beast skidded to a halt. She turned it around to face Reagan writhing like a worm on the cold sand. "What do you think you're doing?"

Reagan thrashed harder, feet scrabbling for purchase on the sand. The woman dismounted and strode over to Reagan, her cloak flapping open behind her and revealing thick robes beneath. Not one inch of her skin was visible, only her bright, purple eyes that stuck out above her bandana.

"Please," Reagan pleaded as the woman drew closer. "What do you want?" Reagan could not help but think the worst. She had been snatched off Galabear's back with such expertise it could have been a choreographed dance.

Her captor stood over her, reached down a gloved hand, grabbed Reagan's shoulders, and hoisted her up to her feet with ease. Reagan gulped. She looked to the woman's eyes, but found they were fixed on the stone around Reagan's neck.

"Do you want it?" Reagan offered, trying to point at the necklace with her chin. She was desperate for freedom, even if it meant giving up the only thing she had left to remind her of her father. "You can have it. Please, take it!" Her captor shook her head and scoffed, then proceeded to drag Reagan across the sand back to the beast.

"What do you want with me? Please, tell me, I'll do anything. I don't even know how I got here," Reagan pleaded. *Anything to get back to Bea.* What had the woman done with Bea and Alpin? Did she go back and kill them? Where were they now? Were they okay? She had to find Bea and get out of this place. Reagan felt her heartbeat speed up and she glanced around for any means of escape.

Her captor ignored her question, lifted her at the waist, and set her back on the beast with the rest of their luggage.

"Would you quit your whining already?" the woman hissed. "You're making it hard to want to help you."

"Help me?" Reagan said. "You kidnapped me and slung me

over your…your whatever this thing is like a dead deer!"

As if the beast could understand, it perked up and bleated like a sheep.

"It had to be done," the woman said, staring at her again with her penetrating purple eyes. "You wouldn't have listened to reasoning."

"You didn't give me a chance!"

The woman sighed. "Like I said, you wouldn't have listened."

"All right, then, how about you give me the chance now? Please, just tell me what you want from me."

The woman glanced around and put a hand on what Reagan assumed to be a weapon hidden beneath her robe. "Not here. At least not until I'm completely certain that we're alone."

Reagan joined her in peering at the endless plain of sand. There was no hope of rescue for her out here. Rolling dunes stretched as far as she could see, the occasional cactus or tumbleweed dotting the land. Not a single, breathing soul, save for her captor and the snorting beast below them, was anywhere to be seen.

"You'd be surprised where they've got ears these days," the woman said. She kicked the beast into a trot again.

Either her captor had an eye for abandoned campsites, or she had been camping out in the desert for quite some time. They stopped next to a tall jutting stone, wind worn almost into the shape of a tree, with a drooping, torn tarp tied from its top to a stake in the sand. From another line hung several cloaked hoods like the one the woman wore. Beneath the tarp were enough supplies to last a cabin at Tossbridge at least a week. There was also a makeshift bed with dirtied sheets, a wash bin, and a blackened fire. Reagan thought it looked like just about every site a murderer would conduct their business at—far enough away from civilization that no one would hear her screams.

Reagan's captor jumped down from the beast and led it over to what appeared to be a tripwire rigged with bells. The contraption surrounded the small camp, evidently to scare away whatever wildlife might try fleeing with any of the food or supplies.

Once the woman had tied up the beast to the tree rock and put a pail of water out for it, she began unloading the boxes and sacks attached to its sides, first grabbing a large, blue chest with gold engravings which stood out among the rest of the beige and brown sacks. She carried it with both hands over to the bed and set it down lightly, then came back to retrieve Reagan and set her down beneath the tarp.

The woman pitched a fire and placed the dead animal from the beast's back on a stick above it.

"What are you going to do to me?" Reagan asked. The fire crackled and tiny flecks of ember floated into the air near her head. She leaned to the side to avoid them.

Her captor ignored her question and shook off her hood. At first glance, there was nothing extraordinary about the woman. She had short black hair curled tightly on top of her head, but the more Reagan focused through the flames, she realized that her dark face was covered with purple scales, and matching purple fins grew out the side of her cheeks where her ears ought to have been.

"Here." The woman ripped a charred piece of meat off the cooked carcass with her bare hands and held it in front of Reagan's mouth. "Eat." Steam rolled off the meat and up Reagan's nose. She hesitated and looked up at the woman's face.

"What? You think I'd poison it?" the woman said. Reagan thought she just might. "It's rabintail. Only a fool would waste that kind of meat. Now eat."

Even if she wanted to, her hands were still bound behind her back. "Would you—uh—please untie me?" Reagan asked while the woman bit into the hunk of meat.

"No," she said while chewing. "I won't risk chasing you out there. It's far too dangerous at night."

"If I were to run, where would I go?" Reagan said. "I don't even know where I am."

The woman thought for a moment, then nodded. "All right." She stood and walked over to Reagan, but instead of untying her, she tied another rope around her waist: a leash. *So, what? I've moved from prisoner to pet?* Then the woman pulled a dagger from beneath her cloak and sliced at the thick twine between Reagan's wrists. The rope snapped and her hands fell free. Though it wasn't exactly what Reagan had hoped for, it was a step in the right direction. She rolled her shoulders around to loosen them up.

"Thanks," Reagan said. She massaged her wrists, which were scratched red and bruised purple.

Not wanting to offend the woman's cooking skills, Reagan bent down, picked up the darkened meat. She grimaced and tossed it in her mouth. It was tough and chewy. She swallowed, and the pieces scratched her throat as they went down. One stuck there, and she coughed and choked until tears ran down her cheeks. At last, it loosened, and she swallowed it. She wished she had eaten more at Tossbridge. Though the camp food was borderline inedible, it was still better than whatever her captor had cooked up.

The woman watched her as if waiting for Reagan to compliment her cuisine. Reagan half smiled and turned her eyes back down toward her "dinner", though dinner did not feel like the right word for the meal she was suffering through. "Are they okay?" she asked, picking at the meat. "Bea and the gopher, I mean. You didn't, uh, go back for them, did you?"

"No, I didn't go back to kill them, if that's what you mean. I have no use for them. Just you."

Reagan closed her eyes and exhaled. "Oh, thank goodness." She placed a greasy hand on her heart.

"I wouldn't be too relieved if I were you," the woman said. "If I'm not mistaken your friends have a Shadow Reaper on their tails. Haven't seen one of those in a while."

"You mean, you've seen one before?"

"Unfortunately, yes. They used to serve Obellius. Though, fortunately for us, most, if not all of them, were killed in the war. Poor things are probably lost without him—scum's been locked away in Morgaedion for about as long as I can care to remember."

Reagan stared into the twilight that was slowly descending on them and took another bite of the meat. "Hmm."

"The name's Tab," the woman said. Reagan looked up. She had already figured the woman would never tell her. *Finally, something.* "And I'm here to protect you."

Reagan gagged on the bite of rabintail in her throat. "Protect me?" she said through a cough.

"Good. You're not deaf."

"Protect me from what?"

Tab scoffed. "But you might be an idiot."

"Excuse me?"

"That stone—the one you wear so carelessly around your neck—do you know what it is?"

Reagan lifted the stone off her chest and brushed its surface with her fingers. "An amethyst?"

"Wrong," Tab said. She stood and walked around the fire, holding Reagan's leash in her hand. "So very wrong. It's almost embarrassing."

"Well, then what is it?" Reagan sighed. She was sick of the woman's insults over a stupid stone trinket. Her father had given it to her when she was a baby and that was all she cared about.

"That is the Eyearke stone."

"The what?" Reagan furrowed her brows.

"You think I'm wrong, do you? Think I'm crazy? Well, good, then you can join the rest of 'em. Those fools claimed its existence was a myth!"

"I'm sorry, but I don't know what you're talking about." Reagan thought the woman may have spent a little too much alone time in the desert.

"Well, then that's why I'm here. I was on my way back from Treenode when I saw the stone." She took another bite, chewed and swallowed. Then she pointed her chin at the necklace. "You can't just be wearing it around like it's…an amethyst or whatever."

"Well, why don't you just take it?" Reagan suggested. "Then

you wouldn't need to protect me anymore." Her stomach growled and she forced herself to take another bite.

"Ain't that easy," Tab said. She ripped a chunk of meat off her bone with her teeth, chewed, and swallowed before continuing. "If anyone other than you touches that stone, they're dead."

Dead? Surely the woman was a nutcase, Reagan thought as she tried to chew through the tough meat. But, then again, she could not remember anyone else having touched the stone. "So, what? You're going to keep me as your prisoner forever?"

"Not forever," Tab said. "We'll deliver it to the Rulers during the High Moon Festival. In the wrong hands, that thing could bring the end of Eslura."

"I thought you said anyone but me who touches it would die?" Reagan thought she had the woman cornered with that one. "So how could it possibly fall into the wrong hands?"

"One way, which won't happen while you're under my guard," Tab said. "Someone kills you."

"You didn't kill me. You don't want its power?"

"No. As much as I hate you having it, I do not want to kill you. Its power was not intended for me."

"Who was it intended for?"

"The Sacred Head, the true descendent of Aezaros," Tab said.

Bea. Reagan recalled their conversation in the not-so-tiny house. Bea was the Sacred Head, at least according to the lizard guy. "All right, then, where is this festival?"

"Galecrest," Tab said.

"Perfect," Reagan said under her breath. *That's where Bea'll be too.*

"What?" Tab said.

"Nothing." Reagan shook her head. The woman could believe whatever she wanted about the stone as long as she brought her to Galecrest. *To Bea.*

"Whatever." Tab rolled her eyes. "First light. Like I said, it's too dangerous at night. Lie down. You'll need the sleep."

CHAPTER ELEVEN

BELLBOUR'S STRAIT

Barnaby turned just short of the bridge before the statue and ducked into the shadows of an alley near the growing line of people gathering to cross. Two Sacred Guards stood underneath Bellbour's massive body, searching through every cart and under each cloak on their way to mainland Eslura.

He glanced up at the giant statue. Bellbour Polindrad, Eslura and Ovallia's first Sacred Ruler of the Book of Water. Barnaby had heard his tale several hundred more times than he would have wished—Pemadee insisted that he know the history of his own land, even if he may never get the chance to explore it. Many moons ago, when Aezaros had retrieved the stone from the heavens, she gave the power of the elements to the Rulers. Bellbour received the power of water, and thus created his island paradise, set aside from the mainland where the Book would be safe inside the walls of the lighthouse.

"What's all the holdup for?" a new member joined the line and complained while parking his cart. Barnaby thought for a moment that the fuzzy mop on the man's head was just a product of bad bedhead, but it shifted and turned into a full-grown cat.

"The Olphin's escaped," a woman pushing a two-wheeled car announced. "They're checking to see if anyone's trying to smuggle it to the mainland." Her eyes fell down to his cart, which was full of red fruits the size of his head.

"Escaped?" The man furrowed his brow beneath the cat and glanced over toward the building where Barnaby stood in the shadow. For a moment, Barnaby was sure the man saw him. He adjusted his scarf and prepared to run. If he went now, he could make it to the other end of the alley by the time the man alerted the Sacred Guard.

"Well," the man said. "They'd better hurry up and catch him. I've got no time for this."

"Yeah, tell that to everyone else in line," the woman said, shaking her head. She pushed her cart forward a step.

Crossing the bridge was out of the question. Barnaby would have better luck swimming through the Bellbour's Strait than getting by those Guards—but even that was a certified death sentence; its rapids were far too strong for even the fish.

"Peppersnakes," Barnaby sighed and sunk down the side of the wall till his bottom hit the ground. He looked up at the sky between the tall buildings and his stomach grumbled. "What have I gotten myself into?" For a moment, he wished he had just stayed at Pemadee's shop. By now, he would be cooking the old man's dinner. Nothing too fancy, of course.

Barnaby was never that handy with a skillet, but the thought of food fueled his hunger.

"Barnaby." His imagination had exceeded his expectations; he could almost hear Pemadee yelling his name to check if he had set the dining table. *Yes, Mr. Pemadee. I've even filled the glasses three-quarters up like you asked.*

"Barnaby." *Yes Mr. Pem*— Barnaby heard the scraping of wooden wheels from the far end of the alley.

"Peppersnakes! Mr. Pemadee!" Barnaby lurched up from his spot. The old man's hair was slick with sweat and he panted profusely as he rolled his way toward Barnaby. Mauz sat in his lap, tongue hanging limp on his pale-green chest as Barnaby had always told him not to do.

"Mauz!" he exclaimed and ran over.

"Gods, Barnaby," Pemadee said when he reached his side. He clutched Barnaby's shoulders and pulled him into an embrace as he caught his breath. "I'd just about given up looking for you." He looked up into Barnaby's eyes. "You sure have given Ovallia a whirlwind of trouble today, haven't you?"

"Please, Mr. Pemadee, don't turn me in. I can explain. I—"

"Barnaby, stop." Pemadee hushed Barnaby with a shake of his head. He released his shoulders and straightened his back. "I'm not going to turn you in, but I do know that you've gone through my belongings." Barnaby's stomach dropped and he felt his face turning the color of the red fruits in the cat-man's cart. "Which means I also know why you're out here, and I—"

"It was an accident, truly! I never meant to read your note. It fell on—"

"Barnaby, let me speak, *please*." Pemadee took a deep breath

107

and closed his eyes like he always did when Barnaby babbled on. Barnaby gulped, wishing he could sink between one of the cracks below his feet. "Now, as I was trying to say…I agree with you."

"You"—Barnaby paused, wondering if he had heard correctly—"you agree with me?"

Pemadee nodded. "Yes, I agree with you. I think it's about time you leave Ovallia and discover your past for yourself."

Hearing it said aloud, especially from Pemadee, who was supposed to shield him from all things outside the store, felt odd and freeing. Perhaps it was all a big, awful joke. He looked up and down the alley again, half expecting to see the Sacred Guards charging in with weapons at the ready, but there were none. "Uh…what?"

"The letter you found." Pemadee rummaged through the pocket of his vest. "It was written by an old friend of mine who used to be one of the Knowers at Galecrest."

Barnaby had heard of the Knowers before—they spent their lives studying inside Eslura's "capitol of knowledge." They kept safe many of the secrets of Eslura and were said to have a special, god-like power to collect and retain information. It was quite rare to ever find a Knower outside of Galecrest. They spent their lives among the rows and rows of books found within its most famed library. And it was even rarer for them to be released from their duties, as Pemadee seemed to imply his friend was.

"He goes by the name Seely now, and he lives just outside of Treenode—the town your people once governed. He's been closely observing the behaviors of another Olphin—one that escaped imprisonment and has remained in the shadows ever since. No one knows she is alive."

"So, it's true, then. I'm really not the only free Olphin," Barnaby whispered to himself. *I'm not alone.*

"Listen, my son, I'm not done, and I don't have much time to explain. There are Guards looking for you." Pemadee put his hands on Barnaby's shoulders again. "There's something I haven't told you. That Olphin stole something very important from Seely and me, part of a research project we had been conducting—the same project that got Seely stripped of his title and kicked out of Galecrest. Eslura has made a terrible mistake, and its people are keeping it a secret instead of facing up to it. You, and *all* of the Olphins, are innocent!" He stared at Barnaby so intensely that Barnaby thought the man might have finally popped a screw. Nevertheless, Barnaby listened intently as Pemadee continued, "When the Olphins were removed from Treenode and brought to Morgaedion for imprisonment, I found you, Barnaby, but I also found this." He reached into his pocket and pulled out a stone, the same stone that once sat in the glass case in his office. "There were two. One a reactor and one a deterrent, an on and off relationship so to speak. One possessed a powerful spell to control, and the other possessed the power to break such a spell. I took possession of one, and Seely the other. We thought it best to keep the stones apart while we conducted our research—if one of us were to get caught for indulging in such conspiracies, at least the other would still have one of the stones, and we would not be at a complete loss. But, as you know, Seely's stone, the deterrent, has since been stolen by this Olphin. You see, I was not

109

entirely truthful with you, and I know now is not the time for apologies, but with Seely's note in mind, I must request your help." He shoved the letter and stone into Barnaby's hands. "I have heard rumors of a terrible event at Morgaedion and I fear the worst. You must bring Seely the stone. It is our only hope of the Olphins ever being freed. We must work together to fight the evil locked deep within Morgaedion. You simply must find Seely, Barnaby. Unfortunately, I cannot make the trip in this chair." Barnaby unwrinkled the paper and scanned it. *Olphin.* The word screamed at him louder than the sandy-haired boy on the beach.

"Find Seely," Barnaby said. He nodded and tucked the paper into a pocket in his trousers. "Hear that Mauz? Find Seely." The toad floated up and puttered around Barnaby's head, testing the strength of his tiny wings. *One day that toad's stomach is gonna glue him to the ground.*

Pemadee wheeled back a few feet. "Now, I'll go take care of those Guards for you. I'll put up enough of a distraction for you to pass by." He turned to wheel away.

"Wait," Barnaby called to him. "What will happen to you? I mean, I've broken the contract." Pemadee had made the contract with the Sacred Ruler Lumikki the day he found Barnaby in Treenode. She had allowed him to keep Barnaby as long as he never left the bookshop.

"Well," Pemadee sighed. "I suppose I will find out whatever punishment Lumikki and her Guard decide is just for an old man who does not keep his promises." He winked and started to wheel away again.

"Mr. Pemadee," Barnaby called again. *Could this be it?*

Barnaby thought. *Our last moment together?*

"Yes, Barna—"

Barnaby ran at him, wrapped his arms around him, and nuzzled his head into his chest. "Thank you." Barnaby wiped away a tear in the corner of his eye. *Where would I be if not for Mr. Pemadee?* he thought. *Certainly not here, that's for sure.* He hugged him tighter. "Thank you for everything." He felt the man exhale and give into his embrace, clasping his hands around Barnaby's back and letting his head rest on the top of his untamed mop of hair.

"Goodbye, Barnaby," Pemadee whispered into his ear. He held Barnaby out in front of him, gazing at his face one last time as if to remember every one of the features that Eslura hated. Once satisfied, Pemadee nodded and released Barnaby's shoulders. Then he spun his chair and rolled toward the end of the alley near the line. This time, without looking back. Barnaby watched him disappear around the corner.

"Oh, Mauz." Barnaby snatched the toad out of the air and pressed him against his cheek. The toad croaked.

"Someone," Barnaby heard Pemadee's voice. He walked to the edge of the alley and looked out toward the line. Pemadee was lying on the ground next to his overturned chair. "Please help."

"Hey." The cat-man pointed. "That's Pemadee! He caused this whole mess in the first place!" The crowd circled around him, shouting and waving their fists at him.

"Back up, everyone, back up!" The two Guards rushed over and pushed the crowd back with their staffs, leaving an open bridge behind them.

"Well, Mauz, would ya look at that. The old man's done it."
He pulled his hood over his head and bolted across the bridge.

CHAPTER TWELVE

WHAT LIES BELOW

A wintery gust blew over Reagan's body, bit her skin, and forced her to huddle into a chattering ball. The fire had long since died, and only the charred remains of broken logs sat in the blackened pit. The barren wasteland lay all around her unseen in the darkness. It threatened to engulf any creature who dared trek into its uncharted depths. Silence sliced through the night, and she heard nothing but the sound of her own breathing.

She stood and stretched her legs. Pins and needles pierced the bottom of her feet and made her skin crawl in circles. Crusted sweat from the afternoon stuck to her forehead like a thick layer of glue.

She took a deep breath, straightened her back, and groped through the darkness in search of the bean-shaped canteen Tab laid out for her. Although she had downed the last few drops before her first attempt at sleep, her mind still clung to the slim chance of a few more drops.

She pressed her lips, which were cracked like the hardened ground beneath her, to the mouth of the canteen and drew a drop, maybe two, and savored the wetness until it dissolved in her mouth. She thought about waking Tab to ask for a sip from her canteen, but her thoughts were cut short when the ground rumbled beneath her feet.

The sharp tremor rocked the ground and tossed her off her feet. She leaned against the tree rock for support, but found that it, too, was vibrating and swaying back and forth. A piece of rock face cracked off and fell, grazing her forehead. She flinched and reached to touch the wound. When she drew her hand back, there was blood on her fingers, and she gagged.

After a moment, the shaking subsided and Reagan walked toward Tab and her sleeping beast. *There has to be some sort of extra cloth or bandage in one of those bags.*

But before she could reach the giant animal, the ground rumbled again. "Ah!" Reagan yelled. She tripped over her feet and collapsed onto the beast, startling it awake.

"I'm sorry," she apologized as it bleated at her. The sand beneath them ebbed and flowed as if they were sitting on a waterbed. Reagan sat on the sand, hoping the earth wouldn't just split beneath her and drag her down. "Tab!" *How is she still sleeping?*

"What?" Tab grumbled and rubbed her eyes open. "What do you want?" She breathed an exaggerated yawn. Then her eyes went wide, and she grabbed at the sand as if she could stop the ground from trembling.

"There's an earthquake!" Reagan yelled. She had seen them only on the news before, but the shaking could not be mistaken for anything else.

"That's no earthquake," Tab said. She drew both her daggers from their scabbards and held them poised at the growing rupture in the ground.

Before either of them could make a move, the shaking subsided and the earth went still. A moment passed with nothing but labored breaths. Reagan glanced at Tab, whose daggers were still drawn. "Well, we certainly got lucky—"

The earth broke apart and a giant worm jumped into the moonlight like a killer whale launching from the water. Three layers of jaws snapped side to side as it let loose a roar that shattered the tree rock.

"What the—" Reagan was knocked to the ground by the shower of sand and dirt propelled by the creature's massive tail. Tab stood firm, staring at the beast, covered in sand, as it fell back into the crack in the earth.

"Stay down and shut up," Tab hissed at Reagan. Then she knelt by the rubble of the tree rock, clutching her daggers at her hips and motioned her head for Reagan to join her. Reagan hurried over and crouched beside her. She fixed her eyes on the spot where the monster had fallen and prayed that it would stay buried.

"What is that thing?" Reagan said, wondering if *thing* was a strong enough word to embody the horror of the gigantic, toothy creature.

"What don't you get about quiet?" Tab said, shaking her head, but proceeded to answer anyway. "It's a drovig. I don't know what's got it all hot and bothered, but they're sensitive to noise, so clam it."

"What do we do?" Reagan asked.

"We don't stand a chance against it on our own. We'll have to outrun it."

"Outrun it?" The thought of simply outrunning a monster that large seemed unlikely, if not impossible.

"As long as it doesn't charge, we might have enough time to get away," Tab whispered. "So, I'd suggest we get moving. Keep an eye on it while I get the pergonzia."

"The what now?" Reagan asked.

"Gosh, you really are thick, aren't you? The pergonzia. How do you think we rode all the way here?" Tab grabbed her box and limped toward the horse-like thing, which was already standing and digging its hooves in the sand.

"Ahh, the pergo...whatever." Reagan looked over at the crack in the earth. Two tall antennae jutted from the hole and poked toward them. "Wait," Reagan stopped and thought out loud, "those antennae...it's sensing the ground...trying to figure out where we are. Tab! Stop moving!"

Reagan saw Tab's head turn like it was in slow motion. Reagan tried to yell, but the drovig launched itself out of the ground. The tremors sent Reagan crashing to the sand and her tailbone screeched with agony. The sound of the monster hitting the ground was nearly deafening. Sand blew into her eyes and temporarily blinded her.

"Hey!" Tab's voice broke through the roar. "Get up. We've gotta move!"

Reagan looked at the drovig clawing toward them, then at

Tab, mounting the pergonzia.

"You think you've gotta choice?" she snapped from the top of her mount.

Reagan pushed herself up and ran for the mount, stumbling across the shaking earth. She grabbed the saddle and hoisted herself onto its back behind Tab. Once situated, Tab squeezed her leg against its side and clicked her tongue. The pergonzia chirped and sped forward, jerking Reagan's head backwards.

Reagan looked over her shoulder at the drovig. It lashed its long tail, shooting its body forward like a snake. The beast was legless, and its rounded face was bare other than an odd, star-shaped scar and its two antennae which poked at the ground ahead of it.

"It has no eyes," Reagan shouted.

"Nice observation, Red. Now, if you don't have anything useful to say, will you shut it already?"

"I mean it has to know where we are somehow or else it wouldn't be on our tail like that, right? Those antennae. I think if we can pierce either one of them, we might just be able to throw it off...at least a little bit."

Tab nodded and unsheathed her daggers. "All right, then. Do it." She handed them back to Reagan.

"What? Me?" Reagan clutched the knives, staring down at her wide-eyed reflection in the polished steel blades.

"I can't steer and throw," Tab said. "Make yourself useful!"

Realizing she had no other choice, Reagan clenched her teeth and turned to face the advancing drovig. She raised one of the knives and flung it at the monster's antenna. The blade whirled, flashing through the moonlit air and flopped to the ground about ten feet in front of the big worm. Then it disappeared beneath the shifting sands.

"What kinda throw was that?" Tab hissed.

"I don't know! What did you expect?" Reagan said.

"Somethin' a lot better than that!" She grabbed Reagan's arm and jerked the second dagger from her hand. "I'm not letting you waste another one of my blades. We'll have to stick to my plan." She flicked the reins and squeezed her legs tighter, but the pergonzia seemed unable to run any faster.

"There's too much weight," Reagan said. "We have to drop some of these boxes!" Reagan turned to face the drovig. It screeched and picked up its speed, worming its way closer to them.

"What?" Tab snapped. "No way!"

"It's only common sense, Tab," Reagan yelled over the thundering sounds of the drovig. "And that drovig isn't gonna wait until you figure that out!"

Tab grit her teeth and looked over her shoulder. "Fine. Drop 'em."

One by one, Reagan untied the ropes tethering the various satchels, bags, and boxes to the side of their mount, and watched them tumble onto the sand and into the gaping jaws of the drovig. When she reached for the large blue and gold painted box, Tab shouted.

"Hey, hey, hey." Tab grabbed Reagan's arm. "I'll die before I let you chuck this one! Leave it alone. Chuck the smaller sacks." She lowered her face to level with the pergonzia's head, lifted up its droopy ear, and shouted, "C'mon, you're supposed to be the fastest beast in Eslura! Move it!" But the pergonzia wheezed and slowed to a jog.

"Tab! Forget the box! Those sacks are half as heavy as this chest," Reagan pleaded. "What's in it won't matter if we both get eaten along with it." The drovig was closing the gap, its gnashing jaws getting closer.

Tab grit her teeth and glanced back at the drovig. Reagan watched her weigh her options and finally give in. She swiped the thick twine with her dagger. It snapped and the box tumbled to the ground under the advancing drovig.

The creature slowed and examined the box with its antennae, giving the pergonzia time to widen the gap and speed away.

Tab clenched a fist in the air. "You better not lay a single one of those hideous teeth of yours on that box or I'll—" The drovig took no heed of her warning. It opened all three of its jaws and wrapped them around the box, swallowing it whole. Tab's jaw dropped open.

"Look! It's going back into the ground," Reagan hollered.

"Yeah, with all my stuff!"

"But why?" Reagan asked.

The drovig let out a final cry before retreating back into the earth with the box in its mouth. Tab's lips quivered as she watched her treasure disappear from view.

"I don't know, Red," she growled, watching the rupture close, "but act a little more thrilled, why don't ya?"

The two rode in silence, though Reagan's ears still rung with the sound of crunching earth. Her head throbbed and she reached up to find her cut had split open, staining her fingers red. She gagged and felt as if she might fall off the pergonzia but grabbed its saddle tighter and hung on. "I'm sorry," she said, wiping the blood from her fingers onto her jean shorts.

"About what?"

"The box," Reagan said. "I'm sorry you had to lose it like that."

"Yeah, we'll all be sorry one day, won't we?" Tab said to the sky.

"What was in it?"

Tab scoffed. "Doesn't matter now, does it?"

CHAPTER THIRTEEN

LIKE BOY, LIKE TOAD

"Hey," Alpin snapped, "get up."

As much as Bea wanted to, she felt tethered to the ground, held down by invisible roots. "Reagan's gone," she said. "We can't just leave her. We have to go get her. We have to." She pressed her fingers to her temples and stared at the dirt beneath her. If only she had done something. If only she had fought back, not just stood there like a weakling. She was supposed to be the Sacred Head, the guardian of the Books, some grand hero, but yet she didn't move an inch when she could have helped Reagan. And then she was gone, just like that.

"Get her?" Alpin said. "Have you already forgotten what's following us? That Shadow Reaper will not stop until it has its claws wrapped around your neck."

"No." Bea shook her head and stood, breaking free of her trance. "I'm not gonna leave her." *She wouldn't leave me.*

And what would Bea do without her? Though she barely knew Reagan, she was comfort in the strange place with all its talking animals and shadow monsters. Now Reagan was captured by some crazy lady with a knife…*a knife!* She prayed that knife hadn't touched Reagan and was only wielded for threatening measures.

"My duty is to protect the Sacred Head," Alpin said. "Which means my number one priority is to get you to Galecrest without any issues. Unfortunately, that does not entail going on some grand quest to save your friend. Now, let's go." He reached for her hand, but she pulled it away. "You'll be no help at all if you died before you even got the chance to search for her. We need to get going."

Though she did not agree, Bea decided it best to follow the gopher. After all, she would have no way of surviving all by herself.

The two of them walked in silence for what Bea had decided was the most uncomfortable amount of time she could bear before Alpin spoke.

"Being out here in the open is simply asking for death. We'll rest there for the night." He stopped where the dirt path became a cracked grey stone walkway and pointed to a cluster of ramshackle houses along the stretch up ahead, all shrouded in the same, lonely silhouette under the thickening grey clouds. As they got closer, Bea could see that their windows were blown out to only a few, stray pieces of glass, and their doors barely clung to their rusted hinges.

"No Eslurian I know would dare stay in a place this despicable, so I can't imagine we'd have any company." Alpin stalked up to the first house on the left and nudged the front door with the tip of his staff. At his touch, it clattered to the ground and broke in two. A horde of insects fled its rotten insides and disappeared into the cracks in the floor.

Alpin's lips curled with disgust. He tiptoed around the door, hugging his body against the frame presumably so that his feet would not touch where the insects migrated. Bea wondered what sort of dramatic display would follow if the gopher got a bit of dirt on his precious fur.

She stepped over the broken door and followed after Alpin, into the building, stumbling blindly through the darkness. Her eyes soon adjusted as she made her way past what must have been a living room at some point.

Like the life that once gave warmth to the home, the room was absent of furniture, save for two wooden chairs that sat in the far right of the room. Though they remained intact, Bea wasn't completely sure they would hold her weight, so she sat down in the corner, brought her knees up to her chin, and wrapped her arms around her legs. She wished she had worn a sweater but had no luck in willing one into existence with the thought.

"I'll be back," Alpin announced, walking back toward the door.

"Where are you going?" Bea asked.

"Don't play a fool," Alpin said. "I heard your stomach rumble just as much as I did my own."

Bea clutched her gut, which expressed its desires with a low growl. "I'll come with." She could hardly stand the gopher, but the thought of being alone in the dark, abandoned house seemed more awful a punishment than tagging along with him. She started to stand, but Alpin waved her away dismissively.

"No," he said, "I'll be much more efficient on my own. I haven't got the energy, nor the patience, to worry about you on this errand." He left before she could argue any further.

Bea sat in the darkness, thinking about Reagan and where in this strange place she might be. She wanted to get up, run, escape through the door and search until she had made sure that Reagan was safe. She felt terrible about leaving her with that bandit or whoever it was that took her. *Breathe*, she told herself. She closed her eyes and inhaled deeply, listening to the wind rage outside. The house shivered as it blew through the open windows and the cracks in the wood-plank walls, whistling and groaning. Dead tree branches scraped the loose roof panels, startling Bea for a moment. But as soon as she had calmed herself again, she heard a voice outside, and it wasn't the gopher's.

"How long have we been walking?" it said. Bea tensed. "I need a break." It was a young boy's voice. "I think my legs are gonna snap if I take one more step." Whoever it was, they were talking to someone else, meaning that there were two…or more in their crew. Bea knew she could not take on another person by herself, and if it were a group, she might as well have been dead. She looked around for something to protect herself with.

"Whaddya think, Mauz? How about we stop here for the night?" The voice spoke from just outside the open door.

Bea's heart pounded. She crawled toward the window, pulled a shard of glass from the window frame, and hunkered in the shadows beneath the sill.

She heard their footsteps outside the window, not heavy and not a lot. At least it didn't sound like an army or a gang of any sort. Nor did it sound like a monster—the Shadow Reaper had had no feet, at least from what she remembered. She took a deep breath, held it, lifted her head and peered through the broken window.

To her terror, she found herself nose to nose with a boy who looked to be about her age. "Ahh!"

"Peppersnakes!" the boy shouted.

Bea fell over backwards, nearly giving herself a shave with the shard of glass and sending a plume of dust into the air. "Snakes?" she gasped, then coughed out the dust she'd inhaled. She scrambled to stand up, kicking out her legs and arms as if the slimy reptiles were crawling all over her. When she got up on her feet, she held her breath and waited to feel their scales brush up against her skin, waiting for the bite and the terrible pain of poison entering her blood stream. The dust settled and she examined the house, finding no snakes. She exhaled, wondering what "*snakes*" the boy was so afraid of.

"Snakes?" the boy shrieked from outside the window. "Where?" He did some sort of panic-dance, then tensed up like a pole. He flung his hands over his eyes, knocking off his oversized glasses and hood in the process.

If Bea was not mistaken, there was a winged toad of sorts floating around the boy's head. She stared at it. *Yup, winged toad.* It certainly was no human-sized talking lizard, but it was weird in its own, almost cute, way.

"Oh gods, Mauz," the boy pleaded, apparently to the fairy

toad, "please tell me they're gone!" The boy was trembling, his feet and knees moving compulsively like he might have to pee.

"Tell me, are they gone?" he asked his plump companion. The toad responded with a deep *croak*. "Oh, thank goodness." The boy bent down and picked up his glasses, which now had a cracked lens, and put them on. Then he squinted at Bea.

As if out of instinct, the boy flung his fallen hood back over his head and pulled its edges down to cover his face. "Peppersnakes!" he said again and sunk down to his knees, shouting, "I never meant to harm anyone! I—I—"

"What are you talking about?" Bea said, pushing her head out the broken window. "There are no snakes here."

The boy looked up at her with his wide, fish-like eyes and said, "You mean…you don't know?"

"Don't know what?"

Croak.

"Shush, Mauz!" He seemed to think for a moment. "Oh… nothing. Nothing at all." He smiled, revealing two sharp-pointed canines, which might have been the most normal thing about him. The boy boasted more features from his floating pet toad than he did any human qualities, and truly was a sore sight for the eyes. A patchwork of green scales covered his skin, and a pair of fins that grew from the sides of his face where his ears should have been. The rest of his body was hidden beneath his robes, and Bea wondered if the pattern continued throughout.

"Hey"—the boy took a step toward the house—"mind if we join you in there? It's awfully lonely out here, and the wind keeps blowing Mauz into the trees." He gestured toward the fairy toad.

"Uh." Bea glanced around the empty room awkwardly, looking for a reason to say no, but finding none. "Sure?"

"Excellent!" He ran over to the front door and inside the house. "My name is Barnaby Britto," he said, "and this is Mauz." The plump toad sat on the boy's head. Barnaby gave him a little pat and extended his hand. It was quite green even in the dim light of the house, and his long, bony fingers were connected with thin green webbing. Bea cautiously took hold of it, and the boy nearly shook her arm from her socket in his excitement.

"Well," Barnaby said. He dropped her hand and peered around the room. "It's not so bad in here. You know, if you look past all the dust, mold, broken glass, and bugs everywhere, it's actually quite nice! Better than sleeping in a bush, right?" The boy shimmied off his shoes, exhaled as if they were restricting him in some way, and tossed them in a darkened corner. He wiggled his toes, which, like his fingers, were also connected by green webbing and accompanied by scales.

Croak! Mauz said.

"It's okay, Mauz, she's not a Sacred Guard." Barnaby looked at Bea and cupped his hands around his mouth so Mauz could not hear. "You're not a Guard, are you?"

Bea shook her head and wondered what he meant. She was supposedly a Sacred Head, but she didn't know what that meant either.

"See? I told ya, Mauz," he said.

Mauz seemed to be more interested in a fly that was buzzing toward his face. When it got close, he opened his mouth and his tongue flopped out onto the top of Barnaby's head. The fly passed by unbothered and disappeared into the darkness.

Barnaby sighed. "Mauz, how many times do I have to tell you, the bugs won't just *fly* into your mouth?" The boy picked the toad off his head and rolled his tongue back into his mouth. "He's still learning." Barnaby blushed and wiped the grime from the toad's tongue on his robe.

"So, what's your name, then, huh?" Barnaby asked, tilting his head like a puppy.

"Uhm." Bea narrowed her eyes at him, debating whether or not to reveal her true name. "Lea."

"Lea?" Barnaby repeated excitedly. "Like the great warrior Lealyn who defeated the rampaging drovig in Varaar?" He leaned forward, eyes wide, and looked her up and down. When Bea didn't answer he rubbed his chin and tried again, "Hmm, then perhaps like Leatran the Great, who swam across the raging rapids of Bellbour's Strait all by herself." Barnaby looked especially hopeful about that one, swinging his arms around like he was a swimmer, and not a good one.

Bea thought for a moment about how it would feel to be named after such great warriors—those who fought monsters and braved raging rapids...*Nah, I can't live up to that.* She shook her head.

"All right, so maybe just Lea, then," he said. "Just Lea is fine, too." He shrugged. "So, Just Lea, what are you doing out here all by your lonesome?"

"I could ask you the same thing," she said.

"Fair! You see, I'm on my way to Treenode, but I had the grandest idea along the way. Since I'm out here, why not go to Galecrest, too. That's where the Eslurian Opera House is.

It's just the most wonderful thing you'll ever see. A massive, marble building with columns all around it and two golden dragons on either side of the roof; their wings spread high into the sky." Bea could not lie, she found herself wanting to see the building in person too, even with his overly exaggerated arm gestures which she assumed were in an attempt to demonstrate the dragon's pose.

"Ever since I was just a little Olphin," Barnaby continued, "it's been my dream to go to Galecrest." His face lit up despite the darkness of the house, and he closed his eyes. "One day, I'm gonna sit in the front row of seats." He closed his eyes and smiled. "I can already hear the crowd cheering, feel the lights on my face, taste the sweat rolling—"

Croak!

"Oh, yes, thank you Mauz." He opened his eyes again. "It's your turn, Lea. What are you doing out here?"

"I"—she thought for a moment—"I don't really know." There was a bit of truth in the statement. Sure, she knew she, too, was going to Galecrest, but why, she had not even the slightest clue. She was pretty sure it had something to do with a place called Eslura and a Head, perhaps a Sacred one. She hoped she could keep her own.

"Well, that's perfect! Mauz and I could sure use the company if you'd like to join us and—"

"What is that *thing* doing in here?" Alpin stood in the doorway in the dim light of the moon. He dropped the handful of seeds, vegetables, and fruits he'd collected. They scattered across the floor, collecting dust as they rolled and settled. "Stand back, Beatrice!" he shouted. He gripped his staff with both paws and walked toward the boy, making a high-pitched whistling sound. "*Twee! Twee!*"

"Alpin, wait!" Bea yelled, but her words did nothing to slow the gopher or extinguish his rage.

"Begone, you spawn of Nelazgus!" Alpin batted Barnaby's knees with the staff, throwing the boy off balance and onto the floor. The boy tried to cover his head with his webbed hands, but Alpin drove the top of his staff into Barnaby's forehead, and he went limp.

Alpin exhaled and clutched the fur above his heart as if he were having a heart attack. "Beatrice," he said. He poked the boy with the tip of his staff and relaxed a bit once he was sure that the boy was unconscious. "Do you know what kind of *monstrosity* it is that you've so kindly invited into this house?"

Bea took a minute to think about that. *Monstrosity?* Though the boy did not know the first thing about controlling his babbling, Bea would not call him a *monstrosity*. In fact, he seemed kind of nice, like someone she actually might want to try and befriend. He was nothing like the girls back at Mountbridge; he didn't treat her like some sort of freak show.

"No?" Alpin shouted. "That *thing* is an Olphin! A traitor! The enemy of Eslura and all of her subjects! Now, help me lift it. I haven't got the twine to bind it, so we'll have to lock it in a closet until morning." He pointed toward a door on the far end of the wall.

Bea looked down at Barnaby. Mauz was slopping his tongue all over the boy's face, apparently trying to wake him. Bea bent down and scooped up the confused frog and placed it on her shoulder.

"Come over here, Bea," Alpin said. "Help me lock him up."

"But why?" Bea asked. "He didn't do anything wrong?"

"But *why*?" Alpin stepped toward Bea. "This monster is an Olphin! Do you not recall the Olphins tried to eradicate the whole of Eslura? A filthy Nelazgian is what it is. Traitors of the War of Shadows and followers of Obellius. You bear the Sacred Symbol, aye? Know your enemies."

Bea decided against arguing with the gopher since he knew far more about wherever she was than she did, and she'd rather not make any more of a fool of herself than she already had. She joined Alpin at Barnaby's side and helped him lift the boy up and over to the closet.

"That's good, easy now, any sudden movement might wake it," Alpin said. Bea opened the door and they slid him into the bottom below the empty shelves. "Perfect." Alpin closed the closet door, slumped his shoulders, and leaned against the wall beside it. "That was too close." He slid down the wall until he was in a sitting position on the ground. "I should have known better than to leave you alone. You're lucky I came when I did."

"I was fine," Bea said, sitting down herself.

Alpin laughed. "Fine? Do you know what that Olphin would have done to you if given half the chance?"

"He had a whole chance," Bea said.

Alpin grumbled something under his breath about Bea being reckless, then he lay flat on the floor. "We leave at dawn. Haberpaw is a short walk and has a gully post. I will alert the scouts of the Olphin's whereabouts from there." He closed his eyes and rolled to face the wall.

131

Bea sat in the darkness, staring at the closet. After a little while, she began to hear some shuffling and soft moaning from inside. She looked at Alpin, his chest rising and falling, his big-toothed mouth open and snuffling. She stood up and walked across the room toward the door, scooping up a few of the berries Alpin had dropped along the way. Then she opened the door.

Mauz announced her presence with a *croak* and Barnaby lifted his head. He had a lump on his head the size of an egg. He looked at her with wide eyes.

"My name's not Lea," she whispered. "It's Bea." She reached her hand, full of berries, down and dropped them into his webbed hands. "It's not much. Alpin's a terrible scavenger."

He grabbed the largest of the berries and plopped it into his mouth. He sucked on it and smiled. "Nice to meet you, Bea."

CHAPTER FOURTEEN

INTO THE CANYON

Tab pressed the pergonzia forward without rest for what Reagan assumed to be at least two hours—though it could have been longer or shorter, she didn't have any way to know. The scenery had yet to change, and she could have sworn she saw the same cactus at least three times. The sun had risen directly above them and beamed down on their heads and backs, forcing a sweat out of both of them. Reagan's head ached from lack of water—the last of their supply having fallen off in the commotion of outrunning the drovig. She wanted to just lie down and close her eyes.

"All right," Tab spoke for the first time since they had escaped the drovig. She pulled the pergonzia to a halt and kicked her feet out of the stirrups. "Off." Reagan followed Tab's lead, swinging her left leg over the tall beast, then sliding down its side.

"What's wrong?" Reagan asked when both her feet hit the sand.

"What's wrong is that you think you can just dress like *that* here." Reagan looked down at her outfit—striped tee, jeans, and tennis shoes, her usual Camp Tossbridge garb. Tab shook her head at her. "You need to be properly suited before we go in." The woman fished through one of the few remaining sacks tied to the pergonzia and tossed a bundle of clothing and a pair of leather boots at Reagan. "That should fit. We're about the same size." Reagan unfolded the bundle and held it out to look at it. A hooded dress with an ankle-length cloak.

"It's for stealth," Tab said. "It's not meant to be stylish. Now put it on."

Reagan turned to look for somewhere private to change but found none in the open desert.

"Oh, please, Red. You're not my type. I like my women much more feisty."

Reagan ignored the comment, took off her shirt and pants, and slipped the dress-cloak over her head. Though it was slim and hugged every one of her curves, the oversized hood drooped down to her nose and demanded an adjustment every few minutes. "I have a name, you know," she said. "It's Reagan, and I wouldn't mind being addressed that way every so often."

Tab scoffed and tossed her a silk scarf. "Make sure that covers the rest of your face and keeps your hair back. I may not like it, but someone else might take a liking to that red hair of yours, and the last thing we need is to attract any unnecessary attention."

Reagan closed her eyes and fought back the urge to say

something back. She slipped the scarf around her neck and tossed the tail ends behind her back, huffing under her breath.

"Hey, it's not my fault you had to be the one with the stone."

"Are we finished here?"

"No," Tab said. She limped over to Reagan, grabbed the chain hanging between her breasts, and tucked it and the stone attached to it beneath the collar of the dress. "Keep that out of sight, got it?" Reagan nodded. "Good." Tab made her way back to the pergonzia and picked up its reins.

"Tab, you're limping," Reagan said.

"Yeah, what's it to ya?" Tab stopped to look back at Reagan. Her face scrunched up and she looked angry, angrier than before, at Reagan's prodding.

"I don't know...it's just...is it painful?"

"No, not anymore. Happened many moons ago. Little dispute with a past lover, is all. No need to shed any more light on it. Let's just go already."

Reagan glanced around, wondering where Tab might be referring to. There were no signs of any city, or human life, or anything for miles all around—just sand, a few cacti, and a couple of tumbleweeds.

They had been walking for about an hour beside the pergonzia when they came upon a long, wide canyon in the desert. They stopped at the edge and peered down. Hundreds of feet below, a large city had been carved into the cliff walls and thousands of people, some in groups, others alone and toting simple wooden carts, wound through the dense maze of stalls and sand huts. Canopies stretched across outcroppings of rocks and shaded parts of the area from the intense heat.

In the center, a colosseum lay surrounded by a honeycomb of streets and buildings. Though the colosseum appeared to be empty at the moment, Reagan could imagine it full of screaming crowds watching a gladiator battle like she had read about in Mr. Bonham's very boring world history class.

"Welcome to Varaar," Tab said, "Eslura's meeting place for the scum of the world."

Reagan was still too overwhelmed by the view to say anything. She had been to the Grand Canyon once when she was five. They were similar in size and makeup, but this one had a bustling city at the bottom.

Tab led Reagan and the pergonzia down the dusty cliff path and into the base of the canyon. The black cloak-dress was extremely hot with the sun beating down on it, and Reagan thought she might pass out any second if she didn't get some water. She didn't know how Tab and her mount were able to persevere, but she said nothing. She didn't need more insults from the woman who claimed to be protecting her. They slunk into the shadows of the cliffs, which were slightly cooler, and were immediately immersed in a seething mass of sweat-drenched bodies and scantily clad dancers.

The air was thick with acrid smoke and made worse only by those whose mouths were attached to the pipes they held between their lips. People hugged the shadows of the cliffs, their sand-stained faces weighing heavier on Reagan's back than the sun as they watched her follow Tab through the mass. They forced her sight to the ground where she fought for proper footing amidst the hundreds of shoes who trod on top of her toes.

"You." Reagan smelled the liquor on the man's breath before she felt his hands on her shoulders. "Take off those robes and dance for me, woman!" He grabbed her cloak with his filthy hands and pulled her into an embrace.

"Let go of me!" She threw an elbow at his crooked red nose, but he blocked it with his forearm and smiled at her with slick yellow teeth. She pulled away from his hot breath, but the man did not let go of her cloak.

"Mmm." The man leaned in closer and lifted her hood. "What pretty red hair you've—"

Tab thrust her dagger below the man's chin. "Do you wanna see how far I can shove this blade up your skull?" She twisted the tip of her dagger into his chin and drew a drop of blood. "'Cause I sure do."

The man looked down his nose at Tab's dagger and rose to her cloaked face. "Who are you?" he asked, tilting his head up to release the pressure of the blade.

"Don't you know better than to question someone who's got a knife shoved up your throat?" Tab said. She pressed the blade a little deeper. "Now, my friend here said to let go. Are you gonna listen, or should I slit your throat?"

"Vorath," the man cursed. He released Reagan's cloak and threw his hands up in surrender. Tab drew back her dagger, and the man groped about his throat to assess the damage. Before turning to disappear into the crowd, he spat a fat lump of saliva on Tab's boot.

"He's weak," Tab said. She used her clean foot to wipe the goop off her other. "He won't last another week down here." She then sheathed her dagger. "Let's move."

CHAPTER FOURTEEN

Reagan brushed her cloak—as if doing so would remove the man's filth—and followed Tab through the crowd. She went about three blocks, past two taverns each with lines around the corner, a pawn shop, and a second-hand clothing shop with some slightly blood-stained cloaks in its display window until she dog legged into a narrow side street shaded by the canopies stretched between the buildings above them.

The street was lined with dozens of stalls on each side, and there was barely enough room to lead the pergonzia between them. As she followed Tab down the alley, Reagan saw all kinds of unsavory things for sale, everything from drugs and moonshine to animals and even dirty little children. The vendors eyed the two from beneath hooded robes and whistled or made sick kissing noises as they passed by. Reagan's stomach bubbled.

At last, Tab walked up to a stall on the right with a flag depicting a crudely drawn shield hanging over it. She tossed a gold coin that read *kap* on the counter. The vendor appeared to understand her unspoken request and disappeared behind a back curtain. He returned almost immediately with two knives, each half an arm's length long and sharp enough to slice the silence between them. Tab sheathed one in the holster that formerly held the knife that Reagan had so ineptly thrown at the drovig, and handed the other to Reagan, who took it by the hilt and held it loosely in her palm, unsure of it.

"You'll need to defend yourself if I'm unable," Tab said. "So, don't be shy. Hold it like you mean it. Loose fingers won't ever secure the kill." Tab demonstrated with her own, pulling it from beneath her cloak, slicing the air twice, then returning it to her scabbard. All Reagan could do was tuck the blade under her belt and pray that she would never have to use it.

"Whatever," Tab said with a dismissive wave. "Don't go sayin' I didn't try. Anyways, we've gotta move. Never good to stay in one place too long in this dump. Keep that hood up and follow close, got it?" Reagan nodded, adjusted her hood, and double checked her scarf. Tab looked her over. "Good. The colosseum is right around the corner."

The colosseum could have been "right around the corner" from any point in the city. Had she looked up from the alley, she would have seen its tiered arches towering hundreds of feet in the air. Seen the orange flags jutting from its awning flicking in the breeze, and above it all, seen the five great statues standing tall from the top of its wall. Its appearance was nothing short of intimidating.

Tab spat on the ground and flipped her middle finger up at the statues. Their stone faces glared back, impassive and unimpressed by her act of rebellion.

"Who are they?" Reagan asked. She had already ruled out their being Sacred Rulers. Neither Alistair nor Millennium appeared among them.

"The scum that erected this crap-hole," Tab said, "Unlike the rest of Eslura, Varaar was created by the people, *the gangs*. The Rewakan, the Nabagari, the Damaziko, the Khaylant, and the Senadryn gangs. Five gangs, five sleazebag rulers. The very voraths standing above you. The only good thing about 'em is they don't give a flying rabintail's horn who's comin' and goin' through their territory. So long as you have kaps in your pockets, they won't question a thing."

"Gangs, huh?" Reagan said. "We have gangs in Missoula, too, but I guess a bit different." She gazed up at the statues again and noticed their eyes were plated gold and sparkled in the waning sunlight.

"Unfortunately, so." Tab rolled her eyes. "They might not admit it themselves, but they still fall under the rule of the Sacred Rulers. As much as they'll claim independence, they're still part of Eslura. Though, you won't find anything Sacred here—the gangs made sure of it when they laid down the framework for the city. 'Freedom' is what they call it. Nelazgian propaganda is what I call it." Tab balled her fists. "Anyways, enough of them. They don't deserve any more attention than they already get." She pulled the pergonzia to the side of the street and tied it up to a post. "Stay here, you hear?" Tab pointed a finger at her pergonzia. "I'm not tryna wrangle me another one of you." The beast gave her an emotionless blink then dipped its head down to nibble at a piece of grass poking through the sand. "Whatever, let's go."

Reagan followed Tab toward the colosseum. They hugged the curve of its side around to what appeared to be the back. Tab slowed to a halt. "There." She pointed to a stable attached to the colosseum by a bridge. Reagan nodded and the two crept across the gap between the colosseum and the stable.

Tab crouched down by a window on the side of the stable and drew one of her daggers. She slammed its pommel into the glass three times before it shattered, raining shards on the ground.

"In and out. Grab your mount, then mad dash out the front door—things are so fast the guards won't even know what slipped past 'em. I'll make sure the room's empty first, then shoot you a signal." Tab sheathed her dagger, cleared the window of its few straggler shards, then disappeared inside it in one swift motion. A moment later, Reagan spied her hand in the window, waving her inside.

Reagan slid through feet first, hoping that the gap between it and the floor was slim. To her misfortune, it wasn't. Her feet slammed onto hard ground and sent pain and pins and needles up her legs, momentarily paralyzing her in place. She bit her tongue to hold back a groan. Then she glanced around the dimly lit room, first meeting Tab's half-cloaked face, then the hundreds of lifeless eyeballs blinking with confusion. The pergonzias.

Tight stalls confined them with an overflowing food bucket set just out of reach beyond the door, forcing them to crane their necks with no hope of ever reaching them. Untended piles of hardened and rotting manure whose already wretched smell was only made worse by the sweltering heat that radiated off the densely packed beasts. And at the far end of all the mess, a beast too large for a stable sat in a cage chained to the wall.

"What the—" Reagan started.

"Oh, that thing?" Tab tossed a finger over her shoulder. "That's a havarrak. A night hopper. Thing's a demon dressed in black fur." As if the beast understood, it bared its teeth and let out a low growl. "You should see the way it tears up the idiots who are dumb enough to challenge it."

A night hopper. The name rang a familiar bell. Alpin had used the same words to describe his own pet, Galabear. Though the one confined before her was twice the size of Galabear, it seemed no more menacing.

"You mean, they force it to fight?"

"Don't act so simple. The things are natural-born killers. And they put on quite a show too, I'll tell ya that."

"They're not natural-born killers," Reagan said. "They're raised to be that way."

"And you'd know that little tidbit how?" Tab raised a brow.

Reagan ignored her and examined the contraption that held the havarrak in place. Two chains extended from clasps on the wall on either side of the cage and attached to a spiked harness around the havarrak's chest. They were set in such a way that if the beast moved, the spikes would dig into its skin. "It's already in a cage, why do they need all those spikes?"

"I don't know, Red. Who cares?"

"I do. It's not right—it's cruel."

"Oh, for the love of Aezaros, don't get all sentimental on me. We don't have time for this. Just grab a pergonzia and let's get outta here." Tab grabbed Reagan's arm and pulled her back toward the pergonzia stalls, but Reagan shook her off and walked toward the havarrak's cage instead.

She crouched and held her hands up. "I'm not going to hurt you, see?"

The beast reared back, bared its teeth, and hissed like a cat, but when the chains drew taut and the spikes on the harness dug into its body, it whimpered.

"I know, I know. You have to be still, or those spikes will keep hurting you."

"Hey, Miss Havarrak Helper," Tab said, "that thing can't understand a lick of what you're spewing."

"Why do you always—aagh!" The beast swiped a massive paw at her, but it clanged off the thick bars of the cage. Reagan fell backwards and nearly landed in a pile of dung. "Why do you always have to be so condescending?" Reagan stood and approached the cage again, noticing a small plaque nailed to the base of it: *ALOEISSA*.

"Aloeissa, is that your name?" The mention of its name seemed to soothe the beast as it retracted its claws and took a step backwards. "Please stop moving, Aloeissa. You're only hurting yourself." She pulled her dagger from her belt. "I'm going to get that thing off of you, okay?" She reached up for the clasp on the wall, but she was too short to reach it with the blade, even on her tiptoes.

"This is painful," Tab moaned. Reagan lowered her blade and watched Tab walk across the room towards her. She stopped in front of her and bent down, making a basket of her gloved hands.

"What are you doing?" Reagan stepped backwards.

"Would you shut it? I'm trying to help you. Now, let me lift you up, so we can get the heck out of here," Tab said. Reagan nodded and set her boot in Tab's hands. She hoisted Reagan up against the wall. "Can you reach it now?"

"Almost." Reagan grit her teeth. The tip of the blade just barely scratched the metal of the clasp. "A tiny bit higher." She felt Tab thrust her up, and she clicked the contraption with the tip of her blade, setting it loose. "Got it." Reagan exhaled. "We'll need the other one too." She pointed to the other side of the cage where the second chain held tight onto the wall.

"All right, all right, just give me a second. You're not as light as you look." Tab carried Reagan to the other side and held her as she loosed the second bolt. It fell to the ground, and with it the chain.

The havarrak whimpered softly as the harness fell forward off its chest. It licked the wounds on its chest, then lifted and tilted its head at Reagan. It stepped toward the bars, pressed its nose through an opening in the metal, and sniffed her. Big, yellow eyes stared her up and down. Reagan could have sworn she saw a smile on the beast's face, but she hadn't enough time to look for the door of the room swung open with a bang.

"Aye!" a deep voice bellowed. Reagan turned to find a broad-chested man with a thick black beard standing in the doorway. "What are you doing here? This area is strictly off limits!"

"Good question," Tab said, stepping toward the man. "Care to answer that one, Red?" Reagan stepped back toward the grunting pergonzias.

The man did not wait for a reply. He unsheathed his sword and advanced toward them. Tab stepped in front of Reagan and mirrored the man, pulling her own weapons into view. "I'm not lookin' to drag this little trip out any longer than we already have. Let's just get this over with."

The man agreed with a yell. He lifted his sword above his head, charged, and swung down at Tab's head. She caught the man's blade between her daggers with a clang of metal against metal. He struggled to free his blade from her trap. While distracted, Tab booted him in the chest, loosing the sword from his grip. He flew backward wheezing, and his blade clattered onto the ground. Tab kicked it across the room, out of his reach.

"While that was fun," Tab said, stepping toward him, "I think it's time for you to leave us be." She pressed a dagger to his stout chest and pushed him back toward the door. He resisted for a moment, eyeing his blade on the ground, then fled out of sight.

Tab sheathed her weapons and turned back toward Reagan. "Gods, you're causing me more trouble than I bargained for."

"Well, I didn't ask you to kidnap me," Reagan said, dipping and pulling her black cloak into a curtsy.

"Whatever, Red. Now that you've completed your little act of justice, we've got one last errand to run before we ditch this sorry sack of a town. Grab a mount. It's time to pay a visit to an old friend."

CHAPTER FIFTEEN

THE GULLY POST

Bea woke to screaming, her back pressed against the ground. Shrill cries filled the ashy air, and feet clapped on stone around her. Shadows scurried past her, scrambling to escape, murmuring.

Bea raised her head and massaged her temples. Her body ached; her head ached. She smelled smoke; orange light flickered through the broken windows.

She stood, turned to look for Alpin, for Barnaby, but found neither. She walked toward the window. People gathered in the street outside, standing around a burning structure. She stared at it. It looked like…it *was* the symbol, five interlocking rings shooting flames into the night sky, crumbling and collapsing piece by piece onto the ground.

The crowd of around thirty people stood mesmerized, staring at it, their backs to Bea in the window as its golden rings fell under the heat of the fire.

A tall, thin man emerged from the flames, his black-and-gold robes burning and then fizzling out. Heavy strides led him toward her, toward Bea. Bea inched backward, not sure if he could see her. But he walked right up to the broken window and stopped before her, head cloaked in shadows, tufts of white hair falling from his hood.

"We'll rebuild this land," he told her. "You and I. Reclaim what was stolen." He reached his hand through the window and waited for her to take it.

"No," Bea shouted and swatted his hand, but the man grabbed her wrist, his sharp nails burrowing into her skin, tearing it apart. She tried to pull away, but he was too strong. "Let go of me!" she screamed. He did as she requested and released her. She fell backwards, tripped on one of the two chairs, and tumbled onto her back on the floor. She gasped for the air that was knocked from her lungs and stared at the ceiling, then clambered to her knees, but the flickering orange was gone, the window was dark, and Alpin stood next to her.

"Let go of you? I haven't set a paw on you," the gopher said, staring at her with furry furrowed brows.

"Where did they go? The symbol, the fires?" She sat up and glanced around the bare room. "There was a man…outside the window." Bea rubbed her eyes but there was nothing except the pink of dawn.

"What man?" Alpin looked around the room. "Is there a man here?"

"I-I don't know." Bea shook her head. She recalled the man, tall and lanky, hair almost too white.

"Right." Alpin rolled his eyes. "You had better come to terms with this *man* soon. We haven't got the time for him with our added stop."

Bea stared at the ground, knowing she appeared foolish. She was unfortunately quite familiar with bad dreams. She had been suffering through them—waking up in cold sweats, screaming herself awake—ever since her mother disappeared, but never had she had ones so vivid, so horrifying.

Bea looked up and Alpin directed his sight toward the closet. "Olphin! Get up and show yourself, you're coming with us."

Barnaby rolled out of the closet, a big purple welt on his forehead. "Me? Coming with you?" Mauz sat atop his matted hair, yawning, eyes swiveling twice before settling in their crossed positions.

"Did I not just say that?" Alpin blinked and rolled his eyes again.

"Thank you so much, Mr. Alpin! Mauz and I will be on our very best behavior and—"

"Oh, please. There's no need for that." Alpin dismissed the boy with a bat of his paw. "I will be announcing your whereabouts by way of gully at the Haberpaw post. The Sacred Guard can deal with you from there." Barnaby's shoulders slumped and his gaze shifted to the floor. Alpin tapped his staff on the doorframe. "It's not too far by foot, but we had better get moving. We've already lost enough time with Galabear tramping off."

They left the old house and continued down the stone path, which soon turned to dirt again. Bea still could not shake the feeling of dread from her dream, looking right and left and into the woods for any sign of the man or the burnt symbol while Alpin tapped along silently, and Barnaby alternately lamented his plight and chattered about the remarkable scenery to his croaking friend. Around mid-morning, they arrived at a small town Alpin announced to be Haberpaw.

Its main stretch seemed a lot like Mountbridge's main road. Squat homes stood along both sides of the well-maintained dirt road. A few blocks farther, they came to some shops, one of which Bea determined was a bakery, based on the sweet sugary smells of confections and the enticing aroma of fresh bread.

"Alpin?" a voice called. Bea turned her head, searching for who it belonged to, and found a giant dog-like creature standing on hind legs in the doorway of the bakery, his sharp-toothed smile as grand as the pile of muffins he held between his paws.

"Keep moving," Alpin hissed, head tucked deep into his chest.

"Alpin Loomin? Is that truly you?" he called again. The creature emerged from the doorway and met them on the dirt road. The large, brown beast had four long arms in addition to his hind legs and was more than two heads taller than Bea. He wore an old patchwork cap on the top of his head, positioned between his pointed ears.

"Gods, spare me," Alpin huffed. He rubbed his temples and turned his head away from the dog.

"Who is that?" Barnaby whispered to Bea through cupped hands.

She shook her head and shrugged. "No idea." Though she more so wondered *what* it was. Four-armed dogs with muffins? She wasn't even going to try. This place was getting weirder and weirder.

"Well, I'll be darned!" The creature beamed, struggling to hold his mountain of muffins in his four paws. "I knew my nose hadn't failed me. You've really come back for a visit!"

"I have not come back for a visit, Bowmidge." Alpin tried to scurry by, but the dog hopped in front of him, smiling like he had just been given a big bone…and was not holding a pile of delicious-looking muffins.

"Oh, no need for excuses." The creature—Bowmidge—dismissed Alpin with a wave of one of his four paws. "We all get homesick at some point or another." He patted Alpin on the back, nearly knocking the gopher to the ground.

"I do not miss home." Alpin caught his footing and grit his teeth. "We are merely stopping to use the post."

Bea wasn't so sure if she was homesick or not. In what felt like the blink of an eye, her life had suddenly changed so much she didn't know what to think, other than perhaps it was all some horrible fever dream. She was surrounded by creatures she never even knew existed, or even thought could exist, and she, herself, was supposedly some kind of Head, though which kind she wasn't sure. And she seemed to be on the run from something very dangerous, though she wasn't sure what that was either. On the other hand, at least she wasn't at the Dildeckers, which was deathly boring, and she wasn't at Tossbridge with the clones, and she certainly wasn't at Mountbridge Psych Ward…or at least she didn't think she was.

"…just happen to be head of the post here in Haberpaw," Bowmidge said proudly.

"Head of the post with that pea brain of yours?" Alpin scoffed. "By gods."

"Ha! You old jokester, Alpin." Bowmidge slapped him on the back again. "Well, are you going to introduce me to your friends or not? It's a bit awkward, don't ya think?" Bowmidge pursed his lips and looked at Barnaby, whose hood was pulled down and his scarf pulled up. "Mysterious one, aye?" Bowmidge rubbed the white stubbles on his chin with one paw, while meddling with the boy's hood in another.

Alpin leapt up and swatted his paw away. "Would you stop it, already. The sun—it…uh—gives him hives."

Now you're helping him? Bea wondered what sort of agenda Alpin had running through his mind. One moment he was knocking the boy out cold with his staff, the next he was defending his identity. Perhaps he was a little madder than she had originally thought.

"Funny fellow!" Bowmidge laughed.

"Bea, Barnaby"—Alpin gestured to each of the two respectively—"this is Bowmidge." He rolled his eyes at the dog.

"He's right, that's my name! Bowmidge Talorn, at your service." He bowed, holding the muffins below his chest.

"Bowmidge and I grew up together in Haberpaw," Alpin explained. "*Unfortunately,*" he added beneath his breath.

"Right-o-right, old pal!" Bowmidge flipped his cap back on his head and gripped Alpin's shoulder with a paw, shaking him till his eyes spun in circles. "And boy-o-boy have I missed you. This town has been ever so lonely since you left."

"I don't doubt that," Alpin said. "It was never all that exciting to begin with."

151

"Why don't you come up and write that letter, hm? I'll even brew us some tea, how 'bout that? The home is a bit of a mess, but I'm sure we can make do. The gullys will be delighted to have some new faces around."

"The gullys?" Bea asked.

"Well, of course! The gullys," Bowmidge brimmed.

"We have no time for tea, Bowmidge," Alpin said. "We're just here to send a quick letter and that's all. No need to waste any of your tea on us."

"Oh, you can spare a moment for your old pal, can't ya? C'mon, I'll make your favorite. It'll be splendid I swear it! And you can send your letter too." Bowmidge placed a paw on his chest and pounded over where Bea assumed would be his heart. "Digguno's honor." Bowmidge pulled Alpin down the road, leaving no room for argument. Bea and Barnaby shared a look and followed along. Mauz croaked.

The road soon became a path that led them up a hill to a crooked wooden house situated at its peak. Dozens of wooden posts jutted from its side, on which strange little fist-sized creatures that looked like cats crossed with birds, or perhaps the other way around, were perched. They made little sounds, halfway between a squawk and a meow, as they flocked down toward Bowmidge, shedding feathers and fur in their haste.

"Hello, hello, my babies," Bowmidge said. He handed the mountain of muffins to Bea and held three arms out for the tiny creatures to settle on. "Why you act like I've been gone for ages!" He nuzzled his face against one of the creatures, and it lifted its beak and nibbled at his ear.

Bea couldn't contain her smile. She wished to have one for

herself, but she couldn't imagine the Dildeckers would be too thrilled about the idea of adding another member to their household—no matter how cute that member was.

Alpin cleared his throat and gestured toward the door, which, like the house, was severely crooked. "Bowmidge, if you would."

"Right, right." Bowmidge walked to the door and twisted the knob with the most delicacy Bea had ever seen, his arms full of cat-birds...or perhaps bird-cats. The door popped open and about a dozen more of the tiny creatures fluttered out and up into the sky. Alpin ducked and covered his head with his staff, while Bea and Barnaby watched in awe as they disappeared into the clouds. Bowmidge, whose cap had been knocked off in their sudden escape, held the door open. "Well, then, come on in, won't ya?" He allowed them entry first, carefully picked up his cap, and followed them in.

"Hello, my gullys!" he sung up to the rafters, where hundreds of the tiny creatures perched on cross beams. They chirped and meowed and flew in circles, long tails flailing behind them. "Are you hungry?" They swooped down en masse and started to nibble at his cap. "Good!" Bowmidge took the muffins from Bea and tossed them up toward the ceiling. The gullys snagged them midair, fighting over every last crumb until nothing remained.

"Quite the place you've got." Alpin nodded at the meager living room, which also seemed to double as a kitchen based on the sink, stove, and large table. In the far corner, a staircase led upstairs to where Bea assumed his bedroom would be, and a single open door branched off from the main living space,

where another room full of gullys chirp-meowed and an array
of box-shaped holes stuffed with rolled-up parchment lined
the far wall. A mailroom.

"Nothing compared to yours, I assume." Bowmidge winked.

"We all can't be blessed by the gods, can we?" Alpin pursed
his lips and stuck his nose up. Bea rolled her eyes.

"Well, sit down, sit down, please do make yourselves at
home, would you?" Bowmidge gestured to the table. Bea,
Alpin, and Barnaby took up three of the four chairs while
Bowmidge busied himself with a kettle over a small fire on
the stove.

One of the gullys fluttered down and hovered by Barnaby's
head, hissing at Mauz. The hair on its back rose in tiny spikes.
Mauz blinked, unbothered or oblivious to its presence, Bea
could not tell.

"Nepsa!" Bowmidge howled. "We treat our guests with
respect in this house." He left the kettle and snatched the
gully out of the air, drawing it back toward his chest, and
locking it in an embrace. "Please do forgive Nepsa. He seems
to have forgotten his manners." The gully opened its beak
and hissed at Mauz then squirmed free of Bowmidge's grasp.
He flew up into the rafters and joined the other gullys, who
shuffled to make room for him on their perch.

Bowmidge approached Barnaby. "May I take your cloak?"
Barnaby shook his head, and Bowmidge drew back his paws.
"Hm, *real* mysterious one, aren't you?" He placed a paw to
his chin and raised his brow. The kettle screamed and he
spun to attend to its boiling water, pouring four cups full of
the green liquid.

"Bowmidge," Alpin said, shifting in his seat, "a piece of parchment, if you would."

"Ah, right!" Bowmidge stuck a claw in the air and scurried off into the mailroom, returning with a sheaf of about twenty or so sheets.

Alpin rolled his eyes. "I'm not writing a novel. One will do just fine." He drew the top piece from the stack and shoved the rest back in Bowmidge's paw. "And a quill?" Bowmidge nodded and picked one up off the floor below the table.

"So"—Alpin looked up from the paper at Bowmidge—"you've stayed put all these years?"

"Well, of course! What else would I do? Give up on the family business? I could never!" Bowmidge brought the tea from the stove to the table. He handed a cup to each of his guests, then sat down on his chair backwards and leaned two of his four arms on the chair; the other two he used to hold his teacup.

"Hmm," Alpin huffed, "how very...*exciting*," he said sarcastically.

"Quite so!" Bowmidge said cheerily. "Tell me now, what is this letter you are sending so urgently?"

"None of your business," Alpin snapped. He covered the page with his paw and leered up at Bowmidge, then at Barnaby. "Just a little letter for someone who might be able to—"

The house fell dark, and a cold chill swept in from under the door, whisking out the oil lanterns hung from the walls. The gullys above started to stir, their light chirps now loud and urgent. Bea looked out the window. Though it had been bright and sunny only moments before, it was suddenly dark outside. Black smoke filtered in below the front door, covering

155

the wooden floor.

"Twee!" Alpin said. Bea and Alpin exchanged a wide-eyed look.

"My gullys please!" Bowmidge stood from his chair and looked up to his pets. They had taken off from their perches and were flapping around in the darkness, squawking and squealing and shedding feathers to the floor. "What in the name of Aezaros is going on in here?"

"Twee!" Alpin chirped again. "Bowmidge, I'm afraid there's no time to explain, but we must not be seen by the creature who is about to make its way into your home."

"There." Bowmidge pointed to the mailroom. "Go on while you can, hide if you must!"

Before Bea even knew what to do, Barnaby bolted into the room, holding Mauz close to his chest. Bea and Alpin followed him, shut the door behind them, and hid amongst a horde of terrified looking gullys. A pounding rattled the front door and Bea put an eye to the crack between the door and the frame.

Bowmidge smoothed the fur on his chest and opened the front door.

A man with no eyes welcomed himself into the home and lumbered into the center of the living room, smoke trailing his footsteps. Robes, long and black, flicked up in the wind, revealing grey accents beneath. His brown hair was tied in tight braids that fell from his hood over his muscular shoulders.

He turned to face Bowmidge. "Why the blank stare?" he said in a low growl. "Don't you know how rude it is to stare like that?" The man walked to the table, pulled a chair, and sat down. He kicked his feet up on the table, knocking two teacups off. They shattered on the floor, causing the gullys to stir and squeak.

"I will not tolerate such disrespect in my household," Bowmidge said.

"Well, isn't that great for you and your 'household'? The wonderful thing is that no one ever said you had to," the man said. "And since we're going on talking about tolerating, I'll add in that I won't tolerate any more musings from you. Now that that has been settled, my name is Demise. I am a chosen servant of Obellius Kalaar, the rightful king of Eslura, and I believe that you are hiding someone I've been looking for. Would you like to spare me the trouble of finding her?"

"I don't know what you're talking about," Bowmidge said, but Bea could see his paws trembling.

Demise laughed and clutched his stomach. He carried on the act till it grew close to awkward, then he wiped away a fake tear from below his empty eye sockets. "Ah, I have not felt the joy of laughter in years. Thank you for that." He laced his claws over his lap. "I see you are not going to make this easy for me. Lucky for you, I came prepared for that outcome." Demise stood and held his hands at his side. "Mayna! Ariz!" called, and his hands began to vibrate. Black smoke poured from his claws and pooled on the ground, slowly forming into two, wolf-like creatures. Their eyes glowed red and their fur spewed smoke across the floor.

"You dare summon demons in my house!" Bowmidge, too, stood from his chair and stepped back toward the mailroom door.

Demise ignored him and raised his claws above the two

wolves' heads. "Bring her to me," he commanded. Bea watched the wolves sink into the floorboards and, like fish in a pond, swim through the floor around the house. They circled the table, then advanced toward the mailroom door. Bea leapt back from the door. She felt the blood drain from her face and froze.

A moment later, a wolf head popped up from the floorboards in the mailroom, mouth open, black teeth dripping with smoke.

"Mr. Alpin!" Barnaby lurched forward and knocked Alpin from the grasp of the wolf's jaw, but it clamped its teeth down on the boy's arm and an inky blackness seeped under Barnaby's skin. The boy howled in pain and jerked his arm away.

"You idiot!" Alpin shouted. He whacked the wolf on its head with his staff. "What have you done?"

"It was going to bite you." Barnaby clutched his arm and grit his teeth. Mauz drooped his tongue onto Barnaby's cheek. "It's all right, Mauz, I'll be okay."

"I had it under control," Alpin hissed.

"Hey," Bea shouted. "I don't think that really matters right now." She pointed at the shadows circling them in the floorboards, their low growls vibrating through the wood.

"Excellent, my darlings," Bea heard Demise reward the wolves through the door, then footsteps crossing the living room, but all she could see was Bowmidge's back through the crack in the door. "Would you mind stepping aside?"

"Sure," Bowmidge said. A high-pitch whistle pierced the air. Bea covered her ears, but even so, it threatened to burst her eardrums. The gullys squawked and meowed, flapping their wings and zooming around the room. The door flung open and the gullys flew out straight at Demise's face. His claws stopped smoking and he covered his face. The wolves disappeared like smoke in the wind.

"The window," Bowmidge shouted. "Go, now!" He pointed to a small window in the corner of the mailroom. Alpin nodded and smashed his staff through the glass.

"Go." Alpin gestured toward Bea and Barnaby.

"Me too?" Barnaby asked, grey hand to his chest.

"Are you wearing earplugs under that scarf?" Alpin snapped. "I said, go!"

Barnaby smiled and leapt through the window; Bea clambered after him, but Alpin stopped halfway through the frame and turned his head around. "Bowmidge!" he called.

"Go on now," Bowmidge said. "I'll be all right." Bowmidge reassured him with a wink, and Alpin jumped down from the window to join Barnaby and Bea in their sprint down the hill, away from the house.

CHAPTER SIXTEEN

AERO ELLISVAT

Tab led Reagan and their pergonzias to a dilapidated wooden shack at the edge of the city, pierced with rot and painted by sand. It struggled to hold a roof shot full of gaping cavities. If not for the smoke billowing from its chimney, Reagan would have assumed it abandoned.

They dismounted and led their mounts next to a stable beside the house. Unlike the house, the stable was in almost perfect condition, built of sturdy wooden planks and roofed with tile shingles. Inside the stable was a single stall, which, judging by the silver plaque nailed to its door, held a horse named Sela. They tied their pergonzias next to Sela, their beasts' heads towering above the horse's, and headed toward the house.

An uneven path led the two across a field of rubbish and broken glass. Tab stopped in front of the door. It hung loosely on rusty hinges, and its handle lay on the dirt near the threshold. Tab banged a fist on the door, and it fell off on the dirty ground. She walked into the dim interior. "Oh, good, you're still alive."

Reagan followed her in and found a handsome man sitting at a table reading a large book and sipping on steaming tea. Brown curly hair fell over his shoulders, and he quickly tossed it up into a bun upon seeing them. The top three buttons of his shirt hung open, and Reagan caught a glimpse of his tightly curled chest hair beneath. She looked away, afraid he might catch her unbuttoning the rest with her imagination. A perch stood beside his chair, and on it was a small, hand-sized creature that looked halfway between a bird and a cat. All the walls except for one were covered with stuffed bookshelves. On the free wall was a small fireplace with doors on either side of it. Unlike the muddled state of the outside, the inside of his home was neat and welcoming.

"Tabitha Glowdish?" he said, arching his eyebrows nearly to the top of his forehead. The bird-cat chirped and flew off its perch onto his head. "Mawris, please, not now. We have guests." He laughed, plucked the bird off his head, and carefully set it back on its perch.

Reagan stared at the little creature and watched it cock its head at her, its long and bushy tail swaying back and forth. The thing could have been a stuffed animal.

"Whatever." Tab rolled her eyes. "Just cause ya haven't seen me in a while doesn't mean you get to use my full name." She then glanced at the bird-cat. "Mawris still kickin'?"

"Tab," he corrected himself and shut the book. "A few inches taller but the same attitude. And of course. She's about the best gully I could have asked for. Delivers letters faster than any I'd ever seen." He pat Mawris on the head and she purred. "Come, sit." He gestured toward the other two chairs at the table. "I also wouldn't mind an introduction, if you would be so kind. Strangers in the house feels a bit odd." He glanced over at Reagan, his golden eyes meeting hers. She felt her cheeks flush and she turned to pretend to look around the house. *Eyes. Why is it always the eyes with men?*

"This is Reagan." Tab grabbed her arm and pulled her into the seat beside her. "My new best friend…until I can get rid of her."

"Ah." Aero set his cup down on the table. "Fawn's replacement?"

"What?" Tab seemed taken aback by the statement. Her lip twitched and she blinked several times. "No. And don't ever mention that name again, got it?"

Reagan wondered who Fawn was and if perhaps she had been Tab's lover. She had told her that she wasn't her type. Now Reagan wasn't sure if she should have been insulted.

"Understood," Aero said.

"So, don't tell me you're training to be one of those incredibly annoying Knowers, are you? I mean, c'mon, what's with all this stuff?" Tab waved her hand around the room.

"Oh those? They're called 'books.'" He lifted the one from his lap and showed it to her. "You should try reading one someday. You might not be so foolish." Tab rolled her eyes and Reagan laughed.

"Oh, can it, Red," Tab snapped.

"But no, not a Knower," Aero continued. "The Knower

lifestyle is not for me. I just prefer a more simple, less treacherous, if you will, lifestyle now."

"You're done with it all?" Tab asked.

"Not done. I still have certain…obligations, of course, but I prefer to keep work away from home."

"Well, great, you will come in handy after all."

Aero stared at her a moment, then said, "Okay…should we cut the small talk, then? What brings you to my place?"

"I was getting there," Tab said, wagging a finger at him. "Would you rather I just barge in and demand your service next time?"

"Fair enough." He looked at Reagan. "You two run into some trouble in the streets?"

Reagan wondered what he might be referring to, but then remembered her forehead. She brushed away her bangs, feeling the wound beneath them. A piece of scab flaked off. *I almost forgot…*

"Well, what kind of host would I be if I let you sit around with a gash like that? Come, let me help you."

"I think I'll sit this one out," Tab said. She flapped her hand toward Aero. "But go on, do your thing if you must. I'll stay out here with Mawris, I guess." The little bird-cat chirped and began to preen its feathers.

Oh, god, no, Reagan thought. For once she wished the woman would tag along and not leave her alone with such a hunk. It was the perfect setup for her to make a fool of herself around him.

Aero stood from his chair and led Reagan through the door to the room right of the fireplace.

163

Inside, it was even smaller than the living space, and resembled a kitchen, though much less fancy than any she had seen before. A table with four chairs took up most of the space; pots and pans hung from the ceiling just above their heads; a small sink sat against one wall, and a large fireplace with a row of bottles and miscellaneous knickknacks and books on its mantelpiece took up most of another wall. Aero ducked beneath the pots on his way to the fireplace, grabbed a few pieces of wood from a pile beside it, tossed them in, and lit them.

"Have a seat," he said when he had finished. He pulled one of the chairs out from the table, and Reagan sat down. The twine holding it together was frayed at the edges and scratched her legs. "I know," he said as if reading her mind, "it's not the most comfortable chair in the world, but it does the job." He took a pot from a ceiling hook, put some water in it at the sink, and hooked it over the fire. Then he ran his finger along the line of bottles on the mantelpiece and eventually grabbed one that read *migplye*. He uncorked it, let a few drops fall into the steaming water, then placed it back in its spot.

"It'll take a moment to boil," he said, his back turned to her while he watched the water. She stared at his bun and was envious of how perfect it looked. She had never been able to pull off such a do with her thin locks.

As he had promised, he lifted the pot from the hook a moment later and poured it into a smaller clear container. The liquid now had a yellow hue. He dipped a cloth into it and wrung it out before crossing the room and sitting in the chair beside Reagan. She could feel the warmth of his presence next to her and wanted to scooch closer.

"May I?" Aero gestured toward her forehead with the rag. Reagan nodded and tried to remain still. He wrapped his free hand around the back of her head, steadying it as he patted the rag on her skin.

Reagan winced. Though his touch was gentle, the yellow liquid fizzed and stung. She knew there was no real flame, but it felt as if it were burning her skin.

"I'm sorry," he said, drawing back the cloth and allowing her a moment to recover. "I should have warned you. Migplye does have the tendency to burn, but its healing properties are unmatched."

He held her again and repeated the process, this time very carefully looking at the wound, his head close to hers. His eyes were golden with tiny specks of brown scattered around his irises. His eyelashes were long and curled. Reagan could not help but be envious again—hers needed several coats of eyeliner and a curler to look even as lame as they usually did. And she almost forgot how much the stuff hurt as he held it to her head.

"How's that?" he asked.

"Uh," she mumbled. *He wasn't gazing into your eyes like you were his, he was asking you a question.* She cursed herself for being so painfully awkward and wished she could sink into her chair. "Yeah, uh, it hurts, but it's better." *How stupid!*

"Good." Aero pulled the cloth off her forehead. "Give me a second. I've got some bandages." Reagan looked down at her fists. Her knuckles were nearly popping out of her skin. She heard the door open.

"Good gods, Aero, what have you done to her?" Tab walked

into the room and grimaced at Reagan. "I thought you were going to make it better, not worse."

"It was infected. It had to be cleaned." Aero walked back to Reagan with a roll of bandage in his hand, unraveled it, and wrapped some around her head.

"Well, you could have at least made it a little prettier, couldn't ya?" Tab said.

Reagan wondered what the aftermath of his concoction looked like but decided to stop thinking about it when the images grew grimmer than she could handle. "Thank you," she blurted at Aero. "For helping me, I mean."

Aero smiled. "So…to what do I owe this visit?"

"I need your help," Tab said.

"Hmm…Tabitha Glowdish needs *my* help?" The mention of her full name made her bare her teeth. He laughed and said, "What can I do for you?"

Tab walked to Reagan, grabbed the chain hanging down into her shirt, and pulled it—the stone attached and hanging loosely—up and out of the dress cloak.

Aero's eyes widened. "That's…uh…what is it, Tab?"

Tab smirked and dangled it around a little. "I think you already know the answer to that."

He looked like he was wincing in pain when he whispered, "The Eyearke Stone."

"Like I said, I need your help. Your protection, more so. I guess you could call it a delivery." She dropped the chain. "Call it what you want, but I need you to take us to Galecrest. No questions asked and no problems along the way. Quick and easy, then you're done, and you can get back to burying yourself in your books or whatever it is you think you're doing."

"Reading them?"

Tab rolled her eyes. "If you wanna call it that, sure."

"Right then," Aero said. "What's in it for me?"

"Other than helping out your old friend?" Tab said. "There may be some kaps in it for you."

"I see," Aero said. He stared into the flames in the fireplace, pondering, Reagan assumed, then said, "I'll take you. Mawris'll be alright on her own for a bit, I suppose." He stood up and dusted himself off, though Reagan could see no dust on him. "It's about time I take a few days away from this city. I'm sick of the heat."

CHAPTER SEVENTEEN

A KNOWER OF MANY THINGS

Bea, Alpin, and Barnaby ran across the flat plains, dodging shrubs and jumping over patches of wildflowers until they reached a dense forest. Birds whistled in the branches, critters scurried in the underbrush, and swarms of bugs buzzed around their heads. One flew straight into Bea's eye, and she rubbed and rubbed until it finally fell out in a tear.

They hiked into the woods for what Bea thought was about an hour until they came to a circular clearing where a herd of florahorses grazed in the orange tint of the fading sunlight. They reminded Bea of the grass horse that Alistair had swept them away to Alpin's house on. It already seemed so long ago. The beasts perked up when the threesome—*croak!* foursome— passed by. They flicked their flower-woven tails and chewed mouthfuls of sticks and long grass. One whinnied and the noise almost gave Bea a heart attack.

After the clearing, they passed back into the trees and tramped along. Bea started to tire and felt like she was walking in her sleep. Soon after the trees dwindled, and the path entered a forest of giant mushrooms even bigger than the trees. Their wide caps formed a canopy that blocked much of the sun, leaving them walking in a shadowy twilight. Vines dangled down like tangled hair and curled on the ground. Bea wiped away the sweat that dripped down the side of her cheek and tugged her sticky shirt off her skin.

They paused a moment to catch their breaths, sitting on the cool forest ground. Bea looked to Barnaby, who nursed his oozing wound and flinched each time his finger brushed over one of the wolf's teeth marks. It was the first time she had seen the boy frown, and she couldn't say she liked it. She wanted to get up and help but didn't know how. She specialized in drawing up escapes, not soothing shadow wolf wounds.

Alpin sighed and stood. He walked over to a bush taller than Bea and jumped up to rip a leaf from it. "Come here, boy," he said. He struggled to hold the leaf, which was almost as large and wide as his entire body, between his paws.

Barnaby looked up from his wound and glanced around as if he were searching to find another boy that the gopher could have been referring to.

"Yes, you," Alpin confirmed. "Come. Don't make me wait any longer with this thing."

Barnaby clambered to his feet and made his way over to the gopher's side, and Bea wondered all the while what the gopher had up his sleeve this time.

"Give me your arm," Alpin said. Barnaby did as he said and

offered up his arm, wincing when Alpin wrapped the large leaf around the wound, completely covering the oozing teeth marks beneath it. "Keep it on there, you hear?" Alpin pointed a claw at the boy. "It's a pavlosia leaf. It'll numb the pain."

"Oh," Barnaby said. "Well, I think it's already working. I can't feel anything under there! Thank you, Mr. Alpin."

"Yeah, well, don't go making a big deal of it, all right?" Alpin said. "And don't go throwing yourself in a wolf's jaw again. At least not for me." Barnaby nodded and Alpin turned his attention to Bea. "Up, up. Enough sitting around. It's time to move on."

Bea stood and she, along with Barnaby and Mauz, followed Alpin deeper into the forest.

Another short while passed, and Bea realized they were walking alongside a river about the width of the Dildeckers' dirt driveway. It led them to an abandoned city where it formed a scummy pond with a disused, rusted fountain in the middle. Trees and mushrooms grew out of the pond and the stone walls around it and leaned crookedly over the water, some dipping down into it.

Though the city was abandoned, life thrived within its crumbled remains. Bea heard creatures croaking, much like Mauz, and insects buzzed near her ears. She wished she had worn a hat, fearing whatever tick-like creatures might leap down into her hair.

Beyond the fountain were rows of houses, half crumpled and overrun with bugs and tiny rodents. Pitted steps and staircases led to nowhere, and rotted roofs lay in pieces on the ground.

"Gross," Alpin snarled. He yanked his hind paw out of a puddle of mud. "It's just as horrid as I remember. This muck will suck you down whole if given the chance."

Ahead, Bea saw what must have been a larger building, perhaps an official one, but it was all ruins now and choked out by the vines and roots that grew over its surface.

"Is this—" Barnaby stopped walking and stared at the cracked stones and collapsed pillars. He took a step forward, squeezing Mauz to his chest and making the poor toad's eyes bug. "Is this *Treenode*?"

"Unfortunately, yes," Alpin said. He then proceeded to give his opinion on the place, though no one had asked him. "If it were up to me, I would have burned it all the way to the center of the earth. What a waste of space to keep it around. Especially in this…this state." He spat on the rubble, though nothing really made it past his big teeth.

"Wow!" Barnaby's eyes, like his toads, nearly popped out of his skull. "We made it, Mauz! We really made it!" He tossed the toad lightly in the air so he could have a look around.

"Twee!" Alpin squeaked, his shrill cry startling Bea. He swatted his paws around his head, batting away a tiny, finger-sized creature that hovered by his ear, its fur glowing yellow. It looked to be a very fluffy rat with wings, but in this world, Bea learned, she could have been easily mistaken. "Stupid peepmuk! I forgot these things even existed. What a nuisance!" The little thing hissed and spat a wad of goop at Alpin's face before flying up and disappearing into a tree. His nose and whiskers twitched, the white goop thick on them, and he ran to the swampy water. Before Bea could ask what the big deal was, he plunged his face into it and ran his paws so fast over his face that Bea thought the goop might as well have been poison ivy. He came up for air and looked at Bea, gesturing with his paw to his face. "Is it all off?" She nodded and he exhaled, then adjusted his monocle. "Good. A peepmuk's spit is about the last thing I would want to deal with now. Second to last is this godforsaken city."

"What happened to it?" Bea asked. Had the place not been in ruins, she might have considered living there. Tucked deep in the forest, quiet enough to work on her drawings, and far away from anyone who might disturb...or bully...her. It reminded her of where she grew up with her mother, but much buggier.

"The Olphins happened," Alpin said gloomily. He turned toward Barnaby, who was poking a greasy stone with his finger, paying no attention to him. "They were a hostile, savage race, who lived secluded from the rest of the world—and thank the gods they did. They betrayed the Sacred Rulers and sided with Obellius, who was determined to take back Eslura for his own selfish reasons. 'Restoring Nelazgus's land' he'd claimed. Ha! The Olphins were his evil minions along with all those foolish Nelazgians. No matter what some apologists might say, there was not a single drop of good in their blood. They deserved to be banished for their betrayal, and so they were. The ones still living after the war were taken to Morgaedion. Some of them likely remain alive there."

Banished. Bea gulped and looked around the empty city. *So that's what happened.*

"Hey!" Barnaby said. "Look at this." He pointed to a piece

of blue candy on the ground. As Bea walked over to look at it, she noticed a whole line of the candies, as if someone had put them there deliberately. Barnaby bent down and picked up the candy. He popped the muddy thing in his mouth, making Bea cringe. Then he swirled it around a couple times and plucked it out with his webbed fingers. "This is the same candy that Mr. Seely sent!"

Alpin tried to swat the candy out of Barnaby's hand, mumbling something about how disgusting it was, but the boy pulled it away and ran along the muddy trail of candies. Bea followed close behind.

The trail led them to a giant mushroom. Spiral stairs led up its side to a balcony built on its cap above which Bea could see a wooden roof.

Barnaby climbed up first, leading Bea and Alpin onto the balcony.

Flies swarmed around about a dozen half-eaten scraps of blue-colored candies on the floor. They were slick and worn, which made Bea think that they were recently spat out. A bamboo rocking chair with a pair of binoculars on it faced into the heart of the woods; beside it sat a small table with a saucer full of wilted, brown flowers. Bird-shaped wind chimes hung limply from rusted nails tied to the lip of the roof, and a hand-painted sign held up by loose twine decorated the front door: *Resident Knower*.

Barnaby licked his fingers and ran them through his mop of hair, apparently trying to make himself look more presentable. His curls, however, rebelled and sprung back up.

"All right, Mauz, how do I look?" Barnaby looked at his

173

toad on his shoulder for approval. Mauz croaked and Barnaby
nodded. He took a deep breath, straightened his shoulders,
walked up to the door, and knocked loudly. The sound echoed
back from the surrounding woods. Barnaby waited, staring at
the door with a smile. Though, that smile faded as the seconds
ticked by and no sounds were heard from within the house.
Barnaby gulped and stepped back from the door. He frowned
and looked at Bea and Alpin.

"Well, well, well," Alpin said, arms crossed over his chest.
"What a wonderful host this Seely figure is to keep us waiting
outside his front door like peasants." He uncrossed his arms
and tapped his staff impatiently on the wooden balcony floor.

Bea gawked at the house. She had never even imagined
such a thing could exist, yet here she was. She spotted a hole
about the size of her fist in the wood beside the door, poorly
camouflaged by some dried flowers pinned there. While none
of the others were looking, except maybe Mauz, she walked
over, bent down, and put her eye up to the hole. The inside of
the house was mostly dark, then something wooden moved
just beyond the hole. Bea jumped back and fell on her rear
end. A wooden hand emerged from the hole and made a
shooing motion at her. Then it reached over and tapped Alpin
on the shoulder.

"Twee!" He swatted it away with his staff. "What the heck is
that?" He glared at the hand as it retreated back into the hole
and then turned back toward the stairs. "This is what we get
for following an Olphin! Let's just get out of here while we've
still got some light. The woods are not welcoming to strangers
like us at night."

"B-but," Barnaby bumbled. He held up the letter. "He has to be in there. Mr. Pemadee would not do us wrong!" The boy turned to Bea, as if waiting for her to back him up. She opened her mouth to say something, though she wasn't really sure what, but Alpin cut her off.

"We have no time to waste with this silliness. Alistair told us to make haste to Galecrest, and to Galecrest we must make haste." He started down the stairs, apparently expecting Bea and Barnaby to follow.

Barnaby slumped his shoulders and dragged his feet toward the staircase, joining Alpin.

Bea looked at the stairs, then at the door, then at the very hurt-looking Barnaby. She was about to follow them when the front door creaked. "Wait!" Bea stopped. She turned to the door. The wooden hand was pushing it open. "Look!"

Barnaby rushed back to the door and pushed past Bea, nearly knocking her off the balcony. He set off into the house and disappeared into the darkness. Bea, gripping the balcony rail, watched Alpin follow the boy, dramatically sighing to himself and rolling his eyes, then she followed them into the house.

Inside, the house was dark save for a small candle flame flickering in the far corner of the room. While Bea's eyes were adjusting, she heard the door slam shut behind her, startling her.

Bea had imagined that the hand operated on its own somehow, so she was surprised to see a long narrow shaft leading to a small creature across the room, who seemed to be operating it. The strange thing was about the size of a wild hare and had the big feet for it, too, but it had massive, floppy elephant ears and a protruding hump on its back, which Bea saw as it climbed up a stack of books to reach a chair behind an old wooden desk.

The walls were lined with shelves stacked with jars of blue and green liquid containing little creatures floating limply. Sacks overflowing with the blue candies sat on the floor along with notebooks strewn open next to crumpled parchment.

The three of them, plus Mauz, watched the little creature for a moment as he shifted on his stool, raised a tiny three-fingered paw, spit his candy into it, and tossed it into the metal waste bin in front of where Bea was standing. It clanged off the rim and fell into the bin on top of a pile of similarly half-eaten blue candies. *What a waste*, Bea thought. The creature waggled his fingers, fished out a fresh candy from a sack next to his chair, and flung it into his mouth, slopping his tongue all over its surface.

"Please do leave your shoes at the door. Mhm, yes, yes, please do," he said, his words slurred by the candy.

Bea, the only one of the three with shoes, slid her tennis shoes off and set them on what looked to be a welcome mat near the door.

"A Knower of Many Things apologizes for making his company wait outside. He must be sure of them before he lets them in, mhm, yes, yes. He hopes his company understands." His tiny hands were busy writing what Bea assumed to be a letter. He dunked his peacock quill, the feather of which was larger than his head, in an ink bottle and continued working as if they were not there.

Barnaby stepped forward and cleared his throat. "Excuse

me, are you Mr. Seely?" The boy clutched his letter in his hands and ran his fingers over the ridges of its wax seal.

The creature's ears perked up. He lifted his head from his work, set his quill down, and blinked at them with his beady eyes, one of which was completely white. "Mr. Seely, yes, yes, but a Knower of Many Things does not abide by such formalities. Just Seely is fine."

"So," Barnaby continued, tilting his head at the creature, "you *are* Seely, then?"

"A Knower of Many Things goes by many names, but indeed, you are correct—that is one of his names." The creature nodded, ears flapping up and down like wings.

"Oh, Mauz!" Barnaby said, hugging his toad. "Did you hear that? It really is him!"

"If a Knower's judgement is correct, there is no other name for a creature of your kind than Barnaby. Barnaby Britto of Ovallia. Ah, yes, yes, Pemadee of Ovallia sent you my way, hm?"

Barnaby's expression shifted from excitement, to shock, to confusion in all but a second. "How do you—"

"And you," Seely said, looking at Alpin, "you must be Alpin Loomin of Farenworth. Hmm, a tragedy yes, very much so. A Knower of Many Things hopes Farenworth hasn't gotten too lonely for him. A Knower can only imagine the lengths Alpin Loomin's mind has travelled...oh, the solitude...yes, yes."

Alpin scowled. "Lonely? I'll have you know I've got more than enough friends to keep me company." As if confirming his statement, Alpin counted on his claws behind his back, stopping at two. He blushed and looked at the floor.

"But you." Seely peered at Bea, hopped off his stool, and

limped toward her. "My, my, my. You. Are. *Interesting!*" He cocked his head, which came up to her waist, and rubbed the tiny, grey hairs on his chin. "A Knower's eyes wish to tell him one thing, but his mind...another." He circled around Bea, staring at her right wrist. "Beatrice Tidal, what is it that makes a Knower believe you are so peculiar?" Bea tensed up and grabbed her wrist, hugging it to her chest. *He couldn't possibly know*, Bea assured herself, *at least not just from looking.*

"Ah, a Knower sees his mistake." Seely took a step back, giving Bea room to breathe. "Beatrice Tidal's muscles are tense and she has no words to speak. It almost seems a Knower has made her uncomfortable. Please do forgive him. He tends to fire his questions without pausing to think, mhm, yes, yes." The strange creature limped back to his stool and squirmed his way up. "You see, a Knower of Many Things is an asker of many questions."

"A 'Knower of Many Things,' huh?" Alpin crossed his arms and tapped his staff lightly on the floor. "I will admit I was impressed by the whole name stunt," he said, rolling his eyes, probably still upset about Seely's "lonely" comment, "but, I can't quite wrap my head around why a 'Knower of Many Things' would live all the way out here in this...this mud bog."

"Ah, mhm, yes, yes." Seely tapped a finger on his chin and nodded. "But Alpin Loomin's question begs yet *another* question: why would a Knower of Many Things and an asker of many questions *not* be in Treenode?"

Alpin rolled his eyes and mumbled under his breath, "What have I gotten myself into..."

"Mr—erm"—Barnaby paused under Seely's glare—"Seely,

I—uh—I have a letter." After Barnaby's manhandling of the paper, a corner was now torn off and creases spiderwebbed its surface. Bea wondered whether or not the scribbles on the page were still legible.

"You see," Barnaby continued, "Mr. Pemadee said he got this letter from you, and I—"

"Ah, yes, yes, Barnaby Britto of Ovallia has come to learn about the other Olphin. Mhm, yes."

"*Other* Olphin?" Alpin blinked several times and stared at Seely wide-eyed.

"Please." Barnaby wagged the letter between his fingers, crumpling it even more, and walked toward Seely, stopping only when he was standing right in front of the creature's face. "You simply *must* tell me!" He dropped the letter on Seely's lap like a dead fish.

"If Barnaby Britto insists..." Seely cleared his throat and held the paper up to his face with both hands. "Ah, mhm, yes, yes." He nodded. His eyes scanned the page, then he lowered it back down to his lap and looked over at the door. "A Knower remembers very well the day the purple-finned Olphin broke through his door and pressed a blade against his throat." He rubbed his neck, bringing Bea's attention to a faint scar. "The Olphin threatened a Knower's life, telling him that if he did not give her the object she sought, she would kill him. A Knower had no choice. He gave up his most prized possession, hoping that it would satisfy the knife-wielder." Seely bowed his head and paused a moment. Then he continued, "A Knower wrote to Pemadee of Ovallia, hoping that his Olphin boy might be able to help him find the purple-finned Olphin, but—" Seely stopped mid-sentence and sniffed the air like a dog who had just caught whiff of some sizzling bacon. "A Knower smells something peculiar."

Bea, Barnaby, and Alpin exchanged looks and sniffed the air along with Seely, but the room smelled the same as when they had entered.

"Well, it certainly isn't me," Alpin said with a shrug. "I'll have the Knower know that I bathe twice a day…in *rose* water."

Seely leapt off his stool and crawled on his hands and knees across the floor to Barnaby. He stopped at the boy's webbed toes and looked up at his face. Barnaby blushed but didn't move. Seely jumped to his feet and announced. "A Knower of Many Things suspects that Barnaby Britto is hiding something beneath his cloak." Barnaby's face turned even redder, and he gulped.

Alpin glared at him. "What now? C'mon, now let's see what you've got already."

Barnaby reached beneath his robes and pulled out a translucent grey stone the size of his palm.

"A stone?" Alpin twitched his whiskers and adjusted his monocle as if to make sure he was seeing correctly. Though the room was dark, there was no mistaking the object for what it was. "Well, you've outdone yourself, boy. I truly did not think you could be any more of a disappointment."

"No, no, no, no…" Seely repeated the words over and over again as he walked back to his stool, hands pressed on his temples. "Please do bring it here for a Knower—*carefully*." Barnaby held the stone out with both hands and carefully walked it over to Seely.

Seely, very gently, as if it were a bomb, took the stone in one hand. With the other, he swiped everything off his desk. Then he put the stone down. He observed it for several moments, shaking his head back and forth, before saying, "Alpin Loomin of Farenworth, a Knower of Many Things will now answer your question, mhm, yes, yes."

Alpin perked up and furrowed his brows. "Huh?"

"A Knower of Many Things had come to Treenode to live a life of solitude after being forced from his position in Galecrest, mhm, yes, yes. Is it known to many why a Knower of Many Things was banished from his duties in Galecrest?" Bea, Alpin, and Barnaby remained silent. "No? It is because he sought out information that Eslura would like to keep quiet. Eslura could not risk her people discovering such knowledge. So, when a Knower became curious, he was exiled. But, in his solitude he discovered more than he ever would have at Galecrest. He unearthed something very important about the Olphin race.

"You see, a Knower had a very hard time believing that a race so peaceful, so gentle, could turn to hatred and greed, mhm, yes, he did. So, he set out to research what happened. Well, he did not find anything, only empty theories that even he knew were merely theoretical. But then he learned of the stones. One of which was in his possession before it was stolen. The other Barnaby Britto of Ovallia has brought before him. A Knower had never seen it with his own eyes, only heard of it by word from his dear friend Pemadee, so even he is surprised by its appearance in his home."

"So, what's the deal with it? It's just a stone," Alpin said. He sucked his big teeth.

Bea glanced at the stone on the desk. For once, she

agreed with the gopher. It appeared to be 'just a stone.' A translucent grey stone.

"No, no, no, Alpin Loomin of Farenworth. It is not a simple stone. It is a *weapon!*" Seely pointed a finger at the ceiling and wagged it back and forth. "A weapon from a god!" More wagging. "A Knower believes that this god can be none other than Nelazgus, the god of darkness and despair."

Alpin tilted his head and twitched his whiskers skeptically. "I'm sorry, what? You've just about lost me."

Seely ignored the gopher and carried on. "A Knower had heard tales of Nelazgus bargaining his god-like powers away to those below him. But this—" Seely lifted the stone from his desk and coddled it like a newborn baby, stroking its surface, tracing the strange markings across its surface. "This is only bringing a Knower closer to presenting his theory to the Sacred Rulers. A theory that he and Pemadee of Ovallia had been researching for many moons. A theory that would set the Olphins free of their punishment!"

"So, let me get this straight," Alpin said. "What you mean to say is that the gods are real? And they can just give their powers away to anyone whenever they please? Pardon me for saying so, but I think you may have spent a little too much time eating strange candies alone in the woods."

Bea rolled her eyes. *You can never spend too much time alone in the woods.*

Seely pointed a wagging finger at Alpin. "That is exactly so, Alpin Loomin of Farenworth, mhm, yes, yes."

"You know," said Alpin, "you don't have to repeat my name and where I'm from every single time you speak. It's a little repetitive. We get it."

"A Knower had researched his theory after he heard tales of the people of Veskadoth contacting their god, Nelazgus, and channeling his power through various objects. A Knower did not think much of these stories until he observed the Olphin race go mad and turn on the rest of Eslura. So, he considered the possibility that one of those enchanted objects may have driven them down that path."

"Hmm," Alpin grumbled. "And?"

"Perhaps a demonstration might be of more help to Alpin Loomin. Please do observe." Seely raised the stone and closed his eyes. He rubbed the stone in a circular motion, and it began to glow.

At its light, Barnaby dropped to the floor. He grit his teeth and squeezed his eyes shut. His body shook all over, like he was being electrocuted. Seely rubbed one last circle and lowered the stone, observing the boy and taking notes with his free hand.

"Hey!" Bea shouted. "You're hurting him." She stepped toward Barnaby, but Alpin grabbed her arm and held her back.

"Wait," Alpin said, staring down at the convulsing boy.

"Beatrice Tidal, a Knower of Many Things suspects that Barnaby Britto feels no pain, mhm, yes, yes."

No pain? He was writhing on the floor, gripping his eyes, kicking his feet, clanking his teeth. Bea was pretty sure it looked like pain.

"Barnaby Britto!" Seely stood on his stool and glanced down at the boy, who was worming his way into a ball, hands wrapped around his knees, and twitching. "Please do stand up."

Barnaby opened his eyes and let go of his knees. He looked around the room, no longer twitching or shaking or vibrating, and stood up. He looked at Seely, who stood slightly above him on his perch, and stared at him blankly, silently, as if he were waiting for his next command. Seely spun around, jotted a note, then turned back with a giddy smile on his face. "Barnaby Britto, please do fetch a Knower another of his candies."

Barnaby moved like a robot, eyes absent of his once bubbly personality, mouth set in a firm line, over to one of the very full sacks of blue candies. He plucked one off the top of the pile, carried it over to Seely, and put it on the stool. Then he stood there stiff as a pole and stared at the Knower.

Mauz seemed to be rather confused by his friend's strange, new behavior. The poor toad tried to land on top of Barnaby's curly locks but was swatted away before he could set his plump self down. Mauz whirled through the air and crash landed on Bea's foot. She bent down, scooped him up, his eyes still spinning, and sat him on her shoulder.

"Excellent, Barnaby Britto, excellent! Mhm, yes, yes!" Seely clapped his tiny hands together, picked up the candy, and tossed it in his mouth. "A Knower of Many Things is very satisfied with this demonstration." He picked up the glowing stone again and rubbed circles on it in the opposite direction. The light of the stone faded out, and Barnaby snapped backward and fell to the floor, slamming his head on a pile of books.

Alpin stared at Barnaby a moment, then looked up at Seely. "B-but, what does this have to do with the gods?"

"Ow," Barnaby groaned. He pulled himself up to his knees

and touched the back of his head where an egg-shaped lump formed even bigger than the one on the front of his head. "Where did that come from?" He winced and drew his hand back. "And why am I on the floor?"

"It has *everything* to do with the gods," Seely said in answer to Alpin's question. "There could be only one way that Obellius Kalaar of Veskadoth was able to gain the Olphins' loyalty...and servitude, nothing less. You see, Barnaby Britto of Ovallia has no recollection of his actions while he was under the influence of the stone. A Knower's theory, in fact, might he say *conclusion*, is that Obellius Kalaar struck a deal with the god Nelazgus, as many of his kind did before him, and obtained the power to control the Olphin race."

"Agh," Barnaby moaned and clambered to his feet. "What just happened, what are you talking about? I heard you say Olphin."

Seely grinned and scribbled some more in his notes. "What a day, oh what a day this has been for a Knower of Many Things!"

Bea walked toward Barnaby but stopped halfway. "Are you okay?"

"What do you mean?" He cocked his head and adjusted his crooked glasses. "Is anyone gonna tell me what just happened or—" He looked at Mauz and smiled. "Oh, Mauz! What are you doing you silly old toad? Have you decided that you like Bea's shoulder better than mine?"

"Brilliant! Absolutely brilliant!" Seely cheered and clapped his little hands.

"Oh gods." Alpin sunk to his knees. "Oh gods, oh gods." He buried his head in his paws. "This can't be so."

While Alpin deflated like a balloon and Seely celebrated

with another candy, Bea and Barnaby just looked at each other even more confused than before.

Barnaby cupped his hands and whispered to her. "Is it just me, or is something funky going on?" He touched the back of his head again. "Ow."

Seely cleared his throat to get their attention. "A Knower would like to thank Barnaby Britto for proving his theory. A Knower also suspects that Eslura may soon thank him as well."

"So, the Olphins—" Alpin gulped and lifted his head from his paws. "They...uh"—another gulp—"they were innocent?" The twisted expression on the gopher's face made Bea think that either the statement was a rather hard one to make or he was about to throw up...or perhaps both.

"A Knower of Many Things believes that Alpin Loomin is correct."

Apparently realizing that he was being given a lot of attention for once, Barnaby stretched his arms and said, "You know, I'm not so sure I understand—"

A powerful gust of wind ripped under the lip of the door and howled through the hole next to it, whisking out the candle's flame and engulfing the room in complete darkness. Outside, Bea could hear the wind chimes clacking against the side of the house, caught in the whirlwind of a storm that began to rock the house back and forth.

The shelves broke apart with a splintering crack, jars falling and smashing into a thousand pieces of jagged glass and spilling their blue-green liquids across the floor. Seely tumbled off his stool, stone clutched in hand, and landed head first in the mess. The sacks of candies spilled over him. He covered his face with his ears and was buried beneath a sea of blue. Bea fell against the wall and Alpin wrapped his arms around her leg, squeezing his eyes shut. Barnaby staggered around the middle of the room, holding Mauz to his chest.

The shaking only lasted a minute; then a sweeping silence raked through the room. All Bea could hear was her labored breathing. Seely popped his head out from beneath the candies and surveyed the damage.

Black smoke crept under the door, through the hand hole, and up through the cracks in the floor, pooling at their feet in a murky cloud. Thunder rumbled in the distance, a low growl that raised goosebumps on Bea's arm. Alpin inched closer to her. "Tw—" She put her hand over his snout.

Seely stood, shaking the candies off his fur, and looked out the window. A storm of smoke was approaching. "A Knower of Many Things fears that his new friends may have company."

CHAPTER EIGHTEEN

THE LESSON

"We need to stop," Tab said. For the first time since she had met the woman, Reagan agreed with her. Her back ached from riding, and she wished for nothing more than to get off the pergonzias and rest. They had set out when the sun reached its peak in the sky, rode through the heat of midafternoon, up and out of Varaar under the twilight sky.

Now, parting from the worn path, Tab led them to a small pool of water not far into the brush. "We won't have any chance of making it to Galecrest if our mounts give out on us. They need food and water, and so do we." She slipped off her pergonzia and led it toward the water. "I'll be back." She took off into the desert, sounds of sands shifting following her departure.

"Then, I guess we wait here, right?" Reagan said. She, too, dismounted and let her pergonzia sip from the water while brushing the sand from its grey coat.

Aero laughed. "Not one for much reasoning, that Tab." He led Sela to the water and gave her a scratch beneath the chin. She sniffed his face, then bent down to drink.

Reagan sighed and lowered herself to the ground to rest. She could sit at least, even if she couldn't lie down and sleep just yet. She'd probably be corralling the kids back to the cabin at Tossbridge right now, nothing more than some noisy girls to deal with. Now it seemed like the whole world weighed on her shoulders, and on Bea's head for some reason she still did not understand. She hoped Bea was okay.

"Tired?" Aero asked, sitting down next to her.

"Beyond belief." She lay down on her back and stared up at the sky, counting the few faint stars bright enough to appear in the dusk.

"Enjoy your moment of peace," he said. "She'll be back soon to take it away."

Reagan knew it was true. Everything was always on fast forward with Tab. She wondered if she ever just relaxed. Maybe she wouldn't be as snippy if she learned the importance of self-care. "So, you've known Tab for a while?"

"I suppose you could say that," Aero said. He leaned over toward the water and dipped his hands in it. "Tab and I used to be a part of a group called the Sarakyan many moons ago before our leader, Elmryn, was murdered. Once he was gone, the group fell apart, and so did Tab and I. Painful, but as you know, life is full of many unusual surprises."

"I guess you're right," Reagan said. She lifted the stone from her neck and rubbed her fingers on it. *Many unusual surprises,* she thought to herself. She'd had her fair share of surprises lately. First day at camp and she ended up in an entirely different world where the cheap amethyst necklace her dad gave her held some kind of mysterious and deadly power. Fun stuff.

Aero stood and walked to the water. He bent down and rolled up his sleeves to dip his hands in it, revealing what appeared to be a tattoo gone bad on his wrist.

"Your tattoo," Reagan said, looking at the small, puffy red mark, swollen and slick with pus. "It looks infected." She could make out a few faint circles around what looked to be a split tree, though, before she could make it all out, he pulled his sleeve back down over it.

"Yeah," he said, "it's okay."

It doesn't look okay. She wanted to argue but didn't know the man well enough to be making any suggestions around his tattoo care. "What does it mean?"

"It's a symbol for liberation," he said. Reagan waited for him to expound but he said nothing, and she decided it was better to not prod the man's personal decisions, even if they were oozing.

"Well, then," he said, "if we're going to ask questions, your necklace?" Reagan grabbed it and held it in her hand, but he didn't get the message. "Where did you find such a powerful stone?"

"My father gave it to me when I was little."

"Your father?" He raised a brow. "Such a nice gift for a young child. You must be very special to him."

"I never knew him, actually. He died shortly after I was born, or at least that's what they told me."

"Is that so? I'm sorry to hear it." He bowed slightly. Though she appreciated his condolences, they weren't much comfort. "And your mother?"

"Same as him. I grew up with an aunt."

"Ah, sorry again. Guess my conversation skills are a bit off today."

"It's no big deal. Things could have been a lot worse than they were. I've actually been pretty lucky in life…until now maybe."

"Well, I'm glad to hear that one of us has."

Not knowing what to say, Reagan kept quiet. She pulled her dagger from her sheath and ran her fingers along its hilt.

"You've never held a blade before?" Aero asked.

"Sorry?" Reagan glanced up at him. His eyes were bright gold in the fading sunlight.

"I mean, the way you hold it—like it's some sort of diseased rat—reminds me of the first time I held my own."

"Is it really that obvious?"

Aero laughed. "I'm going to assume Tab never actually showed you how to use it?"

"Yeah, and I wasn't really gonna press her either. I get the feeling she isn't a very *helpful* type of person."

"Well, your feeling is correct. Would you like me to show you?"

Would I? Reagan felt her heart speed up. His arms, those beautifully sculpted arms, helping her? Would he have to hold her up close to show her? She hadn't brushed her teeth in…she couldn't even remember. "Uh…sure."

"Wise decision," he said. "'Round here, you're just as good

as dead if you can't defend yourself." Aero stood and walked over to her. "And you certainly won't be able to do anything from the ground." He reached down and helped her up. His hand was strong and hard. "Show me your stance."

Reagan separated her feet and held the blade out in front of her, pointing the tip at the center of his chest.

Aero chuckled and shook his head. He slapped the knife out of her hand onto the sand. "First thing is your grip," he said. He picked up the knife and stepped behind her. "A blade is no beast to be taken lightly. It's a part of you, and you it." His chin grazed the top of her head, and she could feel his breath on her hair. He wrapped his arms around her, and clasped his fingers around hers, holding the blade between them. "Too loose and you risk losing it to your opponent; too tight and you restrict your own movement, losing yourself to your opponent."

"Not too tight, not too loose," she said, though she wasn't exactly sure why. His skin was soft, warm, and comforting. She adjusted her stance against his chest, felt it rise and fall against her back. As much as she tried to focus on the blade, she could not help but let her imagination wander.

"Exactly," he said. He shifted back to her front and let go of her hands. They fell to her waist and she felt her face flush. He laughed. "String arms won't help much either."

"Hey!" Tab said, startling Reagan. She came shuffling down the path with three rabintails slung over each of her shoulders. "It's getting dark. It's not safe to be out in the open at night."

"Indeed," Aero agreed. "The Avonbourn is just a ways east. If we ride now, we should be able to make it before the moons peak."

CHAPTER NINETEEN

THE AVONBOURN

Reagan could hear the voices rising up from inside the two-story tavern as she made her way down the empty street. They were loud and unapologetic, two very good signs of a night accompanied by the bittersweet taste of alcohol. From the outside, the place looked like something straight out of a medieval picture book with its wooden exterior and log pillars. A chimney puffed black smoke and a weathervane shaped like a rooster swiveled in the light breeze.

The three tied their mounts in the adjacent pasture in the company of about a dozen other pergonzias and horses and walked up the front steps. Reagan wondered if she would get carded. Of course she didn't have her wallet, but would a Montana ID even work in the first place? She feared for a moment that she might get turned away...what an embarrassment that would be, though, knowing Tab, the woman would probably make Reagan wait outside until they'd had their fair share of drinks inside.

Aero opened the front door and let Tab and Reagan walk in before him. To her luck, there were no bouncers checking IDs. In fact, no one even seemed to pay them any attention as they joined the crowd inside.

Candles and oil lanterns lit the room and a fireplace where several of the tavern's patrons huddled around roared in the back corner by a staircase leading up to the second floor. Two long and narrow tables stretched down the center of the tavern, each packed with creatures and people playing cards. Though, instead of the spades, hearts, diamonds, and clubs Reagan was used to at Camp Tossbridge, these had symbols of fire, land, water, and air on them. The bar itself took up the entire left side of the establishment. A large sword hung front and center on the wall behind it. Below it, a golden placard read *The Viper*. Reagan assumed the title came from either its emerald hilt or the snakes etched into the flat of its blade. Perhaps both.

The bartender, whose eyes were frosted with irritation, stood her ground as a bear twice her size complained about his empty tankard while battling his wolf companion in an intense game of cards. Reagan froze for a moment, staring at the bear and the wolf. She had only seen their kind in a zoo where she was safe behind a layer of laminated glass and had no concerns of ever being within ten feet of their finger-length claws. She worried her dagger wouldn't hold up against them if needed, but they paid no attention to her, only to their empty tankards.

"Oie, Keiser! Another round o' ale o'er here," the bear

shouted over his shoulder. Reagan assumed that he was a few too many drinks deep, for his slurry of words barely passed for speech. He slammed a card with a fire symbol down on the table, knocking his companion's tankard over in the process. The wolf bared his teeth—two gold canines sparkling in the light of the oil lanterns—and growled at the bear.

"What did I tell ye about callin' a lady by 'er surname?" the bartender scolded, the mole on her cheek bouncing up and down.

"A lady?" the bear mocked, to which the wolf howled with laughter. Keiser, unamused, threw her dishcloth at the bear's face, sloshing ale over his white fur. They might have been animals, but they sure did remind Reagan of every other obnoxious drunk she'd ever seen at the local dive bars.

"Ye can wait fer yer damned ale," Keiser snarled through discolored and uneven teeth.

"Reslyn"—Aero pulled a chair up to the bar—"glad to see you're still feeding the neighborhood rats." He shot a glance at the card-playing bear and wolf beside them, though it went unnoticed through their intoxicated banter. "And I see you've been keeping the Viper in good shape for me." Aero gestured to the sword above the bar.

"Well of course! I wouldn't dare leave it ta rust in the back. And I ain't gonna be here for long. These pigs be drivin' me up the damned wall!"

Aero laughed. "You've been promising yourself relief from this place for years. Eslura knows you'll burn down with it."

Reslyn cackled, then reached over the bar to clamp him on the shoulder. "Whatta nice ting ta see yer face around 'ere again. And ye've brought company, aye?" She turned toward Reagan and Tab and extended a hand. "Reslyn Keiser, Lady o' the Avonbourn." Her hand was callused and big enough to swallow Reagan's. "Have a seat, why don't ya."

Reagan and Tab sat down next to Aero among the bear and the wolf whose voices escalated in volume with each chug they tossed down their throats. Reslyn scowled, and Reagan hoped that the beasts would leave soon. But, of course, their patronage was valuable regardless of their horrid stench and obnoxious behavior.

Aero flipped a silver coin that read *yerling* on the bar. "We've had quite the journey to get to here, Reslyn. I think a proper round is in order." Reslyn scooped up the coin, poured three large jugs of what Reagan was pretty sure was beer, and slung them on the bar in front of the three of them.

"Oakenale," Aero said, smiling. He examined the brew for a moment before taking a big chug. He closed his eyes and exhaled. "Just as good as I remembered."

Reagan tried a sip. Compared to all the others she'd tasted back in Missoula, it wasn't that bad. In fact, she thought its orangey aftertaste was quite good.

"So"—Resyln laced her hands on the bar—"what brings ye ta bother ol' me?"

Aero put a hand on top of the barkeeps for a moment, and then said, "Can a man not come around to see his old friend without being interrogated?"

"Ye haven't been 'ere since she passed. Six years and three moons, Aero, and ye haven't thought te come around anytime sooner?"

Aero's face paled.

"What he means to say," Tab interjected, "is that we need a place to rest."

"Well, ye've got a bit o' luck on yer side tonight. I've only got two rooms left, so two o' ye'll have ta share." Reslyn nodded toward Reagan and Tab. "Unless one o' ye would rather sleep wit the pigs out back." She cackled again and winked at Aero.

Reslyn led them up the stairs, which led to a short, dark hallway with two doors on either side and one at the far end. At the second room on the right, Reslyn knocked several times and pressed her ear to the door. Reagan hoped that the act was purely routine and not because they would have more roommates than anticipated.

"Aye." She turned and nodded at Tab and Reagan. "Ladies, room's all yers. Ye can claim whatever's left in there for yerselves." Reslyn opened the door, and the two entered.

The room was small and did not account for any personal space. One bed, a nightstand with an oil lamp beside it, a big window with a view of the moons, and a worn-down carpet that looked like it might have been white some time ago. Reagan thought the room had to have been over the bar because it was almost as noisy as downstairs. She could hear the bear and the wolf arguing over the rules of their card game as if they were in the room with them.

"Where's the other bed?" Tab said.

"Oie"—Reslyn laughed—"there ain't no other. Slim pickins when ye don't book ahead."

"You touch me once and you're sleeping on the floor. Got it?" Tab pointed her dagger at Reagan then flung it on the nightstand and collapsed onto the bed.

"Well then, that should do it," Reslyn said. "If ye need anythin', jus' holler. Someone'll hear ye eventually." She clicked the door shut and left them to the darkness.

"Could be worse," Reagan said, hoping there was more truth in the statement than she believed. Tab dismissed her with a huff and pulled the covers over her head. Reagan undid her belt, placed her dagger under the bed, and walked over to the big window. She knelt down, put her arms on the sill, and gazed up at the sky.

The golden moon, no longer blindingly bright like it had been the night of their arrival, was flanked by an army of flickering stars. The second moon, violet and half the size of the gold moon, hung just above the other moon. In one night's time, the two would be aligned, the golden eclipsing the violet, and their time would be up.

Reagan sighed and closed her eyes. She wished to be back home, not in this strange place, wherever it was that this strange place was. She was stuck. Stuck with no control over what she could and couldn't do. Her life was in danger and the one thing she had to protect herself with she had no idea how to use—though she did appreciate Aero's lesson, and thought about it quite a bit...*those arms*. She lost her friend for whom she was *actually* responsible, and her job as a camp counselor was as good as gone if they, by some magical chance, ever made it back home.

Reagan stood and caved into her fatigue, lying back on her bed. She attempted to fall asleep, but instead found herself watching a spider cross the ceiling toward its web. She did not mind bugs all that much. In fact, its presence was oddly comforting and reminded her of her cabin back at Camp Tossbridge.

"I could hit it," Tab said, startling her, "with my dagger, I mean. Those things are disgusting."

"You're still awake?" Reagan rolled to face Tab, whose eyes were glued to the spider.

"I'm talking to you, aren't I?"

"I guess I'm not used to sleeping with so much noise." Reagan sighed and re-fluffed her pillow, the feathers of which had all shifted to one side. She then pulled the covers up to her chin, though they were little comfort in the cool of the room, and she shivered down to her toes, which she could only imagine were blue by now.

"What did you expect? We're sleeping above a bar. This isn't exactly the royal palace." Tab turned to roll toward the wall, but Reagan stopped her.

"Tab?"

"What do you want?"

"Who was she?"

"Who was who?"

"The woman Reslyn spoke about, that Aero had come here to see."

"Oh, Noran?" Tab rolled back on her back. "She was the woman who stole Aero's heart."

Stole his heart, huh? Though she did not mean to, Reagan found herself pursing her lips at the idea.

"Well, don't get all brokenhearted just yet," Tab said. "She's dead. Passed on years ago."

"That's...horrible."

"Yeah," Tab said. "What's it to ya anyways? You got a little something burning for Mr. Aero?"

"No." Reagan turned to face the window and hoped that through the darkness Tab could not see her red cheeks. "I don't."

"Right," Tab said. "Then get some sleep, would ya? I'm not lookin' to deal with any cranky babies tomorrow."

Reagan closed her eyes and tried to will the noise downstairs away but was unsuccessful. Knowing she would not be able to fall asleep anytime soon, she sat up and shuffled over to the window again and looked out. A field of untended crops rolled over uneven earth as far as she could see in the darkness. Once she was bored of that, she went back to her pillow, re-fluffed it again, and lay down. She closed her eyes and felt the darkness come over her.

She wasn't sure how long she had been sleeping when she heard a loud, splintering crack at the window. She jerked herself upright and could feel her heart pounding. She stretched over toward the window to see if perhaps the wind had broken it.

Crash!

A rock smashed through the window and nearly took Reagan's head off as it came through. Shards of glass sprayed across the rug and masked it in a sheet of sharp spikes. A grappling hook flew through the broken window, and Reagan rolled back to dodge it. Its hooks clung to the sill and drew taut.

"Tab!" Reagan shouted and shook her awake.

"What?" she moaned, pulling the covers back over her

head. "Go to sl—"

Reagan ripped the covers off Tab, and she turned to face Reagan with gritted teeth.

"What gives, Red," she growled, reaching for the covers that weren't there. "Oh, gods." She leapt up and snatched her dagger from the nightstand.

"Get behind me," Tab said. Reagan did as she commanded and watched Tab creep toward the hook on the windowsill, dodging the glass in her way, and holding her blade at her side. Reagan heard footsteps pattering up the side of the house. They increased and then slowed to a halt as Tab inched closer to the window and peered out.

"There's no one there," she said at last. "Whoever it was is...gone." She cut the rope and tossed the hook outside the window. It thudded on the ground below.

"Gone?" Reagan grappled with the nasty feeling that this episode wasn't over.

"Look for yourself if you don't believe me."

Reagan walked hesitantly over to the window and leaned her head out its frame, careful to avoid the remaining shards. She looked up and down the side of the building. *Nothing*.

"Idiot must have realized they were bargin' into the wrong room," Tab said. "I'd suspect Reslyn gets all kinds of...*folks* in this dump."

"Tab, I don't—"

A blow dart whistled past Reagan's ear and lodged itself into Tab's throat. Reagan watched in horror as Tab's hands shot up to her neck and her gills flapped for air.

"Tab!" Reagan yelled, though she wasn't exactly sure why.

"Rea…" Tab began, but her voice trailed off into a mumbled mess. Tab fought for her balance while she grasped at the dart unsuccessfully, then collapsed onto the floor.

"Oh my—" Reagan gasped and ran over to her fallen body, careful to avoid the field of broken glass. She got down on the floor and rested Tab's head on her lap, then carefully pulled the dart from her neck.

The dart. Reagan paused, holding the dart in her hand, and glanced around the room. *Someone shot the—*

A dark-green creature emerged from the shadows in the corner of the room. It roared and charged toward Reagan, gripping a shard of glass in its claws like a dagger. It swiped at Reagan, but she ducked her head and jumped away, wincing as the broken glass pierced her bare feet.

"Help!" she screamed. The creature hissed at her and stepped forward on its short hind legs. Its body was tall and crocodilian, knobby and scaled, and its gaping snout was long and lined with sharp teeth. It roared again and lunged, slamming into Reagan and pulling her down to the floor with it. She kicked and clawed, pushed its stinking jaw away from her face. It stood and jerked her up with it, trapped her with its muscular arms. She opened her mouth to yell again, but its scaled hand clamped over her mouth. Reagan bit down on its hand and warm blood spurted into her mouth.

"Grrr!" The croc yanked its hand away and shook a spray of blood on the sheets. Reagan spat out a loose scale and kicked backwards into its groin. The croc reeled and released its grip. She broke for the door.

Before her fingers touched the knob, the croc grabbed her

ankle and pulled her down again, dragging her across the glass. She kicked her other leg, but it hit nothing.

"The *stone*," the croc growled, shifting its weight onto her. It pressed a claw against her throat, choking off her windpipe. She felt its sharp top piercing her skin and she squirmed, pinning her back against the floor, glass cutting through her shirt. She wheezed for air and clawed futilely at its eyes.

"Where is it?" the croc hissed. Its long, hot tongue lapped her face and slithered across the necklace. "Ahhh!" It poked the gold necklace with its claw, pulling the stone up and out of her shirt. "There you are." Reagan struggled to move her arms, but the croc was so heavy she thought they might break. It sat up on her midsection, freeing her arms as it jiggled the chain, examining the stone with its beady black eyes. She reached for it, but the croc swatted her arm away. Then she remembered the dagger under the bed.

She froze just a second. Then, as slowly as she could, she reached her hand across the glass-strewn rug. Her fingers grazed its hilt. She grit her teeth, stretching her shoulder nearly out of the socket.

"Hey," the croc growled. "Don't even—"

She grabbed the hilt and plunged the blade into the croc's neck. A gout of black blood splashed down on her chest. The croc shrieked and dropped the stone. It scrabbled its claws at the hilt of the blade. Blood continued to pour out of the gash onto Reagan and on the rug beneath her.

She grabbed the stone, shimmied out from underneath the croc, jumped up, and backed toward the door, watching the creature scrape its throat with its claws, unable to dislodge the knife. It opened its massive jaw, blood gushing over its teeth, shrieked, and flopped backwards on the floor. Dead.

Reagan felt like puking. She dropped to her knees, clasped one hand over her mouth, the other clutching the stone to her bloody shirt front, and spewed vomit in all directions.

The door opened behind her and Reslyn ran through it. "Good god almighty Aezaros!" Her mouth fell open. Reagan turned to look at the barkeep, her hand still covering her mouth and dripping with bile. The woman shouted, "Yer face! Aero, get 'er a coolin' rag!" Reagan had not noticed Aero in the doorway behind Reslyn and felt embarrassed for a moment that the man had to have seen her in this state. He held a sword—the Viper—in his hands as if it were his own and took off down the hall before she could steal another look at his face. "Hang in there," Reslyn told her. "Help is on the way." She knelt down next to Reagan and shot back up again, picking at her knee. "Bloody golly! There's broken glass all o'er the floor! Aaaaaayyy! And a crocman!"

"I think…it's…dead," Reagan mumbled. She decided she could not hold herself up any longer and fell back on the floor, cutting her cheek open on a shard of glass.

A blur took the shape of Aero kneeling beside her. "Aye! What the—"

"Glass," Reslyn said. "Cool her face," she told Aero. "Deep breaths, my lady." Reagan tried to breathe but her world was spinning. Someone clutched her hand—Tab—and she held it.

"Gods," Tab said. She shifted beside Reagan. "Well, look at that, Red."

"What?" Reagan mumbled, unsure if someone was talking

to her or she was dreaming it.

"You killed that sorry son of a vorath, and a pretty vicious one from the looks of it. I can't lie and say I'm not proud." She shook her hands from Reagan's and patted her lightly on the shoulder. "You're gonna be one helluva fighter."

"Well, I hope not." Reagan felt squeamish again, but she was pretty sure she'd thrown up just about everything she'd had, thanks to Reslyn's foamy brown ale. "I don't ever want to do it again."

"Eh, trust me, one day you'll have to." Tab was quiet a moment, then said, "Where's my blade?" She scrambled about the floor like a blind mouse in search of her dagger. Reagan saw Aero wave it in the air next to her. "Aye! Give it over here."

"Tabitha," Aero said calmly. He held the blade out of her reach. "You're in no condition to be using such a weapon."

"That thing"—she pointed toward the limp creature—"just came in through the window and tried to *kill* me."

"It's dead, Tab," Aero said.

Tab leaned over Reagan at Aero. "I said gimmie th— *hiccup!*" Reagan watched Tab's eyes go wide and started to think maybe she should move. Tab's hands shot up over her mouth, and she ran toward the window. Reagan wasn't exactly sure what happened next, but it involved a lot of gagging and splashing sounds.

"You—" Tab said, turning around and pointing a finger at Aero. She turned quickly to the broken window again and spewed. When she was done, she turned around again, slightly less angry than before and wiped her mouth with her sleeve. "Oh gods, I don't feel so good."

"Whate'er's got 'er stomach in a twist's makin' its way oot," Reslyn said. She patted Tab on the back. "Ye'll be okay."

"It's rhinespire," Aero said, picking the dart off the rug and dabbing a bit of the remaining liquid on the plump of his bottom lip. "You must have pulled it out just in time."

"I don't remember pulling it out at all," Tab said.

"I think I pulled it out of you," Reagan said, "right before that croc thing attacked me." She glanced at its limp body, its arms fallen at its side, and noticed an odd marking on its right wrist: two circles interwoven with what looked to be a *Y* straight down the middle of them. She wondered if the croc was a member of one of the gangs Tab spoke of in Varaar, but they were quite a ways away from the canyon city for her to really believe it. Either way, it had attacked and tried to kill her.

"Whatever, it's out now. What matters is the stone," Tab said, turning to Reagan. "Tell me you've still got it, Red."

Reagan realized she had forgotten the stone when she lay down on the rug. She looked at her empty hands. "Oh no!"

"That it?" Aero said, pointing at her chest.

Reagan looked down. The stone was stuck to the hardening croc blood on her shirt. "Thank god."

"Well, the gods certainly do have strange plans fer this night, don't they?" Reslyn said. She walked over to Reagan. "Me eyes cannot be wrong. That certainly is the Eyearke stone, ain't it?" She bent down for a closer look, then stood and sighed. "Ye'd better come with meh."

Reagan looked at Aero, then at Tab, who shrugged. They all followed Reslyn out of the room and down the hall to the last door. Reslyn drew a key from her pocket and unlocked it. She led them into a cozy room with a bed, a desk, and a fireplace. She lit a small fire, then slid open the top drawer of the desk and pulled out a picture.

"Here." She handed it to Reagan. "This is for you. Ye might want to sit down." Reagan pulled the desk chair in front of the fireplace and sat down. Once situated, she held the photo in the light.

A man, with short fire-red hair, and a woman with blonde hair to her shoulders stood holding a cloth-wrapped, freckle-faced child with its finger in its mouth.

"Who are they?" Reagan asked.

"Those two," Reslyn said pointing at the photo, "would be yer mother and father. And the little babe"—she paused to sigh—"that would be you."

Reagan looked up at the woman. "But that's…impossible."

"I don't wanna admit it," Tab said, "but I'm gonna have to side with Red on this one. Rulers are forbidden from having, y'know, relations, and I can't see Elmryn being any sort of exception to that."

"Oh, I wish it weren't true, too," Reslyn said, nodding. "It'd make things a whole lot easier."

Reagan stared at the picture. If what the woman had said was true, then she was Eslurian.

It made sense in a way. Her parents were definitely missing, and she had to admit she looked like the little kid in the cloth. She had been told they died in a car wreck just after she was born, but she had never seen a single photo of them, and no one seemed to have any memory of them or what they were like. It was almost as if they never existed. But how could it make sense? How could this whole place make sense? There was no place like this. There were no stones with magic power. That was only in books, and not very good books, either. But if they really were her parents, and they'd intended this to be her role in this place, this very strange but very real place, then she had to do what they'd wanted her to do. Or did she? Could she just go home? Go back to Camp Tossbridge? She realized she had no idea even how to go home. Was this supposed to be her home? Was she here forev—

"You'll have to burn it," Tab said.

Reagan had not noticed her hand clamped around the stone so tightly that a red imprint had formed across her fingers. In her other hand, the photo, her new understanding of herself—she found she was crumpling it.

"Burn it?" Reagan blinked. It was the only reminder she had, the only memory, and it wasn't even really hers.

"You heard me," Tab said. She reached down toward Reagan. "Hand it over." Reagan looked at the paper then at Aero, who was seated across the room, then back up at Tab.

"Why?" Reagan shuffled to her feet.

"Tab's right." Aero stood from his chair, its wooden legs scraping across the floor as he slid it back toward the wall. "Unfortunately, nothing good would come out of that picture falling into the wrong hands."

Perhaps it was so. Whomever had killed her father might do the same to her if word of their relation slipped into the streets.

Reagan nodded and loosened her grasp on the paper. She handed it to Tab, who tossed it over her shoulder into the fireplace without a moment's thought. Reagan watched the edges of the paper turn from cream to black and shrivel up. Fire ate up her family, her *real* family, and they disappeared into a pile of smoldering ashes.

"It'll be all right, dearie," Reslyn said.

Of course, it would seem all right to a woman who had experienced some sense of normality in her life, a woman who did not have a stone more powerful than anyone or anything she'd ever known slung around her neck. Of course. But Reagan realized there was no point in arguing. So, she smiled back and allowed the woman to feel as if she had helped in some way.

CHAPTER TWENTY

SHADOWS TAKE FORM

Bea flung herself down the stairs, three at once. Alpin, Barnaby, and Seely followed her, their footfalls and breathing loud behind her. Bea knew what came with the black smoke; she had seen it twice, just enough to scare the crap out of her.

The wind nearly swept her off her feet along with the sticks and leaves that blew past. The trees bent and Seely's house groaned above her, the giant mushroom teetering in the battering winds. A wall of black smoke crept through the woods, eating up every tree, shrub, and stone as it inched closer to them.

"Twee!" Alpin chirped. "Are we just gonna wait around for it to catch up to us?"

"A Knower of Many Things suspects that that smoke is not—"

"Yeah, yeah, yeah," Alpin said. "Does a Knower of Many Things happen to know how to get us out of here? And might I add *quickly*."

Seely nodded and led them around the mushroom, and then in a straight line into the woods opposite the smoke.

"How did it find us?" Barnaby asked, panting. He was running forward with his head turned back toward the wall of smoke.

"Ask the gods." Alpin squinted at the sky. "They don't seem to be on our side as of late. Watch out!"

Barnaby ran smack into a tree, got up and kept going, facing forward.

"A Knower has heard tales of a smoke as evil as the souls trapped in the depths of Morgaedion. Servants who claim a life-or-death loyalty to their named king."

"You think we don't already know that?" Alpin hissed. "The thing's been following us since Alistair brought the girl to my house, which is probably in ruins by now, thank you."

Bea wanted to snap back, defend herself, say it wasn't her fault, but she decided to save her breath for running, though she lost it almost immediately after. Her shoe caught in the mud, and she fell face first onto the ground. Wind knocked out of her, she gasped for air, watching as Alpin, Barnaby, and Seely raced down the path without her. With no voice left to yell, she scrambled to turn around and face the advancing smoke. The clouds closed around her, and she couldn't see ten feet in front of her.

"Bea!" She heard Barnaby's voice call for her in the distance, slightly muffled by the ring of smoke. She opened her mouth to call back but halted when three figures appeared. At first, they were nothing more than a swirl of black smoke, but then, they took the shape of a person and two snarling wolves.

Demise and his hounds.

"There's nowhere left to run, Beatrice," he hissed, emerging from the smoke. He held an axe as tall as he was. "Nowhere left to hide."

The wolves circled around her, smoke cascading out of their mouths. One snapped its teeth beside her face, nearly clipping her ear, and the other swatted its paw at her back.

"Mayna! Ariz! Not yet," Demise said. The wolves took a step back but continued to growl in Bea's direction.

"What do you want with me?" Bea asked.

"It's not what I want, Beatrice. It's what your king requests, and he wants you, though he never did specify whether he wanted you alive or *dead*," he said. "Now!" At his command, the wolves lunged forward and pinned her to the ground. Smoke fell out of their mouths and over her face, blinding her. She threw a hand up to punch either of the wolves' faces but missed.

"Argh!" Bea heard Demise shout. The smoke dissipated slightly, and she saw him step forward, raise the double blades of his axe over his head, and swing down at Bea. The silver blades sliced through the smoke, the wolves disappearing to let his blade down toward her. Bea instinctively threw her right arm up and braced herself for the worst. The blade hit her open hand. A blinding gold light flashed from the symbol on her wrist. When the spots cleared from her vision, Demise was stumbling backwards. He tripped over a root, dropped his axe, and fell back into the brush.

Bea looked at her hand, not even scratched, and the golden circles pulsed on her wrist.

Demise clambered to his feet and stumbled toward Bea, smoke billowing from his eye sockets. He lunged forward and collided with her, knocking her down on the dirt path and landing on top of her. She grasped at the dirt and kicked her foot into his chest.

"There you are," he said, smiling jagged shark teeth. He dug his claws into her wrist and blood streamed from the cuts. Bea screamed and tried to pull her wrist free of his grasp, but the more she struggled the deeper his claws cut.

Bea could feel herself fading. A searing pain crawled up her arm and into her head. The edges of her vision blurred red. She felt dizzy, and the ground swirled beneath her. She tried to scramble back, pull her wrist away, and felt a tree behind her with her other hand. She reached for it, wrapped her hand around its trunk, felt its rough bark...

A green light pulsed in her mind, behind her eyes, and the ground rumbled beneath her. Roots climbed out from the dirt path, crept up toward Demise.

"Well, what have we here, little Beatrice? You think that you can actually use your pathetic powers on—"

A thick root shot up and pierced Demise's chest. It continued to climb, carrying him up into the air as it grew farther and farther. He held Bea's wrist as the root grew, pulling her arm nearly out of its socket until he could hold it no longer. He howled and let go. The roots carried him bellowing up into the canopy.

Bea slumped to the ground against the tree, her wrist and

the symbol slick with blood. Her eyelids felt leaden. She heard heavy footsteps coming toward her. She wanted to scramble into the woods behind her and hide, but she could not make her body move. She was truly spent. She rolled her head to the side and a massive, black-clawed, furry paw was there.

"Whoa, Galabear!" It was Alistair. He jumped down and knelt at her side. "Beatrice—" He grabbed her bloody wrist. "Aezaros almighty! We must hurry. Your symbol is fading!"

CHAPTER TWENTY-ONE

ALBERTUOUS AND COMPANY

"We've gotta go." Tab wasted no time as she turned and headed toward the door. "No use waitin' around here for the scum to come rollin' back."

Reslyn nodded, led them down the stairs, and out the back door of the tavern to where their mounts grazed. Their cheeks were stuffed full of hay. Neither the two pergonzias nor Aero's horse looked particularly excited to see them and be suited up for another day of travel. They turned to face the opposite direction of their approaching riders, as if ignoring them would set them free of their obligations.

Reagan walked up to her pergonzia, stroked its burnt-orange coat, and untied the rope that tethered it to its post. "Well, at least you had a better night than I had." She forced a smile at the creature and pulled her saddle off the rack on the outside of the stable wall. She dropped it onto the pergonzia and a cloud of dust puffed up from the beast's back, making her sneeze. "You haven't had a proper bath in a while either, have you?"

"Quit talking to it like that," Tab snapped. "It's just a beast." She slapped her saddle on her own mount.

"Well, then," Reslyn said once Reagan, Aero, and Tab had settled atop their mounts. She put her hands on her hips and cocked her head at them. "This surely has been one helluva visit, aye?"

"I would go a little further than 'helluva.'" Tab's pergonzia thrashed its head up and down, apparently dissatisfied with the new bit clamped between its teeth, and she tried to calm it.

"Will you be all right here on your own, Reslyn?" Aero brushed his hand across Sela's neck, fingers running through her thick mane.

"Well, now that ye've took yer Viper back I don't know how I'll sleep another night." Reslyn winked at him.

Aero unsheathed the sword and ran his fingers along the snake engravings. "It's been a while since I've held my own blade, but times have changed, and I'll need a way to defend myself. I hope you haven't gotten too attached," he laughed and tucked the blade back beneath his belt. "You'll have to find something else to decorate the space above the bar."

"Aye! I've got meh an ol' drovig's horn that'll do jus fine." Reslyn pat him on the back. "But, oie, dontcha worry about meh. I'll be alright here on me own. Been dealin' wit all sorts o' mutts fer years. I can fare a wee bit longer."

Aero pursed his lips but held back whatever thoughts he had on the matter.

Reagan turned her pergonzia to face Reslyn. "Thank you,

Reslyn, for everything." She smiled and clutched the stone between her fingers. "You've been a great help. If there's anything I can do to repay you, please—"

"Oh, dearie, please stop that right this instant." Reslyn cackled and the sound was a pleasure to Reagan's ears. "Ye jus' get ta Galecrest all nice and safe fer meh, aye?"

"As long as Red here keeps that stone *hidden*"—Tab furrowed her brows probably as deeply as she could at Reagan—"it shouldn't be an issue." Reagan put the stone back inside her shirt. Tab nudged her pergonzia forward with a light kick and looked over her shoulder at Reagan and Aero, her impatient expression urging them forward.

"Right, then." Reslyn nodded, catching onto Tab's cue. "Ye best be on yer way. I wish ye all the—"

"Oie, Keiser!" The back door of the Avonbourn slammed against the side of the building with a heavy *clap*. A familiar furry face popped out, causing Reslyn's smile to droop at the edges.

"Shut yer darned mouth and get back inside!" She snarled through what teeth she had left, and the bear retreated back through the door. Reslyn exhaled and turned toward the three of them again. "What was I sayin'?" She ran a finger through her hair.

"Goodbye, Reslyn," Aero chuckled. "We'd better not hold you up any longer than we already have."

"Aye, no!" Reslyn swatted the air as if there were a bug buzzing around her crooked nose. "Ye'll always be welcomed 'ere, ye know that. But ye best be on yer way. All me luck to ya!"

Reslyn wobbled back up the steps of the Avonbourn, opened

the door, and shouted, "Off the table ye—" The door slammed behind her, rattling the windows on the back of the building.

"Well, she's certainly a"—Tab paused and smirked—"character."

Reagan, Tab, and Aero rode through the desert, over the meadows, and onto the rolling hills. A clearing cut through the uneven terrain, creating a valley. The sun, now halfway through the sky, lit up a hundred or so tiny homes nestled in the flat of the land, all surrounding a larger, circular structure where a mass of people and creatures milled around.

"What do you suppose that's all about?" Tab pulled her pergonzia to a halt at the crest of the hill. Reagan trotted her mount up next to her and peered down the slope.

Aero rode Sela up and dismounted. "I'm not quite sure." He pulled a small scope from his saddle bag and placed it to his eye.

"What do you see?" Tab asked.

"Looks safe enough," Aero said. He lowered the scope, and Tab snatched it from his hands.

"How can you be so sure?" Tab adjusted the scope on her eye.

"Unfortunately, I'm not," Aero said. "But it doesn't look violent or anything. We should be able to make our way past and head up through the opposite side of the valley."

"Good enough." Tab handed the scope off to Reagan, who put it up to her eye.

What at first she had believed to be a small city, turned out to be a cluster of pitched dwellings surrounding one, large round-top tent. Red banners with a swooping embroidered text that read *Albertuous and Company* decorated the strip of land leading up to the main tent where two enormous rhinos standing stiff as stone guarded its front flap. Two crossed axes formed an *X* on the ground in front of them, presumably barring the lingering crowd from entering the big tent.

The hundreds of smaller tents that surrounded the main one looked like a mini village. Each was connected to the main tent by a string of twinkling-colored lights tied from their tops to the top of the larger tent, casting a rainbow glow about the place. Tiny, flickering specks of pink and yellow bobbed up, down, and around the big tent like fireflies.

A flash of red caught Reagan's eye from the side of the main tent where a rotund elephant with gold-capped tusks and a long red cape poked his head out of a hidden flap on the tent. He opened his mouth and spoke words Reagan could not hear toward the smaller tents, from which people and animals scurried over toward the elephant. One of the group happened to be a giant, blue dog with a scruffy white chest. It stood on its hind legs and towered above the rest of the group's heads. Though it was certainly beyond odd, it wasn't the color of its fur that made Reagan raise her brow, it was its four long arms and enormous paws. "What is that thing?" she asked, pulling the scope away from her eye.

"What thing?" Tab grabbed the scope back and put it to her eye. "Well, well, well," she said, "would ya look at that. Aero, come here."

Reagan looked between the two. She wondered what the big deal was.

Aero took the scope and put it to his eye. "Ah, and you thought that I had found an interesting pastime."

"Oh, pipe it," Tab snapped.

"Excuse me," Reagan said, pulling their attention away from the dog and to her, "what the heck is it? Some kind of dog-centipede thing?"

Aero and Tab looked at each other and laughed, the first time Reagan had ever seen Tab that close to a full smile.

"That would be Long Paws," Aero said. "The only digguno I know who dyes her fur blue. Though where do you suppose Piercio is?"

With all these strange names, Reagan thought she ought to start keeping a log of some sorts.

"Probably already in there. The two wouldn't be more than ten feet apart. C'mon, we'll sneak in through the side." Tab nodded toward the same side flap the elephant had peeked out of.

"Sneak in?" Aero asked. Reagan almost asked the same question. The rhinos out front didn't exactly look like they would be too happy if they caught them in their act, and she wanted nothing to do with their axes...or the horns on their heads.

"You got any better ideas?" Tab flattened her brows. "You may think you're charming, but I don't think those rhinos would agree."

"I mean," Aero said, "should we not keep moving forward?"

Reagan thought the same, though she would rather let

Aero challenge the woman and avoid her backlash. Although she wouldn't mind venturing into the circus, she feared for her safety with the stone still around her neck. One close encounter with death was more than enough for her.

"Keep moving forward and miss *this*?" Tab pointed at the blue dog. "I don't think so. Plus, we need all the help we can get."

"If you say so," Aero said. He tucked the scope away in his saddlebag. They mounted and rode down the hill, Reagan all the while wondering what could be so important to the woman to distract her from her mission.

The closer they got to the tent, Reagan realized that the tiny dots were not fireflies, but finger-sized glowing rat-like creatures with fluffy fur and wings. She held out her hand, palm up, and one of the rats landed on it, looking up at her with beady eyes. "You're kinda cute, aren't you?" she laughed. The little thing cocked its head and twitched its nose.

"Red," Tab startled Reagan. She was holding up the side flap of the tent, waiting and tapping her foot impatiently on the ground. Reagan blew the rat off of her hand and jogged over toward the tent.

"Be careful with those little *demons*." Tab clenched her jaw and swatted one that fluttered too close to her pectoral fin. "Peepmuks may look cute, but get some of their spit on your skin and you'll be itchin' for days. Trust me, I learnt that the hard way." Reagan dipped under the flap and into the tent.

It was a sunken amphitheater with two enormous fires burning in circular pits on either side of the center stage, casting bright flickering light about the tent. Below Reagan, rows of crowded seats angled downward toward the stage where people and animals alike snacked on what looked to be popcorn and drank from frothing tankards of yellow liquid. She watched as the elephant with gold-capped tusks wobbled onto the stage, holding back his gut with one hand. His right foot was made of wood, which caused him to stand unevenly and rely on his walking stick as he made his way to the center of the stage.

"I'm not standing for this thing," Tab said. She walked two rows down to a space with three empty seats and sat in the first one. Reagan looked at Aero, who shrugged and descended the stairs to where Tab sat. Reagan followed and the two climbed over Tab's legs to sit in the remaining empty seats.

The elephant cleared his throat three times, each increasingly louder, before the crowd's chattering subsided to a low murmur.

"My fellow Eslurians"—the elephant spread his arms in a gesture of welcome—"you have traveled from both near and far, trekked across the rolling flatlands, hiked over the towering rocky peaks, all for the wonderful spectacle of Albertuous and Company's Circus of Marvels. I assure you, my friends, that your travels were not for nothing; they will be made worth it in due time, for you have not seen the best of it all!" He paused for effect, waiting with a grin as the crowd applauded. He put a hand to his mouth and whispered to no one in particular, "And, if there's one thing to note about Kantankerous Albertuous, it would be that he most certainly does *not* disappoint."

Aero scoffed, and Tab glared at him. "What?"

"Oh, nothing." Aero shook his head. "He's just an idiot."

"You know him?" "We used to be"—Aero paused for a

moment—"partners."

"Partners?" Tab furrowed her brows. "What sort of partners?"

Reagan wondered too. The man was sort of mysterious in a way that had her wanting to know more about him. Though she didn't want to know too much; it might ruin his charm.

"So," Kantankerous Albertuous continued, "without further ado, I present to you our final act, an act no sane soul would ever *dare* attempt—the pyrotechnics of Metal Mouse and Flint Paw." At that, he bowed and limped off behind the curtains to a wave of applause.

"Oh." The elephant poked his head back between the curtains. "And, as always, folks, remember to keep your trunks up! Also, do be sure to leave your donations at the door on the way out." He winked and grinned widely, golden teeth glinting in the firelight, and then waved his trunk in the air. He dropped the curtain and disappeared again. The crowd roared.

"Now, off with the flames, you scum!" the elephant's voice snarled from behind the curtains. The fires cut out, casting a cloak of smoke and darkness over the crowd. Muffled chattering filled the tent until the flames burst to life again. At center stage stood the blue dog, Long Paws, wearing a crimson cloak that matched the bandana around her white, scruffy neck. Reagan wondered for a moment where the second part of the act was until she noticed, next to the dog's foot, the tiny mouse, only a few inches tall, clad in gleaming silver armor and wielding what looked to be a sewing pin.

"Fellow Eslurians." Though tiny, the mouse's voice

resounded throughout the tent, startling Reagan. "You've come here for a show, am I right?" He strutted across the front of the stage, waving his pin-sword at the crowd in the first rows. "Well, fret no more, for I have just what you desire. *Now!*" The mouse snapped his tiny fingers and the flames cut out. "Feast your eyes, my fellow Eslurians, on Flint Paw." At his call, the flames burst to life again, this time surrounding the stage, their flickering casting shadows across the tent. The dog-like creature now wore a blindfold and had dropped her cloak onto the back of the stage, revealing her paws, which held bombs just large enough to fit between her sharp claws.

The crowd murmured and the mouse smirked. "You seem unimpressed, hmm. Then I must prove you wrong! Shall we begin?" He pointed his pin up toward the ceiling and the crowd roared again. "Flint Paw, are you ready?" The dog nodded, and the mouse walked to the side of the stage to retrieve a stick from a hand that reached out from the curtains. Then he strode over toward one of the fires and dipped it into the flames, igniting the tip of the stick.

Tab grumbled, "Bombs? Inside? What kinda ploy is this?" She crossed her arms as the mouse lit the wicks of the bombs. Reagan felt a wave of unease and looked at the exit behind her.

The dog seemed to know once all the bombs had been lit, for she began juggling them between her four paws, their fuses sparkling, then she launched them over the crowd. The spectators screamed and lurched forward in their seats, covering their heads with their hands. Reagan, too, covered her head. But instead of exploding with fire and shrapnel, the bombs popped open and poured out a stream of bioluminescent dots on the crowd. They cheered and reached for the floating dots. Reagan held her hand out and caught one for herself. She laughed and exhaled, placing her free hand on her heart.

"River spores?" Tab snatched one floating by her nose. "Well, okay," she scoffed and released it back into the air. It floated up to join the rest gathering at the top of the tent. "You got me there, Long Paws." The crowd roared as the mouse and dog bowed at the front of the stage. Then the two performers ducked behind the curtains, and Kantankerous Albertuous reappeared.

"And there you have it, folks, our last act of the evening," he said. He bowed, or at least tried to, but his belly was too big, and retreated behind the curtain.

The crowd began to shuffle toward the exit, squeezing through the tight aisles and walking up the steps. Reagan was also ready to leave, but Tab yelled to Aero over the cheering, "Whattya say we go pay our friends a visit, aye?" Aero nodded and they followed Tab around the crowd to a door beside the stage that led to what Reagan assumed would be backstage. Tab wiggled the knob and, finding it unlocked, waved Reagan and Aero inside.

"By gods!" a voice exclaimed. The tiny mouse stood on top of the collapsed blue dog's head in the center of the room and addressed his fellow cast members. "Would somebody get this digguno something to eat! She's about worked to death!" When his request went unanswered, the mouse clenched his fists and opened his mouth to shout again, but Aero spoke first.

"Piercio." Aero walked through the crowded backstage area, removing his hood, and kneeling down to level with the

225

mouse's—Piercio's—face.

"Aero?" Piercio cocked his tiny head up at Aero and scratched between the piercings in his oversized ears. "Tab?" He shifted his gaze toward the woman. He squinted his eyes and blinked several times. "W-what are you two doing here?" Piercio's voice wavered as the dog shifted and groaned beneath him, nearly knocking him off.

The tall dog reached a big paw out. "Mmhmaa," she moaned and panted, her pink tongue lolling.

"Hey!" Piercio snapped again. "Did you all go deaf, huh? I said, somebody get this digguno something to eat!"

Seemingly tired of his yelling, a woman clad in all yellow plucked a muffin from a pile of pastries on a corner table and tossed it over her shoulder. Piercio caught the treat with both paws. "Thank you!" he snarled and lowered it down to the dog's face. "Open your mouth, you big fool," he said. The dog engulfed it in one bite, nearly taking his paws with.

"There." Piercio wiped some crumbs from his paws. "Now would ya get yourself up and quit your darned whining?"

"Well," Tab said, "I can't say I'm not impressed." She leaned against a support pole and smirked. "Nice show, Metal Mouse."

Piercio grit his teeth. "You know what, *Tabitha*," he said, crossing his arms, "I could live without the criticisms."

"'Cio may not like it, but I sure do." Long Paws lifted Piercio off her head, set him on the ground, then stood up, head reaching a foot taller than Aero's at her full height.

Pericio craned his tiny neck up at Long Paws. "How many times do I have to tell you to quit callin' me that?" The dog stifled a laugh with a big paw. "I won't warn you again!"

Piercio pointed his pin at Long Paws's foot, the hair on his back sticking straight up. "And I don't care how much you apologize. One more time and I'll needle you good!"

"Well," Aero laughed. "I will say that I'm pleased not much has changed between you two."

"So," Tab said, looking around the backstage area. Aside from the performers, it was cluttered with batons, balls, bombs, whips, heaping piles of costumes, masks, blindfolds, streamers in all colors of the rainbow, ropes, rings, and even a canon shoved in the corner opposite the muffins, "This is where life took ya, huh?"

"There isn't much of a choice when you're traveling with a big ol' klutz like this one." Piercio holstered his pin, slapped Long Paws' foot, and clambered up the dog's leg, across her belly, and up over her shoulder, scaling Long Paws like she was a great mountain. He plopped down on her head as if it were a seat made just for him.

"Hey." Long Paws furrowed her brows and flicked him off. "I don't see you juggling bombs anytime soon, so I don't want to hear it from ya."

The mouse landed on top of the pastries and scrambled to right himself, waving his fist in the air. "River spore bombs; might I add!"

"Oh, boohoo," Long Paws puffed. "Take your complaints to Tank. I don't make up the show."

As if he had heard his name, the elephant wobbled in from a curtained area, and everyone fell silent. The performers stared at the giant expectantly. Up close, Reagan could see sweat stains soaking through his shirt and the makeup attempting to cover the wrinkles lining his face. What she hadn't seen before were the two leather wristbands he wore. One was pulled up just enough to show the bottom half of a circle tattoo. When the elephant caught her staring at it, he pulled the wristband down and glared at her.

She thought he might put a tusk through her chest, and she stepped back a few feet.

"Ah, Tank." Piercio gulped and gaped up at the elephant, then dodged a massive foot, as Tank pulled his sight from Reagan and walked directly past him to put a hand on Aero's shoulder. The weight almost knocked Aero down.

"Aero Ellisvat," Tank said, "I thought that was your handsome mug I saw in the crowd. You have an unmistakable jawline, my friend." Reagan couldn't have agreed more.

"Kantankerous," Aero said, shimmying out from under the heavy hand, "a surprise to see you as well."

Tank gestured toward the room behind the curtain he had emerged from. "A word, if I may?" Aero glanced toward Tab for approval.

"Whatever." Tab rolled her eyes and Aero followed Tank behind the curtains.

"So," Piercio said, "what brings you to our neck of the tents?"

Tab looked around at the performers lingering around them. They were undressing, removing makeup, chatting, and cooling down. "You got a … *quiet* place to talk?"

Piercio nodded and led Tab, with Reagan following, invited or not since she had no place else to go, out of the main tent and through the tent village to one that was decorated with blue stripes.

"It's not perfect, but it does the job," Piercio said. Long Paws lifted its flap and held it for them to enter.

Inside was a single room with two beds—one of which was smaller than Reagan's foot and presumably belonged to Piercio. A table with two chairs and an oil lantern on it stood between the beds. Long Paws pulled a chair out and sat down, while Piercio climbed up the leg of the other chair and plopped down, his head falling far too short of the table.

Tab looked around the room, roving it with her eyes for a moment. When she was apparently satisfied, she said, "I wanna get the Sarakyan back together."

"What?" Long Paws said.

"I didn't know you were deaf," Tab said.

"Are you kidding me?" Piercio said. "We nearly got our necks snipped the first go around. What makes you think we would even *consider* putting our lives on the line again?"

"Piercio's right, Tab," Long Paws chimed in. "You shouldn't say that name, not even in here."

"Oh, no?" Tab said. "Red."

Reagan realized she had been daydreaming and walked toward them from the tent flap.

Piercio looked Reagan up and down while she stood there uncomfortably. Then the little mouse said, "What?"

"Go on, show him, would ya?" Tab said.

"Show me wh—"

Reagan lifted the stone out of her shirt. In the light of the oil lantern, it shimmered, casting purple rays around the tent.

"Are you—" Piercio stammered. "How is that possible?"

"By gods." Long Paws put one of her paws over her snout.

"All right, all right. Put that away, now. A thing like that should never be out in the open."

Reagan dropped the stone back down her shirt.

"So…Red, here, found our little stone, and get this." She paused. "Red also happens to be our great Elmryn's daughter." She wrapped her arms around Reagan's shoulders and pulled her into an embrace. "Now how's that for fancy?"

"*Daughter?*" Piercio said. "How can that be? Rulers are strictly forbidden to—"

"Well, that doesn't really matter now, does it?" Tab said. "All that *does* matter is that we have the stone. So, whattya say? You comin' to Galecrest with us to deliver the stone to the Rulers?" Tab's smirk looked almost too confident.

"Sorry, Tab, but we can't." Piercio shook his head, straining to keep his eyes apart from Tab's.

"What do you mean you 'can't'?" Tab narrowed her eyes on the little mouse. "What have you got goin' on here that's so important?"

Piercio shrugged. "It's too risky. We've worked so hard to have a decent life. Why take the chance?"

"A decent life?" Tab laughed and gestured around the two-bed tent. "You're circus clowns, for gods' sake."

"It might not seem like the most glamorous lifestyle," Piercio said, "but at least we have a roof over our heads, food in our bellies, and people to call family."

"But you've seen it with your own eyes, how can you say no?" Tab said.

"For all we know—which, might I add, is *nothing*—it very

well could be a hoax"

"You know that's not true," Tab said

"Then what is?" Piercio asked.

"There are people after the stone, we know that for certain. One of them attacked Reagan; tried to *kill* her just to get that stone. They know it's out here and we have to protect it…and her." Reagan knew that by using her real name, Tab meant business.

Piercio leapt off of the chair and slowly walked toward Tab's boot. "Like I said, it's not worth the risk for us right now. I'm sorry, Tab, but we just can't—"

"Let's go find Aero," Tab said, grabbing Reagan by the arm and heading to the tent flap. "No use wasting any more time in this hole."

CHAPTER TWENTY-TWO

THE BOOK OF LAND

"One of these moons you are going to run your lungs dry, old friend." Bea opened her eyes halfway and could faintly make out the two figures kneeling next to her, but she was too tired to move, and the bed she lay on was too comfy to even think about leaving.

One, a lizard. A lizard tall enough to pass as a full-grown male wearing a pristine white lab coat. *Alistair*, she recalled, a warm and welcome thought.

And the other was a short, plump creature with a nose as big and round as a tennis ball. He had scruffy hair, ocean-grey eyes, white whiskers, and a smoking pipe between his thin, cracked lips. His slate-grey skin was withered, and he wore overalls that reminded her of the paint-stained pair Joe Dildecker always wore.

"What lungs?" the old grey creature said. "The things

haven't worked since the day I was born." He coughed so hoarsely Bea thought he might croak on the spot.

"Perhaps it is due to the fact that your lips have yet to part with the pipe that sits between them," Alistair said.

A waft of pungent odor crept up Bea's nostrils, testing her gag reflexes. "Say what you will, Alistair," the creature said, "but you won't change this old troll and his bad habits."

"Unfortunately, I have just about come to accept that." Alistair swatted away a ring of smoke that haloed his snout.

"Doesn't look like she'll be waking up any time soon, huh?" the troll said, taking a loud draw from his pipe.

"I would prefer to think otherwise."

"I don't know, Alistair." The troll exhaled a cloud of black. "I've never seen a mark that dark before." He paused a moment. "You can't tell me that looks normal to you."

"Have hope, Nordwelg," Alistair said. He placed a hand on the troll's—Nordwelg's—shoulder and squeezed. "You will not get anywhere in life without a little bit of hope."

"Yeah." Nordwelg took another puff of his pipe. "Right."

Alistair retracted his hand and tucked it inside his coat pocket. With his free hand, he hoisted himself to his feet, old bones groaning and cracking several times in the process.

"Stay with her," Alistair told Nordwelg. "I must go check on how our other guests are faring." He departed across the room, his claws scrabbling against the stone floor. "Please do call for me if anything changes on your end of things."

Other guests? In her pain and confusion, Bea had nearly forgotten about Barnaby, Alpin, and Seely. She hoped that they were okay.

"Always stuck with the bedside duties, old me," Nordwelg mumbled to himself. "Don't suppose you'd mind waking up anytime soon?"

A surge of pain rushed through Bea's wrist. She doubled over, left hand clutching her throbbing right wrist. She opened her eyes fully. A stream of light, bright and blinding, cascaded through a wall of glass.

"Well, that was quick." Nordwelg straightened up. "Alistair! The girl, she's coming to."

Alistair shuffled back into the room. "Beatrice." He knelt down to her and touched her cheek carefully with his cold claw. "How are you feeling?"

Bea moaned. She felt like death...if that was even close enough to describe her pain.

"Nordwelg, would you mind fetching me a cloth, please?" Nordwelg nodded and lumbered across the room, returning a moment later with a damp rag. Alistair took it from him and pressed it to Bea's forehead.

She winced. Ice-cold water trickled down her forehead. Pain coursed through her, and she clamped her teeth down to avoid screaming out in agony.

"Relax your muscles, Beatrice," Alistair said. "You're safe now."

"W-where am I?" Slowly, carefully, she lifted her head and looked around. She found herself in what appeared to be a greenhouse.

The room was completely full of plants. Sunflowers, daisies, and roses in bright yellows, pinks, and reds grew from equally colorful pots. Vines dangled from the ceiling like loose power lines. A waterfall trickled into a pool in the far corner and spread out in a thin river that circled Bea and her bed. A willow tree took up the corner opposite to the waterfall, its branches weeping toward the ground, sagging leaves hiding its trunk. Various sticks, both large and small, lay strewn about the stone floor, fallen from shorter trees with pink blossoms. Cords of light streamed through the glass walls, making the room exceedingly hot and humid.

"Lie back down, Beatrice." Alistair helped her onto her back. "Your body is weak. It is for the better that you rest for the time being."

"What happened?" Bea asked. "My wrist…" She massaged her wrist where the symbol, once lustrous gold but now turned brown, burned on her skin. "Why does it hurt so much?"

Alistair and Nordwelg shared a look. Both appeared to be displeased.

"You dispelled the Shadow Reaper," Alistair said. "Do you not remember?"

Shadow reaper. The name brought back a shiver colder than the rag wrapped around her forehead. She felt weak: mind, body, and soul. Her hands were white, her limbs shook, and she was sweating profusely.

"A jug of water if you would, please, Nordwelg." Nordwelg seemed to know the drill by now and left the room promptly, leaving Alistair, who tried to comfort her. "Beatrice, rest easy, now." Specks of red and black blurred her vision and she gripped the sheets beneath her.

Nordwelg returned and handed a canteen to Bea. She held it unsteadily and nearly dropped it. Alistair caught it and held it to her lips. She propped herself up just enough to down half the water in one gulp.

"Take your time," Alistair said.

Bea finished off the rest of the water and gazed down the canteen at its now-empty bottom. "And my wrist?" She lifted her wrist with her other hand and winced at the pain.

"Unfortunately, we were not there for the attack, but my understanding is that it had something to do with a certain contact between you and the Shadow Reaper," Alistair said. "Shadow Reapers live by feeding off of the souls of other beings. One touch from its claw could extract half their victim's lifespan and add it to theirs. Beatrice, did this Shadow Reaper ever touch you?"

"I-I…" She looked at her wrist. She didn't want to tell him. It would only make things worse. But she had to. What if he could help her? What if she could help them? "I think so. Demise…he clawed my wrist…the symbol."

"It is as I feared, then," Alistair said. "She must be reconnected to the Books. It is the only way that we can hope to reverse the effects that he has had upon her."

"Effects?" Bea asked, gripping her wrist tighter. "What effects?"

"Like Alistair said," Nordwelg began, "a Shadow Reaper lives by sucking the souls from its prey. One touch could mean death. Fortunately for you, your power is much stronger than his. But you can't fight it off forever."

"You see, Beatrice," Alistair continued, "you are made of the same energies that sustain this world—fire, water, land, and air—your body must be brought back to the source of its power, the very same power that this Shadow Reaper attempted to drain from you."

"Mhm." Nordwelg nodded. "Pesky little demons have the power to insert themselves inside their prey and eat away the energy that lives inside them. I don't doubt for one second that you would be the highest on their list of prey. Now, if I had just one assumption to make, it would be that the reason that symbol of yours has darkened is because part of that Reaper is still inside you. And until he eats up every last bit of your energy, he'll stay inside you, tearing away at whatever life you've got left to offer."

"Do you think you can walk, Beatrice?" Alistair asked.

Bea shifted her weight to the side of the bed. She shuffled her legs off and rested her feet on the tile floor. It felt like ice. She steadied herself on the side of the bed. Her breathing was heavy, and her arms shook under the weight of her body.

Alistair wrapped his claws beneath Bea's shoulder, and helped her up. She felt her body collapse into him. Her head bobbled, her neck went limp, and her legs turned to rubber.

"Careful, now, slow steps." Alistair coached her to her feet, holding her carefully.

Nordwelg picked a branch about half Bea's height and just thick enough to bear her weight from the floor.

"Good thinking," Alistair told him. Bea shifted her weight onto the stick.

Nordwelg grinned. "This old troll hasn't lost all his wits, you see."

"So you say." Alistair smirked. "We must take Beatrice to the Sacred Chamber. There isn't much time left to spare. Her body is growing weaker with each breath we take."

Bea agreed with the lizard but didn't know how any chamber, no matter how Sacred it was, would help. What she needed was a trip to the hospital…if there even were any in this strange place.

Nordwelg nodded and made his way through the door and into the hallway first, turning back to watch Bea struggle over on the makeshift cane. Alistair, a foot behind her, held his arms out, ensuring there would be no chance of Bea falling over again.

Nordwelg led them out of the greenhouse into a glass hallway. Bea shuffled along after him with the help of the cane and Alistair. The hallway was hundreds of feet above the ground, and below her lay a city made nearly invisible by its garden roofs. At the end of the tunnel was a giant tree, its branches stretching high over their heads and its leafy canopy shielding them from the sunlight.

It was no ordinary tree, even Bea knew that from first glance. No tree could grow so immense…or so she had thought before. But, even then, no tree seeped green light from the veins of its bark, shining on her clothes and the city below…far below, almost too far. She felt sick looking down at it and forced her eyes back up to the tree.

"Gewa hosts the Book of Land inside her trunk," Alistair told her. "The Book's energy courses through her, and thus over the city and the land, traveling down her roots and spreading its energy across all of Eslura."

"Gewa?" Bea asked, craning her neck up at the vast spread of its canopy.

"The first settlers—well, the first Sacred Ruler of Blighburrow, more so—were quite keen on naming plants," Nordwelg said. "They believed it to be just as important as naming people. I've no idea why they thought that, though, but they worshipped that tree, and all the plants for that matter, more even than they worshipped Aezaros. They even had naming ceremonies each time a new bud sprouted."

"Our ancestors and their ways are not to be made a joke of, Nordwelg," Alistair said. "If not for them, many of the customs we have come to appreciate today would not be so. Take Gewa, for example, our natural-born protector and home of the Book of Land."

"Say what you will." Nordwelg swished a hand. "But you can't say they weren't a little bit twisted up in the roots."

Alistair ignored the troll's statement, and they continued toward the end of the tunnel where a group of masked figures waited. "Thank you for your assistance, Nordwelg." Alistair halted a few feet in front of the masked figures and turned to his companion. "But we must continue this journey alone. I am certain that you understand my cause for saying so."

"Of course," Nordwelg said. "You know where to find me." The old troll plucked his pipe out of his overalls and packed the chamber full of brown leaves. He flattened them with a chubby finger before sparking a match and lighting them. He took a drag.

"Thank you, Nordwelg," Bea said. She smiled at the troll, who winked and bowed.

"My pleasure." He spun around and walked back down the glass tunnel, rings of smoke following him as he disappeared from sight.

Bea and Alistair continued toward the figures, whose unwavering stances made Bea think for a moment that they could have been statues.

Cloaked in green, the four towering figures stood guard in front of an entrance to another door cut into the side of the tree's—Gewa's—trunk. They held staffs made of spiked wood in their gloved hands. Only their emerald eyes showed through their wooden masks, following Alistair's every movement.

Alistair glanced at each of the guards in turn and nodded his head once, the simple gesture enough to part the foursome and allow them passage into the tree.

As Bea followed Alistair into the tree, she found the guards staring at her through their masks. Though they showed no signs of aggression, she could not help but feel uneasy.

"The Sacred Guard means you no harm," Alistair said as they proceeded down the walkway. "They are trained to respond only to the commands of their Sacred Ruler and, of course, the Sacred Head."

"You mean, they're under my command too?"

"Of course, Beatrice," Alistair laughed. "As Sacred Head you have ultimate control over the Sacred Guard—that is, those stationed in Blighburrow, Galecrest, Ovallia, and Zybersia. Remidigon deals with the Guards on Morgaedion, so, unfortunately, those units are out of your hands."

Bea did not know the first thing about commanding anyone. She could barely muster the courage to raise her hand in class, how could she be expected to give an order to an entire unit? She wanted to ask more, but the lizard kept walking forward.

240

He led her through a tunnel just tall enough for their heads and with walls just far enough apart to accommodate them in a single file. Had Bea been a smidge more claustrophobic, she might not have made it through. The tunnel opened up and the pair entered a circular cavern the size of a football field, or two.

"Welcome to the Hollow of Gewa," Alistair said.

Despite its sheer size, the space held nothing more than a narrow walkway through the vast empty space that led out to a platform in the middle of the hollow. Above the platform floated a book of unfathomable size surrounded by a pulsing green glow. Not just a book, *the Book*. A book, larger than either Bea or Alistair, hovering, as if by magic.

Alistair, seemingly unimpressed by the sight, continued down the walkway to the middle of the tree and stood on the platform beneath the hovering book. Bea, however, stopped before the path, her body paralyzed momentarily by the enormity of the empty space. The walkway had no rails and was so high that she could not see anything in the depths below it...and she thought the glass tunnel was bad.

"Have no fear, Beatrice," Alistair said from the platform, his voice echoing through the hollow. "You are no longer in danger; not in this Sacred space."

Bea took a deep breath and held it. She clenched her fist on the walking stick and tapped the walkway with it. The endless resounding echoes were almost maddening. Her legs still ached. One wrong step would send her hurtling down the hollow to certain death. She took a first step and then a second and before she knew it, she was standing next to Alistair on the platform. She let out her breath.

The book floated over them, about the size of Fran Dildecker's old Dodge Dart; its pages facing down at them coursed with a green light, emitting from an emerald crystal rooted in its spine. Green lightning rolled across its surface and shot up through the darkness into the tree.

"The Sacred Chamber is a very special place," Alistair said. "There are only four like it in all of Eslura. Though, unfortunately for us all, when Elmryn...passed on, the Sacred Chamber of Zybersia was left without its shield, a powerful protective barrier that allowed only those of Sacred titles to enter, the very reason that only you and I are in this hollow right now."

As Bea stared up at the Book, its green glow began to flicker.

"You see, Beatrice," Alistair continued, "the Book of Land suffers a great deal now that the Book of Fire is no longer able to produce its share of energy." As if its fuse just blew, the Book went black and cloaked them in darkness. "The way things are playing out now," Alistair said, seemingly unbothered by loss of light, "the Books of Land, Water, and Air have been forced to produce much more power to sustain the balance in Eslura, and even then, I fear it is not enough." The Book's green glow pulsed to life again, covering them in its green hue.

"What will happen?" Bea asked. "To Eslura, I mean, if they can't keep the balance."

Alistair took a deep breath and bowed his head to his chest before rising to lock eyes with Bea. "The Books will eventually run out of energy trying to fill the void that was left behind when the Heart was stolen from the Book of Fire. Their shields, like the one in which we stand, will fall weak, leaving them vulnerable to attack. And life on Eslura will cease to exist without their power."

"What can we do? What can I do? There has to be something," Bea said. She had nearly forgotten how much her legs ached, and she felt herself getting sick, her knees wobbling. Alistair grabbed hold of her.

"First," he said, hoisting her up, "we must ensure that our Sacred Head does not fall more ill than she already is." He helped her steady herself on the walking stick, then he reached his arms above his head. The tips of his claws emitted a green light that shot up at the book, drawing it down in front of them.

"Place your hand on the Book's Heart, Beatrice," Alistair told her. "Close your eyes and allow its energy to merge with yours."

Bea stepped forward and extended her right hand toward the page, ignoring the pain in her wrist and throughout her body. Her fingers stopped an inch before the crystal, and she turned to look at Alistair. He nodded, urging her to proceed. She touched the tips of her finger to the crystal, the Heart of the Book of Land.

A beam of green light shot out of the Heart and onto her hand, her wrist. It seeped into her skin and turned her veins green. She felt it climbing into her body, through her chest and into her head. It moved inside her, its intense energy warming her blood, coursing through her brain and into her eyes.

All she could see was green, like a thick screen in front of her eyes, and she could not even see Alistair beside her any longer. Everything went completely silent. She was trapped in a vast green emptiness.

Then white. She stood in the middle of a blank white field.

Puffy clouds appeared, so low she could touch them, and hovered around her.

"Hello?" she called into the field of clouds. Her voice echoed back to her. She looked around at the empty white space, wondering where she was, wondering if this was what heaven looked like. Did she die? Could the Book not save her? She called out again. This time, her voice did not echo.

"You've come," a voice said through the clouds. A familiar voice.

Bea turned around and saw her mother walking through the clouds toward her. She wore a golden cloak. Her long, curly brown hair swirled in a non-existent wind. She strode up to Bea and stopped before her, golden eyes glancing down and meeting Bea's.

"I knew you would." She touched Bea's cheek, then turned away, cloak and curls trailing behind her.

"Wait. Where are you going?" Bea called. She watched her mother disappear into the clouds, her body sucked in and concealed by their puffiness. Bea ran after her, ran through the clouds, swatting her hands to part them. The clouds turned grey and then black. Thunder rumbled through them and a storm raged in the distance. Lightning illuminated the same white-haired man she had seen in her dreams. Beside him, her mother lay limp on the ground, her cloak ripped to shreds and her face bruised.

Bea opened her mouth to yell at the man, but her tongue twisted into a knot, barring her speech. She tried to run, to escape, but found herself moving in slow motion.

The man caught her wrist and pulled her toward him. She

fought, but she could not break free.

"Look at us now," he said to her. "Together at last."

Together? No! Bea clawed at his face and he released his hold, dropping her to the ground.

She fell to her hands and knees, vision swirling. Her heart raced and she couldn't breathe, couldn't speak, couldn't scream. She closed her eyes, then opened them and found she had returned to the Sacred Chamber. She glanced around her for the man, for her mother, but could not find either, only Alistair and the Book of Land floating above them.

"What is it, Beatrice?" Alistair said. He knelt by her side on the platform. "Tell me, what did you see?"

Bea looked the old lizard in the eye. She swallowed the fear in her throat. "Him."

CHAPTER TWENTY-THREE

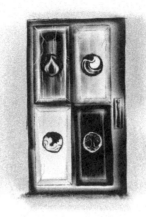

THE DOOR

Reagan, Aero, and Tab left the backstage tent in silence. They walked past the flapping red banners to their tethered beasts, mounted, and took off down the worn dirt path. It led them out of the valley and into the woods, where they weaved through tall trees, ducked under low-hanging branches, and leapt over fallen trunks till it opened to a low, flat plain with knee high grass.

Tab rode about four pergonzia lengths ahead of them. The woman mumbled something to herself angrily, but Reagan could not make out the words. She shifted in her saddle and turned toward Aero. "Will she be okay?" Reagan asked while keeping a side eye trained on Tab's back just in case the woman decided to impulsively throw a dagger at her.

Aero sighed. "Tab doesn't exactly move on from her feelings very quickly, but I assume she'll come around eventually."

Though Reagan did not say it, she hoped he was right. She knew Tab had a short fuse, but she had never seen her this distraught.

"You see," Aero continued as if reading her mind, "although her heart is as cold as Eslura's highest peak, there are still a few things that she truly cares about, one of which is the Sarakyan. It meant more to Tab than it did to the rest of us. Long Paws, Piercio, and I were nobodies, outcasts with nowhere left to go in life. We joined them hoping they would lead us to good fortune, nothing more. But Tab had joined the Sarakyan and found a family...a father. Until his death, that is."

"Her father died?" Reagan asked, looking down at her hand, which was wrapped about the stone.

"Not her real father," Aero said, "but Elmryn. He was like a father to her."

"How so?" Reagan asked. She wanted to know more about Tab, not only to protect herself but also because she felt herself beginning to care about the woman. But she knew Tab would never share her personal story.

"As an Olphin," Aero said, "she faced certain...struggles, if you will, growing up. The whole world hated her for something she knew she didn't do. She hid herself in the darkest alleys of Varaar to escape a life of imprisonment and let no one really know her. Except Elmryn and perhaps Fawn, too."

"My father?" Maybe she had more in common with the woman than she thought.

"That's correct. He took her under his roof, fed her, clothed her, showed her what it meant to be *loved*. Without him, she would not have survived, or worse, she would have been thrown into the ground block at Morgaedion to waste away with the rest of her kind. Elmryn gave her a life, the best he could, and taught her everything he knew about the stone. So, when Elmryn died, Tabitha took it upon herself to avenge him, to bring the stone back to its rightful place, even if she died in the process."

Reagan lifted the stone from beneath her shirt and held it inside her palm. "This silly little thing causing all that trouble?"

"Apparently so," Aero said. The man closed his eyes and fell silent, letting Sela carry him onward. Reagan wondered whether she should speak or let the man enjoy his moment, but he opened his eyes and spoke again before she could decide on her own. "Look"—he pointed into the horizon, squinting his left eye as if to better aim his finger with the right—"just beyond the Meadow of Aezaros."

Reagan hadn't the slightest clue as to what he meant by the name, but she assumed it was in reference to the massive meadow before them. In the distance, beyond its grassy plains, nestled among a range of snowcapped peaks, and below the two moons, was a floating city held down by giant chains. Buildings, topped with silver spires split through a skirt of puffy, white clouds, and all around them were windmills spinning in the high breeze.

"Whoa," Reagan gasped. She halted her pergonzia and pondered how such a thing could even be possible. With no ladder, or stairs, or elevator, she wondered how they would reach it, but her concern did not last long as her awe took over again. "It's beautiful."

"Hey," Tab snapped. She pulled her pergonzia to the side of

the path and leapt off its back. "This is not a sightseeing trip." She knelt behind a line of bushes and poked her head through an opening in the branches, peeking into the meadow.

Reagan and Aero dismounted and walked over to her.

"Stop," Tab hissed. She jabbed an arm into Reagan's stomach to stop her from coming closer.

"What is it?" Reagan whispered, taking a step back.

Tab unsheathed her dagger and held it down by her waist, tightening her fist around its purple hilt. "Quiet." Tab put a finger to her lips to hush Reagan. "Look." She pointed the tip of her dagger through the bushes and toward a grassy field. Reagan squinted through the branches.

Through the light of the golden moon, high in the sky above and nearly covering the purple moon, she could see the field almost as if it were day. Untouched and untamed, the grass was about knee high and dotted with wildflowers of every shade of blue, red, and yellow as far as her eyes could see. A dirt path accompanied by masses of people, made tiny by the distance, followed the tall trees that rocked in the breeze around the edges of the meadow. A stream tumbled down from the mountains that loomed in the distance and snaked through the meadow, pooling into a large lake that took up the middle of the meadow.

Reagan watched as a florahorse and its calf wandered into the grassy bank at the side of the lake, flower-woven tails flicking up behind them. Though the pair was quite a distance away, Reagan could not help but hold in her breath, fearing she might disturb them.

"Tab, I don't—" Reagan whispered, but before she could

finish, she noticed a slow-moving black creature, crouched down and nearly invisible in the tall grass between herself and the florahorses. It crept on all fours toward the city in the sky. As she watched it, it apparently knelt on a stick, which snapped loudly. The florahorses whinnied and galloped away, disappearing into the woods.

"They're here," Tab said.

"Who's here?" Reagan asked, but as she stared at the black creature, she noticed several more crawling through the grass beside it. *Ten, twenty, even more, many more.* She could see at least a hundred, but there could have been more deeper in the grass. The crowd on the path, too far away to notice, inched closer to the city.

"Nelazgians." Tab grit her teeth and jabbed her dagger blade into the soil. "They must have known, but how?"

"What's a Nelazgian?" Reagan asked. With all these bizarre words, she didn't know how to keep up. Soon she'd need a notepad to start writing down what they all meant, or she'd lose her mind.

"The sons of voraths who worship their god's, Nelazgus's, idiotic ideals," Tab said. "Follow him and everything he stands for like they'd die if not."

"We have to go," Aero said. Tab and Reagan turned to face him.

"What?" Tab frowned at him. "Turn back after all we've been through to get here?"

"That is exactly what I mean," Aero said.

Tab shook her head. "What in the name of Aezaros makes you think that we would just turn around and leave? The moons are about to eclipse, this is our only chance to enter that city." She thrust her dagger up to the sky, where the golden moon covered over three quarters of the purple moon.

"The Nelazgians will advance on the city and claim it by dawn. It's too dangerous to go in now. We wouldn't last against a horde that size."

Tab stood and stared up at him. "What are you saying?"

Aero pursed his lips a moment. "I was a part of that plan."

"You—you what?"

Reagan looked between the two, grabbed her stone, and took a step back. She felt her heart drop, and for a moment, thought she was trapped. She couldn't believe what she was hearing. How could she?

"For once, listen to me, Tabitha," Aero spoke. "If you were to walk out into that meadow right now, it would be a certain death for us all."

"*You were a part of what plan?*" Tab spat. She inched closer to him and adjusted her grip on her dagger.

Reagan half-wanted Tab to shove it through his chest right that moment, but then again, he had confessed. Though, for what reason? And why now?

"The plan to intercept Reagan in the city and reclaim the stone," Aero said.

"And why would you do that?" Tab said.

Reagan could almost see the steam rising from Tab's pectoral fins. Her face twitched and her knuckles whitened around the hilt of her dagger.

Aero took a slow step back. "Because I was a member of the Nelazgians—a warrior for liberation. I told them Reagan would be in the city."

Tab's eyes went wider than Reagan had ever seen them. "I'm sorry, I think I got a little fuzz in my ear," she said, sticking her finger in her ear. "You did what now?"

"It's not worth discussing right now, Tabitha."

"Oh, I think it is very much *worth discussing right now*, Aero."

"Not if you want to make it into Galecrest before they burn it to ashes."

Tab paused, lowered her dagger, and stared at the ground, chewing her lip.

Aero waited patiently a moment, then he said, "If you want to make it into the city, there's only one way, but you will have to trust me."

"Trust you?" She glared at him. "Why in the name of Aezaros would I ever trust you after what you just confessed? Why shouldn't I just slit your throat?" She shoved her blade up under his chin, drawing a thin line of blood that trickled down the blade. "Give me one good reason."

As much as she wanted to agree with Tab, Reagan saw no other choice than to hear out the man's plan. If they were to kill him and make haste for the city, the Nelazgians would still launch their attack.

"Tab." Reagan pulled her arm back. "Hear him out."

Tab stiffened and shook Reagan off her arm. "You *trust* him?"

"We don't have a choice," Reagan said. "If we need to get to that room, and he can get us there, then we have to trust him."

"Fine." Tab wiped the blood off her blade with her cloak. "You get us into that city." She spat a wad of phlegm at Aero's foot and turned to look back toward the meadow, brushing the branches to the side with her blade.

"Right, then," Aero said. He wiped his shoe on the grass, then gestured toward his saddlebag. "Reagan, may I?" She nodded and he withdrew a long rope and a blindfold from it.

"What *exactly* is your plan?" Tab asked, her face still flush with anger.

"As I said, we cannot just walk into the city. The Nelazgians believe that I will be bringing Reagan as my prisoner, so that is the plan."

"So, let me get this straight," Tab said, "your grand *plan* is to bring Reagan into the city as your prisoner?"

"*Our* prisoner," he said, forcing a smile. "Yes."

"No, no." Tab shook her head. "Not happening."

"Would you let me explain," Aero said, rolling his eyes.

"Please do," Tab huffed.

"Right now, the Nelazgians still think I am on their side. To them, I am a full-fledged servant of the rightful king, Obellius."

"And how do we know you're not still a 'full-fledged servant'? For all we know you could be tricking us."

"I very well could be, and you have a right to think so, but that evening you came to my home, I had already planned to set out on my own to find the stone. Word had already made it to the backstreets and alleys of Varaar that a certain stone had reappeared. It was hushed speech, no doubt. Only a few dared speak of it, but those who did spoke of a prize no man could resist. Of course, I have nothing but a few presps and some sword tricks to my name, so I decided to set out in search of the stone, working with the Nelazgians."

"How can you be sure this'll work?" Tab said.

"I can't, but is there another way to get into that city alive?"

"And what about me?" Tab asked. "Sure, you take Reagan prisoner, but what am I supposed to be doing here?"

"You are a member of the Nelazgians, of course."

Reagan half expected Tab to stab Aero at that, but she just shook her head, and said, "Okay, let's go."

Aero nodded and tied Reagan's wrists behind her back. Instead of fastening the blindfold over her eyes as she had expected, he tucked it into his back pocket and put a hand on her shoulder. "Are you ready?"

Reagan didn't know if she was ready or not, but she also didn't seem to have much choice. "Yeah."

Tab shot a finger back toward her pergonzia. "You stay here, got it." The big beast was too busy chomping the grass to pay any attention to her. "Oh, whatever. You things don't have half the brain to wander off anyways." She turned to Aero. "Lead the way."

Aero nodded and stepped through the branches, pulling Reagan behind him. "Drayzuzian," he called toward the meadow.

"Ellisvat," a deep voice answered.

Aero jerked Reagan forward and the rope burned at her wrists. She stumbled over a clump of grass and fell flat onto her chest.

"I've brought her," Aero said.

Reagan heard shuffling in the grass and raised her head. The Nelazgian, Drayzuzian, crept up and peered into her eyes. In place of his right eye was a deep, black pit with a cracked red scar running along the skin. The rest of him was covered with splotchy black fur, and black wings rose from its back. His pointed snout bent sideways, and he smiled jagged teeth in her face. "Ah, sooner than expected," he said, his breath hot and stinking like dead fish. "Excellent." He bared his knife-like claws at Reagan.

She wanted to get up and run away but couldn't move with her hands tied behind her back. The creature looked like something out of a horror movie, or maybe more like the creatures her younger campers had always claimed were hiding under their beds or in their cubbies. Not really something she ever thought she would be nose to nose with.

"No." Aero stepped in front of Reagan and put his hand on the Viper's hilt. "She lives."

Drayzuzian batted his eye and bared his teeth as more Nelazgians gathered around. "You defy our lord. Step aside, peasant scum."

"We need her alive," Aero said without flinching.

"Why?" The creature looked at Reagan and then at Aero. "So you can lay with her at night? Funny little thought, Ellisvat. You'd be better off sticking to the brothels in Varaar."

The rest of the Nelazgians cackled, but Reagan could barely see them hidden in the grass.

"She must be kept alive," Aero said. "Without her, the stone will lose its powers. I do not expect Obellius would be pleased to find out that this opportunity was blown by lustful claws."

Reagan didn't know if the man was bluffing, but the cackling Nelazgians fell silent, and Drayzuzian retracted his claws.

"Right then, have it your way." The creature stood up and dismissed Aero with a wave. "The girl is yours to deal with."

Aero pulled Reagan to her feet. "Get up."

"And her?" Drayzuzian cocked his head toward Tab, who still stood near the line of trees. "Who is she? Another to keep you warm at night?"

"Tabitha Glowdish," Aero said. Tab took a step forward. "She has offered her assistance to the Nelazgians."

Drayzuzian looked her up and down before turning back to Aero. "She loyal or what?"

"You blind in the other eye too?" Tab said. "I'm right here. You can ask me, not him."

"Ah, righteous one, aye?" Drayzuzian cocked his head and licked his sharp teeth. "Show me your mark, then, if you're so sure of yourself."

Aero spoke before Tab could. "Tabitha has not been marked yet, Drayzuzian. She has only just joined us."

"So you say?" Drayzuzian scratched his chin with a claw a moment, then snapped his fingers, summoning two smaller, nearly identical Nelazgians from the grass. "She'll be marked now," he snarled.

Tab stepped back, grit her teeth, and placed her hand on her daggers hilt. Aero caught her by her wrist and pulled her forward, shooting her a glare.

"Your wrist," Drayzuzian demanded. Before Tab could offer it up, the two smaller Nelazgians gripped her wrist and raised it toward Drayzuzian. Drayzuzian closed his eye, mumbled something, and thrust his arms toward the sky. Then he lowered his hands and extended them toward Tab. "Give it, now!" The two smaller Nelazgians pushed Tab forwards. She fought them for a moment but stopped when Drayzuzian stood an inch before her face.

"Congratulations," he said with a smirk as he snatched up Tab's wrist and twisted her palm so that it faced up toward the sky. "You're officially a part of the club." He raked his claw deep into her skin, peeling layers of flesh as he embedded the same symbol Aero bore onto her.

Tab grit her teeth and clamped her eyes shut. She collapsed to the ground, head bobbling as if on a spring.

"Do it, *girl*," Drayzuzian coaxed her. He leaned down and clawed deeper into her skin. "Scream. Scream so our god Nelazgus might hear it!"

Tab did not scream. When Drayzuzian released her, she spat on the grass and gripped her bleeding wrist. "I'm no girl," she growled through gritted teeth.

"Righteous *and* tough." Drayzuzian smirked. "You might make a better ally than I thought." He flicked a glob of blood and flesh from his claw into the grass. "Right then, now that that's settled, let's put a little blindfold on our new friend. She's seen enough already."

Aero nodded and reached into his pocket. He pulled out the long piece of white cloth and tied it over Reagan's eyes.

"Let's move," Reagan heard Drayzuzian say.

"Aero," Reagan said. She adjusted her head just enough to allow a small sliver of the blindfold to open next to her nose.

"I said move," Drayzuzian growled.

Reagan felt the rope tighten around her wrists and Aero's hand against her back, pushing her forward. The ground dipped, and she fell to her knees. Aero hoisted her back to her feet.

"You two," Drayzuzian snapped, his voice a few paces

ahead, "Hurry up already. That rock'll be in the ground before we even get there."

Rock? The ground began to shake, and Reagan staggered ahead, nearly falling, but Aero held her up. "What's happening?" she yelled over the rumble of the earth. Her whole body vibrated as the ground shook beneath her. She tried to extend her arms to maintain her balance, but the rope held her wrists tight behind her.

"The city is sinking back into the ground," Aero said.

"Aero," Tab yelled up ahead, her voice barely audible over the quaking earth, "we need to hurry! Pick up those feet and get movin'."

Aero pushed her harder, but he held her up with his other hand under her arm. "Almost there," he said.

For all Reagan knew, almost there could have meant anywhere. She had no idea what she was doing or where she was going and just wanted to slip the stupid blindfold off.

"I'm about to jump," Aero said.

"Jump?" Reagan felt her heart speed up. "What do you mean? Jump where?"

"Don't worry, I've got you," he said. He took his hand from her back, put it under her arm like the other one, and she no longer felt the ground beneath her. Darkness fell over her blindfold, and the slit in the blindfold showed only black. Before Reagan had the chance to question what was happening, Aero's feet landed on the ground with a *thud*.

"You know the way to the castle tunnels, yes?" Drayzuzian said. He was close to her. Too close. Reagan squirmed, hoping to move farther away from his voice.

"Yes," Aero replied.

"Well, then, get a move on!"

Reagan felt Aero push her forward again. She wondered how long until they reached where they were going. How long until she could ditch her blindfold and move her arms once again. How long until she wouldn't have to worry about the stone around her neck.

"Get ready," Reagan heard Aero whisper, his voice almost masked by the claws scrabbling on the stone floor behind them.

"Been ready," Tab growled, her voice close by.

Aero pulled Reagan to a stop. "It's here."

"Great," Drayzuzian said, "open it."

What Reagan assumed to be a door clicked open. Aero pushed her forward. Then the door slammed behind her. Feet shuffled around her and she heard someone grunting.

"Bar the door, Tab!" Reagan heard Aero shout.

"Gah, gimme a sec, would ya?" Tab yelled. "This thing isn't light." Reagan heard the wooden thump of the bar sliding into place. Then she heard pounding.

"You really think that'll hold 'em back?" Tab asked.

"I hope so," Aero said.

"We're gonna need a little bit more than hope," Tab said.

Aero carefully untied the blindfold and then the rope around Reagan's wrists. She took a deep breath, rubbed her wrists, and glanced around the room, eyes adjusting to the darkness.

"Elmryn's old study…how perfect," Tab said.

"It was the only place I knew how to find in the tunnels," Aero shrugged. "I think just about anyone would have memorized the route with all the meetings he'd had us attend."

259

The room had dark stone walls and a low ceiling. A stairway behind her led up to another door barred shut by a wooden plank where she heard heavy pounding on the door. The bar rattled in its clamps. On the far wall was another door, taller than the others, four-paneled, and painted red, blue, green, and grey. Beneath the thick dust on each of its panels a depiction of an element was painted in their respective color—fire, water, land, and air. Reagan walked across the room and ran her hand over the panels, tracing the cracks in the wooden surface. She stopped above the red section. *Fire.* She could almost feel its warmth on her fingertips.

"Red," Tab huffed. "We haven't got all day. Step aside, would ya?"

Reagan withdrew her hand and stepped away from the door. Tab inched in front of her and drew her dagger from her sheath. She drove it under the handle and twisted the blade until it clicked. Then she kicked it open. "All right, in ya go."

Reagan took a deep breath and stepped inside.

CHAPTER TWENTY-FOUR

HIGH MOON FESTIVAL

Alistair clutched Bea's shoulder, claws digging into her skin. "Who is he, Beatrice?"

Who, she thought to herself, sitting there beneath the Book. She didn't know. "The man," she said, trying to remember. "I saw him again. He seemed so familiar. Every other time he's been far away, but this time, he was so close." She wished she could describe him better, wished she knew who he was, wished she could help Alistair help her.

"Okay," Alistair sighed, releasing his grip on her shoulder and rising to his feet. "First, I must say that a Shadow Reaper is not a man, Beatrice. A Shadow Reaper—"

"No...it wasn't Demise." Bea shook her head, closed her eyes. "H-he was different. I've seen him before. It's almost like he's been...been following me."

"Different in what ways? How, exactly, did this 'man' appear to you? Can you describe him?"

Describe him, she thought, *but where do I start?* Everything about him begged for attention. "He had long, white hair, like snow, and red eyes. He was taller and thin, but also muscular."

"Hmm." Alistair smoothed his wispy beard. "I see. The man you describe seems to be none other than Obellius Kalaar."

Obellius Kalaar. That name…she had heard it before used by many to describe the usurper. But why him? Why him in her dreams haunting her, calling for her? She felt an urge to get away quickly but was unable to move.

"Though, what concerns me most of all is your mention of his red eyes," Alistair continued. "Those I have not seen. With the Book of Fire taken from its chamber, I cannot help but piece the two together."

"What do you mean?"

"How are you feeling?" Alistair asked.

"Uh…" Bea suddenly realized the pain in her wrist had subsided. She looked at the symbol. It was no longer brown, but now a rusty orange, closer, but not quite its original gold. "Better, actually." She held her wrist up so he could observe the color for himself.

"Good." He nodded. "The symbol works on a spectrum. Assume gold as full and black as empty, in the terms of your energy and connection to the Books.

"So, I'm halfway?"

"I suppose you could say that. It's a good start. The symbol will recharge itself now that it is out of the brown zone, and it should give you enough energy to make it to Galecrest. Now, to answer your first question, we must leave immediately.

Come, follow me."

Bea and Alistair made their way out of the Sacred Chamber and back into the glass tunnel, Bea too distracted by the mentioning of Obellius's name to notice the hundred or so feet drop below her. They walked down the hallway toward the greenhouse but turned down another hallway just before it.

"Whoa, whoa," a voice said from behind them. Bea turned and saw Nordwelg rush out of the greenhouse, pipe in mouth, and hurrying to catch up to them. "You just gonna leave without checking in?"

"There's no time," Alistair said, halting not one step to make eye contact with his companion.

"Hey, what happened in there?" Nordwelg asked, evening his stride with Alistair's.

"Beatrice has seen him," Alistair said.

Bea felt a tightness around her chest. She wanted to stop, but the lizard kept moving forward.

"Would you slow down a second?" Nordwelg begged, almost tripping over his overalls to keep up with the lizard. "He? 'He' who?"

"Who do you think, Nordwelg?"

"Well, gee, I don't know. A third of Eslura is 'he.'"

"I hate to admit it, but your foolishness pains me, Nordwelg." Alistair sighed. "Obellius. That's who."

Not again. She wished they would stop saying his name. Stop connecting him with her. Why did it have to be her vision?

"*My* foolishness? Oh, c'mon, I'm not the one who just openly announced that the Book has shown her that monster." Nordwelg threw his arms up, nearly dumping the leaves from

263

his pipe. "Have you lost it?"

"I speak with as much candor as I can muster. The Book of Land does not lie, and its message to Beatrice must be heeded."

"Message to Beatrice?" Nordwelg shook his head. He turned to Bea, fell behind a step, and hustled to catch up to Alistair again. "Alistair, would you please stop for a second and talk to me?"

"As I have said, we have no seconds to spare, Nordwelg."

"I think you do for your old friend." Nordwelg leapt forward, grabbed Alistair's wrist, and pulled him to a stop.

Bea bent over and exhaled, her heart hammering in her chest. She wanted to savor the moment of pause but couldn't through her growing fear.

Alistair struggled to free his hand from the troll's grasp but failed. He clenched his jaw and glared at Nordwelg. "Pardon my behavior, old friend," Alistair said after a moment, his voice no longer hurried or panicked. "You see, this situation seems to have gotten the best of me."

"There we go, thatta lizard," Nordwelg said, releasing his wrist with a pat. "Now, can you tell me what happened in there?"

Alistair nodded and told him about Bea's vision. She winced at the recounting.

"Hmm. Well, I can definitely understand why this bothers you." Nordwelg rubbed his chin. "So, what do you think?"

"We must go to Galecrest immediately and meet with the other Sacred Rulers."

"Sure, but if Obellius has the Heart of the Book of Fire, don't you have bigger problems than meeting with the Rulers? Bigger problems like protecting your own Book's Heart so it doesn't get stolen too?"

"I have no qualms about the safety of our Sacred Book. The Hollow of Gewa retains its power as long as I am still breathing, and my life is not in danger at the moment."

"But didn't you just say—"

"We must make our way to Galecrest to pass this news to the other Rulers. By then we may also have a better understanding of the threat."

"All right, then," Nordwelg said. "But you might want to deal with her little fan club outside first."

Fan club? Bea looked up. Who…how could she have forgotten! "They're here?" she said, fighting back a smile. "You mean they're okay? Barnaby, Alpin, and Seely?"

"Well, of course they are," Alistair said. "As unfortunate as I assume it is to hear, that Shadow Reaper couldn't have cared less about their presence in the scene."

"Can we go see them?" Bea said.

"That's where we are headed, yes," Alistair said. He led Bea and Nordwelg outside to where Bea's companions—accompanied now by Galabear, who sat tall beside Alpin—waited kicking their feet around in the dirt. Behind them lay a city almost invisible through the lush flora its houses were built into.

"Would you stop that already? How many times must I tell you—" Alpin stopped scolding Barnaby and turned his attention toward Bea as they walked through the door.

"Bea!" Barnaby leapt up from his seat, ran over to her side, and wrapped his arms around her shoulders, nearly squeezing the life out of her. "Good gods, you're alive! I mean, of course you're alive, hah! It's not like Mauz and I thought otherwise or anything. We were just so worried, all that smoke, I mean, you can't blame us for being worried, can you?"

"Mr. Britto, please." Alistair detached the boy from her waist. "Beatrice is still recovering from her encounter. At this moment, she needs space, if you would be so kind."

"Oh, yeah, of course! S-sorry about that." Barnaby's cheeks flushed as he stepped back and ran his fingers through his hair. She almost wished the boy would keep hugging her...anything to momentarily distract her from thoughts of Obellius.

"Alpin," Alistair said, bowing, "good to see you again."

The gopher rolled his eyes, crossed his arms, and leaned back into his beast. "I wouldn't necessarily say 'good', but yes, I suppose so."

"And I see you've been reunited with Galabear?" Alistair smiled.

"Well, as you already know, that would be thanks to you." Alpin pat the giant beast on her snout. "You sure did have quite a run on your own, huh, girl?" he said to his pet as if he were talking to a little baby. Bea cringed at the unnatural sound, not sure she would ever want to hear him use that tone again.

"Ah, yes," Alistair said, "poor thing had quite a few burrs sticking in her fur when I found her trudging through the woods. I suppose she must have been following your scent. She was right on your tail. Lucky I found her when I did, the smoke would have sucked me whole had she not given me a ride."

"She's quite the savior when she needs to be," Alpin said. "But most of the time just lazy." He booped her on the nose and she sneezed.

"And Seely," Alistair said, "it has been quite a while, has

it not? A pleasant surprise, might I add. Glad to see you are faring well these days."

"A Knower of Many Things would consider the phrase 'faring well' to be inaccurate given the findings of his latest research."

"Ah, yadda yadda." Alpin swished his hand at Seely. "You'll survive…probably."

"Alpin," Alistair said, glaring at the gopher, "if you must be so rude, please keep your thoughts to yourself. What are these recent findings you speak of, Seely?"

Seely explained his findings to Alistair and Alpin begrudgingly confirmed the story.

Nordwelg almost choked on his pipe. "Well, we know you've been expelled from the Knowers, but have you really gone completely mad?"

"Now, now, Nordwelg," Alistair said. "We mustn't be so quick to dismiss his research." Alistair bent down to level with Seely. "Please, continue."

"You see, a Knower believes that there is another piece to Mr. Britto's stone. A piece that would restrict its power and save the Olphins from their ailment. A Knower urges his friends to find the other Olphin who had so viciously broken into his home and retrieve the stolen piece."

"There is not much use making a plan until we speak with the entire council in Galecrest," Alistair said. "But, if what you speak of the Olphins is true, then I must say that there is no reason they should be imprisoned any longer."

Barnaby, who had previously been staring down at a strange lump on his toad's leg, perked up at the statement. "You mean I'm free?" The question came with raised brows and a contorted face. Bea could tell that even Barnaby did not believe the words he spoke.

"Well, that is what he said, isn't it?" Alpin said.

Barnaby smiled so wide Bea thought for a moment his lips might split at the ends. He squeezed the toad and kissed his head.

"Don't go celebrating yet," Alpin said. "You've still got the whole of Eslura to win over before your kind is accepted in the streets again." The gopher paused to close his eyes and exhale. "Though, I *suppose* you could stay in Farenworth until they do." If Barnaby wasn't at his maximum smile before, he was now.

"A Knower of Many Things must bring the attention back to himself. He fears Eslura and her people's time is running far too short," Seely said, his ears sticking up on his head.

Alistair shook his head. "There is no sense in making any such plan without seeing them through with the council; even you, Seely, should know this much."

Seely began pacing in tight circles and biting his fingernails.

"Where's the candies when ya need 'em?" Alpin rolled his eyes at Seely.

"With that being said," Alistair said, "we had better move. Luck will favor us if we are quick on our feet."

"Hey," Nordwelg grabbed Alistair's arm. "You be safe for me, all right? I don't want you coming back in two pieces—I can barely handle one." He shook his stubby finger at the lizard's face.

"Will do, old friend. As for you, do not let your lips get too accustomed to the pipe between them."

"Hah"—Nordwelg laughed and clutched his gut—"they already have."

"All right, then," Alistair said. "We move north."

The crew, half carried by Galabear, traveled north through the forest and its maze of trees until they came to a vast meadow. A sprawling lake lay at the center of its rolling green hills and sparkled in the light of the golden moon. Beyond the lake, spires of a city poked through a layer of low hanging clouds, their metallic tips twisting into coils.

"Is that it?" Barnaby asked. "Is that...Galecrest? All the books say that it's a floating city. Doesn't really look 'floating' to me. Maybe it sprung a leak?"

A floating city? Bea had seen a lot of strange things in this place, in Eslura, but she couldn't picture such a bizarre sight. Though, with her fear of heights, she was sort of grateful that it hadn't been floating at that moment.

"It is the floating city, you fool," Alpin said. "All that huffin' and puffin' about your 'favorite city' and you don't even know that when the two moons align it sinks into the earth? Have you never heard of the High Moon Festival?"

Barnaby's cheeks flushed and turned the opposite direction.

"Indeed," Alistair said, "and we are quite lucky it is in the ground, for if what Millennium said about her dragons is correct, we would have no way of flying up to the city if it were in the sky."

"Flying?" Bea gaped into the sky. She hadn't even ridden in an airplane, so how could she expect to ride up on the back of a dragon? Wouldn't they rather eat her than take her for rides in the air?

269

"A Knower of Many Things suspects Beatrice has never ridden on top of a dragon?" Seely said, his ears flopping as he walked up beside her.

Bea shook her head. "No, I definitely have not." *It would be kinda cool, though,* Bea thought to herself. *As long as they don't get hungry along the way.*

"All right, all right, quit daydreaming already." Alpin pushed her forward. "Once the moons pass by each other, the city will rise again."

"Indeed," Alistair said, "Lumikki and Millennium will be awaiting our arrival as well. It would be best not to make them wait any longer than they already have."

Alistair led them around the lake and into the bustling heart of Galecrest where what Bea assumed had to have been the High Moon Festival was in full swing. Gold balloons were tied to each lamppost, with matching banners strung between them. Fireworks shot up into the air, scattering golden light over the city as they crackled and fizzled out. People sat back in chairs, munching on baked goods while they stared up at the colorful display, oohing and aahing at each burst.

They hurried down what appeared to be the main street of the city, edging their way through an almost-immovable crowd. The cafes were crammed with mingling people and animals alike dressed in gold silks and sipping golden-colored drinks. They were clearly not aware that Obellius Kalaar was on the rise. Bea wished to join them in their oblivion, to sit back and forget about everything that was going on around her...just for a moment, at least. But Alistair pulled her forward, away from that thought.

The wide cobblestone street poured into a vast, red brick plaza, where a gold dragon statue stood as tall as a four-story building. Its mouth was open in a roar and its wings were spread out over the people lingering below it and letting loose floating lanterns into the sky. On a hill in the distance beyond the city, stood an impressive castle with high gables and a balcony that overlooked the city. Bea could see a line of people forming up the hill toward the castle. Its lights were on, so Bea wondered if perhaps part of the festival was held inside it. She wanted to go see for herself, but there was no way she would suffer through a line that long and boring, even if they weren't in such a dire situation.

They walked to the center of the plaza, near the dragon statue. Bea recognized the building to the left as the Eslurian Opera House that Barnaby had so vividly detailed to her in the abandoned house, and his expression only further confirmed it.

"By gods we've done it, Mauz," Barnaby shouted, tossing his webbed hands in the air. "Look at it! It's absolutely gorgeous! Even better than the photos." He took a step toward the opera house but Alpin grabbed his arm.

"Aye," Alpin snapped, "have you forgotten who you are beneath that cloak? The whole of Eslura doesn't know the truth yet. Don't forget that. Besides, you haven't come this far with us just to dip off into the opera house. You're just as much a part of this whole situation as I am."

Bea saw the longing in Barnaby's eyes as he stared at the beautiful, ornate opera house. "We'll get you there," Bea whispered to him, "I promise." Barnaby perked up and nodded.

Across the plaza from the opera house, Millennium waited alone at the top of a flight of marble stairs to what looked to be a library from the large, stone statue of an open book beside its front door. Her hands were crossed behind her back and her scarf was nuzzled so far up it covered her mouth.

Alistair led them toward her. Halfway up the stairs, he addressed her, "Millennium, how nice of you to wait outside for us. I suspect Lumikki is inside already?"

Millennium lowered her scarf to speak. "Something is horribly wrong, Alistair."

Alistair frowned, paused a moment, then continued up the stairs. "What do you mean?"

"It's Lumikki," she said. "I could not find her when I arrived in Ovallia. I spoke with Harp, but even he was uncertain of her whereabouts. In fact, he said it's been several days since she was last seen there."

"S-several days?" Alpin stuttered and hurried up the stairs beside Alistair. "What is that supposed to mean?" He looked between Millennium and the lizard, who paid no attention to him and his worry. Bea wondered who Lumikki was, and why the gopher seemed to care so much about her being absent from her city.

"Is that so?" Alistair combed a claw through his beard. "That is quite unlike Lumikki. Something has drawn her out of her city then."

"I am certainly just as baffled as you are," Millennium said.

"Well, what are we doing standing around here, then?" Alpin tossed his paws in the air. "We need to go find her!" He paced tiny circles like Seely had, sucking on his big teeth and twitching his whiskers. Bea thought the gopher might fall apart. It was the first she had ever seen him more concerned about another being than himself.

"Hmm," Millennium said, "I sure do hope nothing has happened to—" The woman stopped halfway as the ground shook.

Bea fell to her knees. The others staggered on the trembling cobblestones. The top of the library shuddered, and stones and debris began to rain down on the square. Bea covered her head with her arms. Then, just as suddenly, the shaking stopped. Bea looked up to face Alistair.

"Beatrice." He walked toward her through the dust and rubble. The roof of the library had crumbled onto the ground, spreading stone and broken tiles on the marble steps. "Are you all right?"

"Ah," Bea moaned. Her left arm was bleeding. A shard of stone tile had evidently sliced a deep, finger-length gash down her arm. She felt herself sinking and dizzy at the sight of the gore.

"I'm okay," she mustered, though she wasn't quite sure.

"What in the name of Aezaros was that?" Alpin asked, knuckles white on his staff. Galabear stood trembling beside him, and he tried to soothe her by scratching under her ear.

"A Knower of Many Things suspects that an earthquake has struck the city of Galecrest." Seely, unscathed, propped himself up on an upturned piece of roof.

"An earthquake?" Alpin furrowed his brows.

"Mauz? Mauz? Peppersnakes! Where's Mauz?" Barnaby called through the dust. He patted his head in search of his

273

companion, eyes wide with horror upon realizing his toad was missing from his normal spot.

Croak!

"Oh, thank the gods," Barnaby sighed. The toad sat covered in dust on a pile of rubble just beside him. Barnaby bent down, scooped him up, and brushed him off, then placed him back on his head.

"Millennium," Alistair said again. She stood in the doorway of the library, peering up at the now gaping ceiling. Smoke billowed into the sky, painting the golden moon with a smudge of grey.

CHAPTER TWENTY-FIVE

ELMRYN'S STUDY

Darkness engulfed the room, so much so that Reagan could not see her hand. She heard sounds of shuffling footfalls around her.

"Agh," Tab said. Some sort of metal clattered to the floor. "Where's the darned light in this place?"

"Working on it," Aero said.

A moment later, a spark ignited in the far corner of the room. Aero held a lantern with one hand, a burning match in the other. He lit the lantern, illuminating the room in a dim yellow light.

The space looked nothing out of the ordinary: a proper office with a large oak desk, a chair, a rug, floor-to-ceiling bookshelves, and miscellaneous paintings and framed documents on the walls. A chandelier hung above the desk, its mismatched candles unlit.

Aero placed the lantern on the desk and pulled the chair out from under it. He climbed on top of it, its uneven wooden legs wobbling and threatening to send him off balance. He lit each wick, brightening the room.

Reagan wondered what sort of business her father carried out inside the room, and she wished he was there to tell her all about it himself. With as many books as he had, she could only assume he spent many hours studying them. She would have liked to share her similar love of reading with the man, though he seemed to be a bit more into history than her own favorite genre, fantasy.

"We'll have to seal the door," Aero said. He stepped down from the chair and shoved it back underneath the desk.

"With what?" Tab asked.

Aero looked around the room, then back at the desk. "This." He slapped the top of it. "Help me move it." Tab and Reagan nodded and helped Aero drag the desk in front of the door. Once in position Aero gave it another pat. "That should hold them off for long enough."

"Right," Tab said, rubbing the oozing symbol on her wrist.

Reagan walked over and put a hand on Tab's shoulder. "Hey, I'm sorry about—"

Tab shook her hand off. "Just make this worth it, Red," she hissed and stalked to the other side of the room.

Reagan took a deep breath. It wasn't her fault. None of this was. Though, she did feel horrible about the woman being branded...especially with such an awful symbol.

"We should probably start looking for another way out," Aero said. "As much as I'd like to believe it, I can't imagine the Nelazgians will sit around waiting patiently until we've safely escaped."

"Yeah, sure. This is all part of your grand plan, isn't it? Lock us in a room and have us wait for death to come breaking down the door," Tab said. She fingered through a shelf of books, tossing every other title to the floor in the process.

Reagan lifted the corner of the center rug but set it down when nothing out of the ordinary jumped out from beneath it. She turned to face the wall opposite the door where a hand-painted portrait hung slightly askew. Though she had never met him, she recognized the face almost immediately as her father's. "So, that's really him?" She walked over to get a closer look at the man and his freckled face.

"Of course it's him," Tab said. "Have you ever seen a man with such red hair?"

Reagan ran her fingers along the surface of the painting until she found a small lip at the bottom. She narrowed her eyes at the piece and toyed with the bump. With each stroke, the glass rattled in its frame. "Hey," Reagan called over her shoulder, "I think I found something."

"What?" Tab rushed over to her and bumped her aside.

"Look." Reagan pointed to the lip. "Do you think there could be something inside the picture?"

"I don't know, Red. Why don't you quit standing there and check?"

Reagan nodded and lifted the picture off its hook. She carried it over to the center of the room and sat down, holding the large frame in her lap. "All right, here we go."

Reagan used her nail to lift up the glass. Then she carefully removed the painting and set it on the floor beside her. As she suspected, a small piece of paper lay hidden beneath it. "It's a letter," Reagan said. She lifted up the piece of paper, which was folded in two, and showed it to Aero and Tab.

"A letter?" Tab's brows arched. "Okay, well, what does it say?"

Reagan unfolded the paper and squinted at the tiny script. It took her a moment to make out the words which were scribbled in such a way it made her think they were written in haste.

Reagan, I do apologize that this is our first official meeting, but I have no other choice than to write to you. If you're reading this, I must assume you already know about the stone around your neck. The Eyearke stone is no myth. Though Eslura may try to cover up its existence for the safety, and sanity, of her people, you must believe me in my words that it is not some children's fable. The stone and its power must not fall into the wrong hands. Obellius will pursue it until his death; that is for certain. Although I fear the worst in handing the stone over to you, I have no choice. I'll place it so far out of his reach that he will never find it. That is, until you return to Eslura. You must keep it safe and deliver it to the Sacred Head. I have little time left to cover up the rest of my research. Obellius knows I have it and will come for me. Know now that this was for the best. Tabitha, please make sure this letter gets to my daughter. Best, Elmryn.

Reagan held the letter out and flipped it over, but the back was blank.

"May I?" Aero said. He reached a hand out, and Reagan gave him the letter. Tab leaned over his shoulder and scanned the paper with him.

"He never got to give me the letter," Tab said.

"Obellius killed my father," Reagan said to the ground. She didn't know what to think...she couldn't think. This man, Obellius, had taken her father away from her all for what, a stone? She clenched her fists.

"Sure seems like it, doesn't it?" Tab pulled away from Aero and shook her head. "Obellius gains the trust of the Rulers, finds out the secrets of their world, and betrays them. Classic. How could they have been so stupid?"

"We weren't there." Reagan looked up. "We can't judge them."

"There you go again." Tab rolled her eyes.

"We just have to move forward from here, right?"

"Tell me, then, Red. Where exactly is forward?" Tab swung her arms open and glanced around the room. "Last time I checked, we were trapped behind a door holding back Nelazgians waiting to get their claws on us."

"We'll have to fight our way through," Aero said. He drew the Viper from his belt and walked toward the door.

"Are you mad?" Tab said. "There's about a hundred or so Nelazgians out there and three of us. I know you like to think your sword skills are unmatched, but why don't we just take a step back, aye?"

"Do you see any other options? Waiting any longer will just

put us in an even bigger—"

An explosion ripped through the room, shaking the books off the shelves. The ceiling quaked above them and bits of rubble rained down, cloaking the room with dust. A high-pitched ringing filled Reagan's ears. She squinted through the dust.

"Oh, thank the gods, we're not too late." Long Paws stood in front of a hole in the wall.

"I told you we wouldn't be too late," Piercio said. He scrambled down Long Paws' chest and jumped to the floor.

"Long Paws? Piercio?" Tab said, her voice cracking in her dusty throat. "What are you doing here?"

"Eh, we made a last-minute decision." Piercio shrugged. "One that most certainly did not directly involve Tank firing us."

Tab leaned over toward the little mouse. "Tank fired you?"

"Well," Long Paws said, "let's just say he didn't agree we deserved a raise."

"He might be an elephant, but he sure is as greedy as a pig," Aero scoffed. "Always has been, always will be."

"Never mind that," Tab said. "How did you find us?"

"Simple." Piercio pointed his finger toward the door, which rattled with the pounding from the other side. "We just followed the trail of Nelazgians. Darned things have lined themselves up, down, and around the streets, settin' fire to nearly everything in sight!"

"So, they've already begun?" Aero said.

"Already begun what?" Long Paws cocked her head.

"Nothing," Tab snapped, looking at Aero sidelong. "Let's just get out of here while we can. We got what we came for. No point in waiting for the Nelazgians to come crashing through."

"Right." Piercio nodded. "Follow us."

Reagan, Aero, and Tab clambered over the rubble and followed Long Paws and Piercio out the hole into the hallway. The pair led them through the darkness, through a maze of intertwined tunnels, then stopped at a fork in the path. Long Paws started down the tunnel on the left.

"What are you doing, get back here," Piercio snapped.

"What do you mean?" Long Paws said. "This is the way we came from."

"No, you big klutz," Piercio hollered, pointing to the tunnel on the right. "It's not that way; it's this way!"

Long Paws brushed her paw against the wall. "We came through this way. Remember this little indent?"

"This little indent?" Piercio rolled his eyes. "There's about a million little indents on these god forsaken walls."

"Hey," Tab shouted. "You just came through here. Do you remember the way or not?"

Piercio sighed and looked up at Long Paws, who stood firm in the tunnel on the left. "All right, fine. Follow the big mutt."

They proceeded down the darkened hallway but stopped after a moment.

"Hey," Piercio said, "what's that?" He sniffed the air. Reagan paused behind him and glanced around but saw nothing.

"What's what?" Tab asked.

"You don't smell that?" Piercio said. He glanced back to where they had come from.

"I certainly don't smell it, but I hear it," Long Paws said. Her ears perked up and she spun to face the sound.

Reagan paused and listened. She heard claws clicking over

stone, lots of them.

"The Nelazgians," Aero said. "They've broken through the door."

"Gee, thanks, genius." Tab rolled her eyes.

"Stand back," Long Paws said. She stepped forward and opened her cloak. Under it, she wore a belt strapped with bombs similar to those she had used on stage, but much smaller.

"Sorry to ruin all your fun, but river spores won't help us here," Tab said.

"No," Long Paws said, unclipping a bomb, "not river spores."

"Oh?" Tab arched a brow.

"You're gonna want to plug your ears," Long Paws said with a smirk. She flexed her claws and snapped them at the wick of the bomb, igniting a small flame. "Bombs away!" Long Paws hurled the bomb in the direction of the Nelazgians and then turned around to shield her head with her paws. The bomb exploded midair, shaking the tunnel and nearly knocking them off their feet. The ceiling cracked and collapsed, filling the tunnel with stone and blocking the Nelazgians from advancing.

"I'll stay behind with Long Paws and Piercio," Aero said. "You two go on ahead and search for an opening. The last thing we need is to be trapped on both ends." He placed his hand on the hilt of his blade and nodded toward Tab. "We'll hold down this side. It won't be long till they break through."

"Right," Tab said. "See you soon, then." She turned and took off down the hall opposite Aero, Long Paws, and Piercio. Reagan turned toward Aero, who mouthed some words she couldn't make out, but she assumed they were some sort of confirmation, then took off behind Tab.

"That vorath makes me sick," Tab mumbled over her shoulder.

"Aero?" Reagan asked. "He hasn't done anything but help us." *Well…kinda.* She didn't exactly know why she was defending the man after what he had done…but something inside her urged her to.

"Oh, right, and also work behind our backs the entire time. Don't try to defend him."

Reagan shook her head and followed Tab through the tunnel until they met two Nelazgians standing in their path: one small, black and furry, and the other tall and lanky and so hunched his head was practically dragging on the floor.

"Ah, finally." Tab stopped and put her hands on her hips, just above where Reagan knew her blades would be hiding. "It was getting a little too quiet down here."

"So, this is the one Drayzuzian spoke of," the smaller Nelazgian said. "The one with the fins."

"Yeah?" Tab snapped. "Cute huh?" She batted her eyelashes and cocked her head.

"Quite the opposite, actually," the creature said.

"Right," Tab said, "well, then he can join the rest of Eslura, I suppose."

The taller Nelazgian stepped toward them. "Make this easy on all of us and surrender your weapons."

"Ha, funny!" Tab laughed. "You idiots don't know who you're messing with." She drew both her daggers from her hips as the pair advanced toward her. Then she let out a low growl and charged toward them. They raised their claws, ready to strike, Tab whipped her blades so fast, they probably didn't even see them. The sharp metal struck their throats, forcing their hands up to their now gaping wounds. They collapsed to the stone floor, eyes rolling back into their heads. Tab turned to face Reagan, her cheeks splattered with blood. "Don't just stand there. Let's go."

Reagan nodded and they sprinted down the tunnel. It was so dark she could barely see where her feet fell. The Nelazgians could have been anywhere waiting in the shadows to take them off guard.

And yet, they were.

They came upon a short, scaly creature standing guard in the center of the tunnel. It stood waiting for them, claws drawn and ready.

"Just you?" Tab scoffed.

The creature, who stood barely up to Tab's chest, opened its mouth to show off its jagged teeth. "Confident, are we?"

"You could call it that," Tab said. She flipped her daggers in her hands and charged the creature. It side-stepped her lunge, stuck a clawed foot out, and tripped her. Then it knelt over her and spun her into a headlock.

"Tab!" Reagan exclaimed and placed her hand on the hilt of her dagger.

"Quit standing there and help me out, would ya?" Tab elbowed the creature in the gut and freed herself from its grasp. It tried to claw her face, but she knocked its hand away with the hilt of her dagger.

Reagan drew her blade and rushed to Tab's side. The creature locked eyes with her and snarled. She hesitated, holding her blade toward its head as it grabbed Tab's neck in its claws. Reagan squeezed her eyes shut and thrust the blade forward. The creature howled. She let go of the blade and opened her eyes. Her dagger hilt was jutting from the creature's head, and black blood spewed all around it as it collapsed.

She felt bad for a second, staring at its lifeless body, thinking about the family it could have had waiting at home, but pulled herself away from her thoughts. The creature would have killed them both without a moment of hesitation.

"Nice one, Red," Tab said, patting her on the back with a bloodied hand. "But we've got more comin' down the back." Reagan stood and wiped the sweat from her forehead. Tab handed Reagan her gore-stained dagger.

The two raised their weapons and held them toward the figures advancing down the tunnel toward them, but lowered them when Long Paws, Piercio, and Aero emerged from the darkness.

"Path's cleared behind," Aero said, tucking the Viper beneath his belt. "At least for now."

"Tunnel's safe over here too," Tab said. "Only ran into a couple."

"Well, then," Long Paws said, dusting off her paws, "that should do the trick!"

"No. It won't be enough," Tab said, to which Long Paws frowned and lowered her ears. "As long as we're inside, there's still the chance that they'll come back in and trap us. We have to get out of here. Staying any longer is just a certified death wish at this point. We have both ways cleared. Pick one and let's get outta here."

"Tab's right," Aero said, his agreement seemingly irking Tab as she grit her teeth and glared in the man's direction.

"The exit is just up ahead," Piercio said, sitting on Long Paws' shoulder and pointing in the direction Reagan and Tab cleared.

"You sure about that?" Tab asked. "You didn't seem very confident with the tunnels."

"Did we lead you wrong?" Piercio huffed. "No, so pipe it. That's the way and I'm sure of it."

"All right, then. Go on." Tab gestured for Piercio to take the lead.

"Onward, Long Paws!" the little mouse shouted, his back straightened as they marched forward.

Reagan squinted into the darkness, wondering where they were and where they were going.

They emerged from the tunnels on a rocky hillside. The purple moon was edging out from behind the golden. The sky was clear and full of stars. The air smelled like fresh grass, but a hint of smoke lingered there, too. The city lay spread out below them, and Reagan hoped there was a hamburger or some sort of food down there somewhere.

"Feels good to be out, doesn't it, Red?" Tab said. She took in a breath of fresh air and patted Reagan on the back, a little harder than necessary, Reagan thought.

She would have agreed with Tab had she not smelled smoldering ash wafting through the air.

"Is that fire?" Long Paws said. She stuck her snout up in the air and sniffed. "Smells close."

"Whattya think, Aero?" Tab said.

Aero ignored the jibe. "We'd better leave the city before things get worse."

"Yeah, ya think," Tab scoffed. "Go on, then. Lead us to safety."

FLAMES ACROSS THE NIGHT

A scream ripped through the city. People and creatures alike ran across the plaza, covering their heads. Mothers dragged screaming children, merchants scrambled to pack up their street-side booths, and Sacred Guards attempted to corral the crowd, but with little luck. Broken glasses lay in puddles of golden liquid and balloons floated into the smoke, away from the people who once held their strings. The crowd pushed and shoved at each other, fighting to escape the plaza and knocking one another down, trampling folks to get away.

In the distance, stone walls and cliffs cracked, the earth rumbled, clouds of black smoke and sparks billowed into the sky, blotting out the stars.

The High Moon Festival seemed to end all at once, and the gold that once decorated the city now fell dark to the smoke.

Behind Bea, a Sacred Guard flung the front doors of the library open and rushed out of the building. He found Millennium on the stairs and bowed. She nodded for him to speak. "It's the Nelazgians, my lady. They've started a fire on the east side." Through his mask, Bea saw terror in his silver eyes.

"Go," Millennium said. "Take the rest of the Guard with you. Clear the people from the area and stop as many of them as you can."

The Guard gave a sharp nod and retreated back into the building, his grey cloak whipping behind him.

"We must defend the city," Alistair said. "The Nelazgians cannot be allowed control."

"Agreed," Millennium said. "I must go help my Guard." Alistair nodded and she closed her eyes. A grey light surrounded her, so bright Bea had to cover her eyes. Then the Ruler shot up into the night sky, no longer a human, but a serpentine dragon, her long tail swirling in the air as she disappeared behind the buildings.

"Alpin," Alistair said, "take Beatrice somewhere safe. The Nelazgians must not know she is inside the city. Galabear can help with evacuating the citizens, yes?" As if the beast understood, she blinked and nodded her head slightly.

For the first time since their meeting, Alpin did not argue with the lizard. "Come on, quit standing there."

Bea followed Alpin, and Barnaby and Mauz joined her, but Alpin stopped after a few steps to squint at a group of people.

"Well, would you look at that," the gopher said. He pointed to a group of five rushing across the center of the plaza. Three humans, and two animals, one of which was a big blue dog with four arms, reminding Bea of Bowmidge, but taller. The dog's head rose above the people around it, and a mouse rode on its shoulder. "That's your little friend, isn't it? The one with red hair? What was her name again?" He tilted his head and scratched between his ears with his staff.

Indeed, it was. Reagan hurried across the cobblestone square, and Bea shouted to her, "Reagan!" Reagan stopped.

"Bea?" Reagan squinted at her. "Bea! Oh my gosh!" Relief washed over Bea; she ran to Reagan and threw her arms around her. Reagan almost squeezed the breath out of her.

"I can't believe it!" Reagan said. She pulled away and smiled down at Bea. "Are you okay? You're not hurt, are you?" She held Bea out at a full arm's length, looking her up and down. "Your arm! What happened?"

"It's okay," Bea laughed. "It's…nothing really." At least compared to what she'd suffered through with the Shadow Reaper…

"Oh my gosh, you're not okay, though! It's deep. Look at it. You're gonna need stitches!" Reagan frowned and placed a hand on her forehead. "Camp Tossbridge is gonna throw the biggest fit ever if I bring you back like this. I'll be out of a job!"

"Reagan, I'm fine. It's just a cut."

"I am so sorry, Bea," Reagan said. "I should have come looking for you the second I was able. I just—"

"Hey, stop." Bea forced a big smile. She really was overjoyed to see her friend, but so much was happening, and they were still in grave danger, both of them. "We're okay now, right?" She laughed. Reagan smiled and laughed with her.

"Well, well, well, look what the cat dragged in. Alpin Loomin, it's been a while," the mouse who rode on top of the dog said, chest puffed out defiantly.

Though Bea had grown quite used to the idea of talking animals, something about the mouse surprised her. Perhaps it was his unusually deep voice, his full suit of armor, or the sewing pin he wielded like a sword.

"Piercio," Alpin growled through clenched teeth. His whiskers twitched as he stepped forward to meet the mouse.

"That's what they call me." The mouse smirked, cocking his head arrogantly. He leapt down from the dog's shoulder and strode over to Alpin. "It brings warmth to my heart to know that you have not forgotten."

Alpin spat a wad of spit onto the ground, just an inch in front of the mouse's steel-toed boots. "Scum. Of course, I hadn't forgotten the name of the pest who tried to steal Farenworth from me."

"Well, when you've got an abandoned town, it's really up for anyone to take, isn't it? Can't blame me for tryin', can ya?" He shrugged.

A strong-looking woman in a black cloak walked up behind them, the man at her side. "Aye, enough with the pleasantries, already," she said. She had fins growing out the sides of her face and scales grew across her skin. Bea realized that she was no ordinary woman; she was an Olphin. "In case you people haven't noticed, the city is very much under attack."

"A Knower of Many Things would not consider his reunion with the Olphin before him to be classified by the word 'pleasant,'" Seely said.

"Great gods," the woman exhaled, "you're here too?"

"Y-you…" Barnaby stepped forward, holding Mauz to his

chest. "You're a...you're an Olphin. You're *the* Olphin."

"Congratulations." The woman rolled her eyes. "You're not blind. Now, as much as I am enjoying this little reunion, I think we've got more important things to deal with. The massive horde of Nelazgians trashing this city, for example."

"I must say I do agree with you, Tab," the man beside her said.

"Wow," Tab said. "I'd love to savor the feeling I've got from you saying that, but time's a-wastin'."

"Tab, yes?" Alistair said. Tab nodded and he continued, "A pleasure to make your acquaintance." He held a claw out. She hesitated, looking down at his claw, then up at his face. Then she gave in and shook his hand. "Well, then, Tab here is right. We had better put an end to this chaos."

"We, as in you," Alpin said. "I've got a Sacred Head to babysit, yes? I would prefer to stay as far away from any trouble as possible." He stuck his nose up.

"Yes, *you* do," Alistair confirmed, "but there are quite a few able bodies here that I might request assistance from, though I would assume Reagan will be joining you, Alpin." He looked at Tab, the man whose name Bea did not know, Piercio, and the big blue dog, and all of them nodded. "Excellent. It appears their attack is centered around the castle. We'll head there now." Alistair led the group down the library steps and into a side alley where they disappeared.

"Just because they're gone does not mean we get to stand around and wait," Alpin said. "Let's go."

Bea followed Alpin into the dense crowd, but soon she bumped into Alpin's back and they were unable to move any farther. People stepped on her feet, yelled over her head, grabbed at her shirt and attempted to push her aside. Alpin, whose head barely reached her knees, squirmed through the mass, between legs, and under vendor stalls being pulled from the square. He looked back and yelled something through the shouting, screaming, and crying, that Bea understood loud and clear. "Move!"

Reagan elbowed an opening between a woman carrying a baby and a tall lion with a tray of tobacco and pulled Bea through. Barnaby followed, lips trembling, Mauz clinging to his hair. They broke through the crowd and into an alley, pausing only a moment to catch their breaths.

"What madness this city has descended into!" Alpin hissed.

Reagan looked at Barnaby. "This might not be the best time"—she laughed through heavy breaths—"but you've got a cute frog." She stared at Mauz, who held one wing up in the air and the other to the side.

"Sorry, me?" Barnaby seemed to come out of a terrified trance.

"No, the other boy with the winged toad riding on top of his head," Reagan teased. "Yes, you!"

"Oh, well, I'm not very used to people talking so nicely to me," he said to the ground. Then he looked up at her with a wide grin. "But his name is Mauz! Isn't that right, buddy? And he's just the best! A little heavy on my head sometimes, but we make do. I couldn't imagine a day without him."

"That's enough babbling out of you," Alpin groaned. "I've had more than enough Olphin to last me the rest of my life. So, cut it out, would ya?"

"He hasn't changed all that much, has he?" Reagan whispered to Bea through a cupped hand.

Bea shook her head and mouthed, "Nope."

Alpin opened his mouth to respond, but the ground rumbled again. Bea fought for her balance, stumbling into Barnaby, who fell sideways into the wall of the alley. Smoke rose into the sky, and the shouting and screaming intensified in the square behind them.

"We'd better move," Alpin said. He ran down the alley. Bea, Barnaby, and Reagan followed as closely as they could. When they got to the next cross street, four creatures jumped out and blocked their way.

"Hello, there, friends," the largest of the group said. He was at least seven feet tall and towered above his comrades, whose backs, unlike his own, were hunched beyond any measure Bea would have considered healthy. His biceps were as big as basketballs and bulging with tension. And his snout, long, sharp, and scaled like an alligator's, hung open to show his mangled jaws. He had wings with more holes than skin, and his right eye was nothing more than a scarred empty pit. "Why the rush?"

"That's their leader," Reagan whispered to Bea. "Drayzuzian."

He raised his arms in the air and the three smaller creatures bolted forward. Bea readied herself for the attack, but to her surprise, they ignored her and went straight toward Reagan, Alpin, and Barnaby, and seized them by the arms. Mauz, however, escaped unharmed and flew up where their prying claws could not reach him.

Drayzuzian stepped toward Bea. "Ah, so there you are. My

senses never fail, and I knew I smelled a special kind of *freak* in this city," he said. "The famed Sacred Head, yes? What luck! Both the stone and the Sacred Head. Obellius will give me a whole kingdom of my own. Perhaps even this one. Though, you know, I must admit I had expected a bit more of a, hmm, powerful, impressive, perhaps formidable-looking creature. But who am I to judge the almighty and powerful Book's decision?"

"You don't know me," Bea said.

"Aye," Alpin shouted. "Don't act so righteous. Don't you see his—" One of the creatures threw a hand over his mouth.

"You're right, I don't," Drayzuzian snarled. "And to be fair, I don't really care to either. I'm an honest worker. Got only one job and no real room to get to know, or care about another. So, if you don't mind, let's just get this over with."

"Don't even think about touching her." Reagan stepped in front of Bea.

"Reagan," Bea gasped. She looked behind her and saw that the creature who had previously restrained Reagan lay limp on the ground, his neck slit open above a growing puddle of blood.

"Oh, how cute is this!" Drayzuzian said. "I wish I'd brought my mother...if I'd ever had one."

"Reagan, stand back!" Bea grabbed her arm and tried to pull her back, but Reagan fought her grasp and stood firm.

"And let him take you, no way. I'm not losing you again." Reagan held her dagger out in front of her chest.

Drayzuzian feigned a yawn. "As much as I simply adore your little friendship, I also find it quite pathetic. Step aside."

When Reagan didn't move, Drayzuzian bared his claws and lunged at her.

Reagan parried his first strike with a sideways slash of her blade, but he swept under her arm and caught her chest with his other claw, tossing her aside with little effort. She hit the ground, rolled into the wall of a nearby building, and fell limp.

"Reagan!" Bea shouted. She rushed toward Reagan, but Drayzuzian blocked her path. Bea clenched her fists, knuckles white beneath her skin. She stared down at a tuft of grass growing between the cobblestones, and it seemed to stare back at her.

"Now, now," Drayzuzian said, wagging a bony finger at her. "Take it from your little friend over there. It's best not to mess with an angry Nelazgian."

It's best not to mess with Beatrice Tidal, either.

Bea felt the warmth in her hand before she looked down to find the green glowing between her fingers. She glanced at the grass and found that it too, was glowing. She flexed her hand and, as if they were a dozen swords, the blades of grass surged up and pierced straight through the center of Drayzuzian's chest, carrying him up into the air like meat on a skewer. Blood bubbled from his mouth and rained down on the cobblestones. He let out an ear-piercing roar that echoed through the city, shaking the nearby buildings before his cry cut out to cough up a mouthful of blood.

Bea turned to face the other two creatures, her hand still glowing green. She spread her fingers and a blade of grass twisted up and wound around their necks. They released Barnaby and Alpin and clawed at the tightening grass to no avail. Their faces turned blue, and their arms fell limp. At last, the only thing holding them up was the blade of grass.

She heard the sounds of claws scraping against stone coming up behind her and prepared to fight, though, instead of running towards her, she watched as the dozen or so Nelazgians rushed past the alley, away from the castle. She wondered for a moment what had caused them to flee then remembered Reagan. She rushed to her side. "Reagan?" She shook her lightly. "Reagan!"

Reagan's eyes blinked open. "Hey," she coughed and grabbed at her side, which was soaked with blood.

"She's bleeding!" Bea called over to Alpin and Barnaby. They joined Bea at her side.

"Here," Barnaby said. He shook off his cloak, exposing his fins and scales, and handed it to Bea, who grabbed it without a second thought and pressed it to Reagan's side.

"She needs help," Bea said.

"I'm fine, don't you worry." Reagan rolled her head to face Bea. Her skin was pale and sweat beaded on her forehead. "A counselor never leaves her camper behind."

A gust of wind stirred over Bea's head, pulling her attention to the sky. "Millennium," Bea shouted. The dragon paused her flight a moment to glance into the alley, then she swooped down in a bright flash of grey, and the old woman rushed to kneel beside Reagan.

"You're lucky you caught me," she said. "The Nelazgians have left the city." She looked around at the four creatures. "Ah…" She stared at Drayzuzian. "I've seen that one before. He put up quite a fight in the War of Shadows. What a powerful one to be able to call a full retreat with just a roar. So, what's happened here?"

"One of them got her in the side," Bea said. "It's bleeding bad."

Millennium lifted Barnaby's cloak and then Reagan's shirt to look at the wound. She dropped the shirt and placed a hand on Reagan's pale cheek. "Do you think you can stand with me, Reagan?" Reagan moaned and rolled her head in a circle. "That's the spirit." Millennium helped her to her feet and put Reagan's arm over her shoulder. "You don't mind if I take her from you for a moment, do you? I promise I'll give her back." Reagan's head fell limp on her shoulder like a broken bobblehead, and her body went slack in Millennium's arms. With a flash of grey, Millennium transformed back into a dragon and took off into the sky, cradling Reagan like a baby.

Alpin twitched his whiskers. "Are my ears not working or did she say that the Nelazgians left the city?"

By dawn, the smoke had dissipated, and the sky glowed pink with the rising sun. With the moons sunken beneath the mountains, the city began to rise back into the sky, slowly raising them above the earth and into the clouds. Civilians returned to their homes and the aftermath of the battle was cleared from the streets. The city slowly returned to normal, bringing with it the smell of baking bread and other sugary delights.

Bea, Alpin, and Barnaby returned to the library and found the rest of their group waiting on top of the steps. Alpin immediately ran to his pet and collapsed into her side. Reagan stood beside Millennium, her waist wrapped in a thick, white cloth, but her face was back to its natural peachy color.

"Reagan!" Bea called out. "You're all right."

"Ha," Reagan laughed, "by the grace of a dragon's spinal fluid, I guess."

"Indeed"—Millennium smiled—"a dragon's spinal fluid has near-magical healing properties."

"Well," Tab said, "I hate to admit it, but I never thought I'd see you again, Red." She put a hand on Reagan's shoulder and laughed. "But I sure am glad to."

Alistair smiled broadly. "Millennium is ever so trustworthy, Tab. If there are any hands to be safe in, they are hers. And of course, Alpin's paws as well." He winked at the gopher.

"Heh, whatever you say," Alpin said.

The sun rose and Millennium led them up the hillside and into her castle. By that time, Bea thought she might keel over and die of hunger on the spot. She could have eaten anything at that point, even Fran's eggs. Millennium led them through the castle to a room that could have been an art gallery based on the number of paintings decorating its velvet walls. It had a long table, long enough to fit all eleven of them with room to spare, and vaulted ceilings. A little placemat had even been set out for Mauz next to Barnaby and a much larger one for Galabear beside Alpin. Luckily for Bea and her grumbling stomach, the castle staff had been busy cooking up the largest array of food she had ever laid eyes on: bacon, steak, chicken, roast beef, mashed potatoes, rolls of fluffy bread, carrots, tomatoes, squash, salads, cupcakes, chocolates, cookies, blue candies, and many other strange foods that Bea had never seen before. She didn't know where to start. Seely, however, immediately reached across the table for one of the blue candies and shoved it in his mouth.

They sat at the table, stuffed their mouths till their stomachs could handle no more, and spoke loudly across the food between them. Long Paws and Piercio ranted about their time in the circus, Barnaby told jokes no one seemed to find funny, though Bea forced a few laughs. Tab and Aero continued to glare at each other for reasons unbeknownst to Bea, and Reagan tried profusely to diffuse the tension between the Olphin and the man, but with no luck. Bea had almost forgotten about Obellius until Alistair spoke.

"On a more serious note"—he cleared his throat—"there are some matters that must be addressed this afternoon. First, we must discuss what to do about Seely's discovery." The lizard gestured at Seely, who stood on his seat and bowed awkwardly, large ears flapping downward.

"Agreed," Millennium said. Bea assumed the two had already conversed, as the woman did not appear confused by his statement.

"While there is much to be done here with Beatrice, I believe that a crew must be sent to Morgaedion immediately to free the Olphins of their confines. Of course, there will be backlash from the kingdoms, but it—"

The door to the dining hall swung open and smacked against the wall.

"Twee." Alpin leapt from his seat. He glared down the table and adjusted his monocle. "I never really considered that I could be blind before, but is that Officer Kazke? Where are his cloak and mask?"

Bea spun to look and saw a big gorilla making his way across the room towards them. One of his eyes was swollen and caked with dried blood. He cradled his left arm with his right, and his thick, black fur, mottled and burned, exposed his red, seared skin.

"Officer Kazke?" Tab said, her mouth full of grapes. "You mean that son of a vorath from Morgaedion? I swear, you give someone a lick of power and they think they're all that. Just wait till he sees that one of his most wanted subjects is still roaming free and standin' right before him. Hah!" She slapped her knee and shook her head.

"Alistair, Millennium," the gorilla addressed the two Rulers with a bow, but he nearly crumpled to the ground. "Please do pardon my appearance. It is my own fault that I have lost my mask and cloak. I do hope you understand."

"There is no need to apologize," Alistair said. He stood from the table and placed a clawed hand on the gorilla's shoulder. "What is it that brings you all the way to Galecrest?"

The gorilla looked around at the group, then at the paintings decorating the walls. As if he had realized something of utmost importance, his eyes widened. "Galecrest was the nearest city I could drag myself to. I had no other choice than to leave Morgaedion. You must understand that I—"

"Kazke, please," Alistair said. "There is no need for such ramblings. You are hurt and need medical attention. What has happened in Morgaedion?"

"It's Obellius." He paused. Alistair and Millennium shared

a look. Bea felt her heart skip a beat and her throat tightened.

"What about Obellius, Kazke?" Millennium said. Though no window was open, Bea felt the room grow colder and goosebumps rose on her skin.

"He's escaped Morgaedion and he's coming for the girl."

EPILOGUE

THE LAST CELL ON THE BLOCK

Dark clouds lingered above Morgaedion, above the thick brick walls surrounding the island. A single dock stretched out into the ocean, with several, large ships tied to it, which Lumikki assumed to be the transports for the island's prisoners. Unlike her city's sprawling and vibrant, ocean-inspired palette, the prison island was absent of all color save for the blacks and greys of stone walls and lookout towers.

Lumikki pulled her wave up to the dock beside a ship branded with the name The Last Stop. *You poor, unfortunate souls*, she thought to herself.

She stepped onto the dock, feeling as if she had entered a new world. She walked to the shore and stepped off onto the rocky beach, making her way toward where the inky-black grass tickled her paws.

She followed a worn, black dirt path to the front gates

of the prison. To her surprise, the gate was unguarded. She remembered the face of the friendly, old guard, his beard hanging nearly to the ground, but could not recall his name. *Oh, Lumi.* She bonked herself on the head, *Why have you gotten to be so awful with names?* She walked through the open gates and into the enormous field behind it.

Curiously, there were no guards on the wide field either. Lumikki felt a twinge of discomfort. Though she saw no one, she couldn't help feeling that someone was watching her.

She came upon a puddle of water, which was peculiar because as Ruler of the Sacred Water, she knew it had not rained here recently. She followed the trickling stream that pooled at her feet all the way to a well-kept two-story log cabin. Water leaked out from under the door and down the front steps.

Lumikki knew the house. Ever since his promotion, Remidigon had been living in what he referred to as 'his new castle', a humorous comparison to her own home. He had even put up little flags around it, hoping to give it a more regal appearance.

Lumikki made her way up the wet steps and knocked on the door. When no one answered, she wiggled the knob and pushed it open.

What in the name of Aezaros…

Water overflowed from the kitchen sink, its nozzle pouring a steady stream onto the floor with a droning whirr. She stepped into the house and the soaked floorboards bent beneath her feet. The wallpaper had mostly peeled off, and the house was in disarray.

She lifted her paw and flung a blue light at the sink, stopping the faucet, and another at the floor. The water quickly evaporated. Then she walked up the stairs in the far-right corner to Remi's room.

"Remi?" Lumikki called at the top of the steps. Hesitant, she lifted her paw and rapped twice on his bedroom door. At the second knock, the door creaked open on its own. Lumikki gulped and stepped through the frame.

He was not there.

Oh, Remi—Lumikki doubled over and placed her paws on her kneecaps—*where are you?* She exhaled, wondering how long she had been holding that breath inside her cheeks.

The small bedroom had maroon walls decorated with numerous gold, silver, and bronze awards. An unmade bed sat by a dresser whose drawers overflowed with dozens of the same official-looking garments, and a desk—messy as she expected—was propped against the opposite wall beneath more awards. A metal rod with white curtains leaned up against the window. Lumikki shook her head. *Come on, Remi.* The curtain rod had been in the same spot collecting dust ever since her first visit. Though, she should not have been surprised. It was very much like Remidigon to push off even the simplest of chores; he had been doing it ever since they were little.

A silver key lay beneath the desk. She bent down to pick it up and found a vault painted a brownish-red in an attempt to blend in with the wall it was built into. Remidigon had shown her the vault once before. It was the proudest she had ever seen him.

She remembered Remidigon kneeling down to tug at

whatever was hidden inside the vault, needing his full body strength to do so. "Do you happen to know what is hidden behind the door of this vault, Lumi?"

"No," she'd replied with a shake of her head. "What is it, Remi?" He'd stopped tugging and grinned at her.

"This," Remidigon groaned, pulling again, "is the only thing that separates us from Eslura's *demons*." The giant object fell out of the vault and onto the floor with a thunder-like clap. Lumikki jumped back.

"An *S*?" She furrowed her brows. The metal twisted to form an *S* and was so heavy he could barely pick it up.

"Oh, Lumi," Remidigon chuckled and gave the *S* a pat with his paw. "Must you ruin *all* my fun?"

Lumikki snapped from her memory and opened the vault. It was empty.

With the *S* gone, it could only mean one thing: Remidigon had opened the door to the prison's ground block, the block that held Eslura's most vile criminals. She gulped and closed the door of the vault.

Lumikki crawled out from under the desk and stood up. A large bottle of ink lay, overturned, spilling its contents all over a piece of weathered parchment.

Two words lined the top of the page in a familiar elegant script. "Dearest Lumi." Lumikki felt her heart drop. She did not want to read any further, but she could not stop her eyes from crawling down the page:

As much as I love our monthly get-togethers, I will admit that I have never been as eager to meet with you than I am whilst writing this letter. In fact, I might dare to leave here earlier than I had planned (that is, of course, if you do not mind; please do let me know in your correspondence). Strange things have been happening around the island in these past few moons, and I don't quite know what to think of them. Our special guest seems to have been in high spirits lately, which, as you may understand, is rather out of sorts for him. He has even taken to casting threats on my Guards as they make their rounds, claiming that they will "fall at the feet of their rightful king in due time." Though this is not entirely unexpected behavior, I will say that it is odd for not having talked in nearly a hundred moons...

The rest of the letter was covered by the blob of ink. Lumikki cursed her brother for being so careless and lifted the bottle upright.

She tried to make sense of the note. *Special guest*, she thought to herself. He had said it before in reference to Eslura's most despicable prisoner, Obellius, but could that truly be what Remidigon had meant? Lumikki shook her head, not wanting to believe...

The sound of a shattering plate echoed up the stairs. Lumikki jumped and stood, frozen, staring at the open bedroom door. She wished she would have closed it when she entered. Down below, she could hear footsteps moving around the kitchen. Someone was downstairs. *Someone was inside the house.* Her eyes widened and her heart kicked her chest so hard she feared it might break through.

Coming to her senses, she inched toward the window, grabbed the rod, and slid the curtains off. Wielding it like a double-edged sword, she crept forward toward the door.

On her way up, Lumikki had not noticed how the old steps moaned with each foot fall. Now, as she descended the flight, she cursed the wood for being so loud, gritting her teeth with each shriek they sent through the house.

With a great big leap, she jumped off the final step and landed in the middle of the kitchen, ready to fight. She thrust the rod out and swung it back and forth, but, to her surprise, there was no one there.

After a moment of standing, staring, and waiting, she lowered the rod and walked around the room. Near the door, she found a shattered plate on the floor. She bent down and picked up one of the larger pieces and held it up to her face.

A light thump made her let go of the piece and fly into the air with fright. She gripped the rod tighter and looked at the front door. She was sure she had closed it on her way in, but it was now swaying loosely in the wind, clapping against the side of the house. Lumikki left the house and headed back toward the field.

Dark clouds swirled in a circle high in the sky, chasing each other around and making her dizzy from staring at them. A strong cool breeze swept across the grounds, rustling her fur and tossing her robe about behind her. Had there really been anyone inside the house with her? Had she imagined the sounds? Surely there had been someone there. The plate could not have broken itself, and, of course, she had heard footsteps. Someone was there; someone was following her.

Out the corner of her eye, she saw a large, black figure galloping across the field on all fours. She whipped around to face it, pointing her rod toward where she could have sworn she saw it. Before she could make out anything of its appearance, it disappeared into the shadows of the wall.

"Hello?" she called, squinting into the shadows and shrinking backward.

No one answered.

Knowing that she had no other choice than to enter the prison in search of her brother, Lumikki walked across the field, up the prison steps, and into the great marble hall. Lining the walls were dozens of finely chiseled marble statues modeled after the island's previous captains of the Sacred Guard. Each held its own lit torch. The ceiling stretched high above her head, losing itself in the shadows not even the torchlight could reach. Lumikki walked down the line of statues and stopped at the smallest one, the one that looked just like her brother. *Remidigon Otsby* the plaque read.

Lumikki placed her hand on the statue's paw and bowed. She rubbed it and looked up to meet his lifeless eyes. "I will find you," she whispered, then unhinged the torch from his hand and headed down the hall to where the steps descended into the ground.

After stepping over the first of what she assumed to be many steps, Lumikki entered what she had envisioned Morgaedion to look like from all she had heard. Hundreds and thousands of cold, dark steps spiraled deep into the earth, connecting the Guards to the countless cell blocks. Lumikki had heard rumors that the farther down you went, the more your soul clawed at your chest, itching to break away and race back up to the surface. Lumikki could not agree more; even with her first step, she felt the heavy weight of the darkness descend over her.

The deeper she crawled, the more she noticed a strange scent. At first, it did nothing but tickle her nose, making her wrinkle her brows, but soon it became too strong to ignore, too awful to breathe. She began to gasp, then choke, then suffocate. Lumikki fell to her knees, dropping the torch to brace her fall. She watched helplessly while it rolled into the shadows and puttered out. When she caught her breath, she clambered to her feet and grabbed a handful of her robe, bringing it up to her face and shielding her nose from the noxious odor. She moved on without the light, feeling her way along the wall and down the stairs.

On the next flight of steps she found the source of the smell; she stepped on it with a *crunch*. She looked down on the step, letting her eyes adjust. Then she screamed. A charred body, its arms stretched out in such a way that made her think that it was crawling to get away, lay on the steps. Around it, a dozen more lay in the same, fervent position, all desperate to get away from *something*.

She stepped between the bodies and came to the bottom

landing, where a door to a hallway lay on the floor, blown off its hinges and steaming. Below it, another cluster of charred bodies lay crushed beneath it. Lumikki felt her heart drop in her chest. She knew what was hidden behind that door; nearly every living being in Eslura knew of the prisoners kept in the ground block. With the door off, there was no telling where the prisoners could be…where her brother could be.

Something shifted behind her. She braced herself against the wall, readied the curtain rod. She heard footsteps shuffling and listened intently, gripping the bar tighter in her paw and raising it above her head. Her heart thumped in her ears as she strained to listen.

A ball of black and grey crept out of the darkness. Lumikki jumped. *A fat rat.* Lumikki exhaled and lowered the bar. The obese grey vermin stood on its hind legs and trained its beady black eyes on her. Then it twitched its nose and scampered away, seemingly dissatisfied with her scent.

When silence took back over the cell, Lumikki crept through the open door and into the ground block. She walked down the line of empty cells. Something moved in the third on the right, and she stopped.

"Remi!" She dropped her rod clanging to the stone floor, thrust the cell door open, and flung herself onto her knees before her cowering brother. Lumikki wiped back a tear and embraced him, digging her face into his white chest.

After a moment, she pulled away and stared into his eyes.

"Remi?" His eyes, once a deep blue, were now a dull grey and lacked the life they once had.

Remidigon mumbled something, but Lumikki could not

311

make it out.

"What is it, Remi? What are you saying?" She grabbed his limp hand and watched his head roll back and forth, staring off into the darkness. Lumikki let go of his hand and dropped her head toward the ground, tears blurring her vision.

Remidigon mumbled again, drawing her attention back up to him. She blinked away the tears. He had lifted one shaky finger and pointed down the hall to the last cell on the block, the smallest out of the many along the corridor. Lumikki nodded and got up. She walked toward the cell, stopped halfway, and turned to look back at her brother, whose finger was still in the air, shaking.

Lumikki reached the last cell and pushed open the door. It screeched along the stone floor.

A giant hole was cut deep into the stone floor. Lumikki picked up a loose stone from the ground and dropped it into the hole. She watched it fall into the darkness, clicking between the walls and echoing itself away without plunking down on the bottom. She stood up and felt a warm breeze against her back.

She peered down into the hole again and saw a tiny red dot far, far down, so small she nearly missed it altogether. She watched it expand, grow bigger and brighter. She leapt back as fire erupted out of the hole, shooting against the ceiling, and creating a canopy of flames above her. She tumbled backwards onto her bum, raising her hand up to shield her searing eyes. The fire danced across her fur, burning the tips of her brown coat black and lighting her robe on fire.

Lumikki rolled backwards, patting out the flames but

stopped when she felt her back rub up against something hard and scaly. She looked up at two bulging, black eyes and an open, jagged-toothed mouth wide enough to swallow her whole. The creature smiled, bent down over her, and grabbed her neck with its sharp claws, digging into her skin and lifting her off the ground. Lumikki did not have time to shout for help before the creature flung her into the flaming hole.

PRONUNCIATION GUIDE

CHARACTERS

DEMISE – Duh-mize

REMIDIGON (REMI) OTSBY – Reh-mih-dih-gon (reh-me) Ots-bee

OFFICER KAZKE – Kahz-key

OBELLIUS KALAAR – Oh-bee-lee-us Kuh-laar

BEATRICE (BEA) TIDAL

FRAN AND JOE DILDECKER – Dil-deck-ur

DR. LIZZAR – Liz-aar

BARNABY BRITTO – Bar-nuh-bee Brih-toe

MAUZ – Mouse

PEMADEE – Peh-muh-dee

REAGAN HIDEAWAY

CELINE TIDAL

WREN GROUT

AVA GROUT

KRISTA LETTING

MILLENNIUM LOFTWIND – Muh-leh-knee-uhm Loft-wind

FERHANT – Fair-hant

KUMA – Koo-mah

ALISTAIR ARCHIBALD – Al-iss-ter Are-chi-bald

ALPIN LOOMIN – All-pin Loo-min

GALABEAR – Gala-bear

AMELIA LUNALA – Uh-me-lee-uh Loo-nah-lah

AEZAROS – A-zar-ohz

NELAZGUS (NELAZGIAN) – Nuh-laz-gus (Nuh-laz-gee-ann)

LUMIKKI (LUMI) OTSBY – Loo-me-key (Loo-me) Ots-bee

HARP

TRELLUBY – Treh-luh-bee

TABITHA GLOWDISH – Glow-dish

BELLBOUR POLINDRAD – Bell-boar Pole-in-drad

ALOEISSA – Aloe-ee-suh

BOWMIDGE TALORN – Bow-midge Tah-lorn

NEPSA – Nehp-suh

SELA – Say-la

AERO ELLISVAT – Arrow Ellis-vaat

MAWRIS – Maw-ris

SEELY – Sea-lee

RESLYN KEISER – Rez-lyn Kai-zer

NORAN – Nor-ann

KANTANKEROUS (TANK) ALBERTUOUS – Can-tank-ur-us Al-burr-choo-us

LONG PAWS

PIERCIO – Pier-sea-oh

NORDWELG – Nord-wellg

DRAYZUZIAN – Dray-zoo-zee-ann

ELMRYN NEZFARR – Elm-rihn Nehz-far

PLACES

MOUNTBRIDGE – Mont-bridge

CAMP TOSSBRIDGE – Toss-bridge

ESLURA (ESLURIAN) – Ez-lure-uh (Ez-lure-ee-ann)

OVALLIA (OVALLIAN) – Oh-val-ee-uh (Oh-val-ee-ann)

BLIGHBURROW – Bligh-burr-oh

TREENODE – Tree-node

GALECREST (GALECRESTEEN) – Geil-crest (Geil-crest-een)

ZYBERSIA (ZYBERSIAN) – Z-eye-burr-shuh (Z-eye-burr-shian)

VARAAR – Vuh-raar

FARENWORTH – Fair-en-worth

HABERPAW – Haburr-paw

MORGAEDION – More-gay-dee-on

VESKADOTH – Ves-kuh-doth

MEADOW OF AEZAROS – A-zar-ohz

THE SACRED CITY

THE KELLA DESERT – Kell-uh

THE AVONBOURN – Aa-von-born

CAPE HELADRIA – Hel-aa-dree-uh

BELLBOUR'S STRAIT – Bell-boar

SPECIES

FLORAHORSE – Flora-horse

DROVIG – Drow-vig

PERGONZIA – Purr-gon-zee-uh

DIGGUNO – Dig-goo-no

OLPHIN – Ole-fin

HAVARRAK (NIGHT HOPPER) – Havur-rack

RABINTAIL – Rah-bin-tail

PEEPMUK – Peep-muck

OTHER

EYEARKE STONE – Eye-are-key

REWAKAN – Rue-ah-kahn

NABAGARI – Nah-bah-gah-ree

DAMAZIKO – Dah-mah-zee-kOH

KHAYLANT – Kay-laant

SENADRYN – Zen-uh-drIN

SARAKYAN – Sara-key-ahn

GEWA – Gee-wuh

DRINGRYS – Drin-gris

VORATH – Vo-wrath

MIGPLYE – Mihg-plye

PAVLOSIA – Pav-low-see-uh

KAP – Cap

PRESP – Press-puh

YERLING – Yur-ling

DEAR READER,

You're done! You finished the book *insert mega gasp here*! I really hope you enjoyed your adventure through Eslura. I just wanted to take the time to thank you once again for picking up a book from a new author and sticking through it till the end. It really means the world to me (and my characters) that you took a chance on this read. If you enjoyed this story, I would really appreciate if you took the time to leave a review; either on Goodreads (a social media site for voracious readers) or Amazon, or if you are feeling super ambitious, on both!! Also feel free to share this story with anyone you feel might be interested, my characters and I would greatly appreciate any exposure we can get.

Thanks again for taking a chance on me and my world,

M.C. BEELER

LOOKING FOR MORE ADVENTURES IN THE WORLD OF ESLURA?

Subscribe to M.C. Beeler's newsletter for a FREE short story

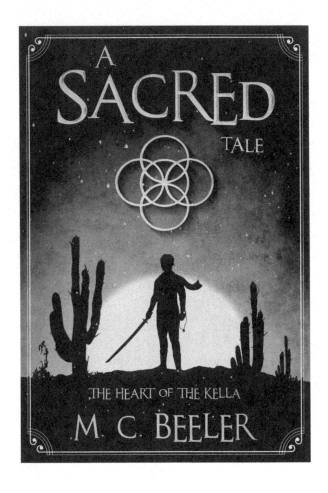

A DYING WOMAN. A CLEVER THIEF.
ONE FINAL MAGICAL MISSION.

For Aero, one letter changes everything. He never expected to hear from Noran again—not after what happened. But the woman who holds his heart after all these years is on her deathbed. And he has a new vital mission. Find what was so viciously stolen and return it to her...before it's too late.

It won't be an easy task. A vicious gang holds the Heart of Kella in a dark and dangerous territory. Even with all his skills and tricks, it may not be enough. Yet, failure isn't an option. He must save the Heart—at any cost.

This short story in the Sacred series can be read at any time as a stand-alone or as a part of the series.

ACKNOWLEDGEMENTS

Often times, you hear that writing is a solitary act. In its most basic form—the initial writing of the story—it is, of course. But there is so much more that goes on behind the scenes that is often overlooked, more so, the "other people" of the process. Without them, I cannot say for certain that I would be where I am now.

Hart S., who encouraged me at such a young and eager age to pursue my passion for writing. Never did I think that on our walks around the lake that I would be holding this book in my hands. Your words moved me to reach for the stars—and here I've found them.

Susan E., who also played a large part in my passion for writing. You listened to me talk about my story over weekend lunches and cared just as much about my world, my characters, my passion, as I did. Thanks for being there.

Jacob H., Brad B., and Danni H., my first readers who talked about my world like it was a real place and my characters like they were real people. Your passion for Eslura fuels my flame.

To my dream team—the ones who worked so tirelessly with me to bring this book to life. Mike Myers, Emir Orucevic, and Alex Wiersum—my editor, cover designer, and cartographer respectively—working with you has been the most amazing treat I could have asked for. You brought this story to life, and I could not be more thankful for having stumbled into your expertise. A special thanks also to Celestian Rince, Tandy

Proofreads, and Fantasy Proofs for helping me work out the kinks in my prose and catching those pesky spelling errors.

To my beta readers, who so generously offered up their time, energy, and amazing feedback on this story at its earliest, most vulnerable stage...I owe you everything.

To my family and friends who have supported me and my career every step of the way.

And, of course, to you, dear reader, who has taken a chance on me and my story—Eslura lives within you.

ABOUT THE AUTHOR

M.C. BEELER, raised in northern Indiana, lives in a small city just close enough to be considered a part of the Chicago-land area. A student at Marquette University, she is studying business with a concentration in Marketing and Entrepreneurship in hopes to use her skills to not only help herself, but also other authors to pursue their writing careers.

On the off chance that she isn't stationed at her writing desk, she can be found glued to whatever Nintendo console she can get her hands on working to sustain her self-proclaimed title of "Pokémon Master." You might also find her hitting the slopes during the winter season (aka her favorite season) either snowboarding or skiing.

For more updates, follow M.C.Beeler on social media:

INSTAGRAM

www.instagram.com/margaretcbeeler/

FACEBOOK

www.facebook.com/margaretcbeeler

WEBSITE

www.margaretcbeeler.com/

YOUTUBE

www.youtube.com/channel/UCWki05KCcNcQRcEsuIlqzvg

And be sure to subscribe to her newsletter for
exclusive content and a FREE short story!!

Made in USA - North Chelmsford, MA
1320050_9781736123836
06.29.2022 1041